EYESHOT

TAYLOR ADAMS

Published 2014 by Joffe Books, London

www.joffebooks.com

© Taylor Adams

ISBN-13: 978-1503245174

ISBN-10: 1503245179

DEDICATION

For Mom, Dad, Riley, and Jaclyn. Thanks for everything.

1

For a killer, William Tapp looked pretty stupid right now.

He cut a shaggy brown silhouette of twigs and crunchy grass. Like the Swamp Thing, dried out and crispy after a trek in the Mojave sun, half-walking and half-climbing over a current of loose rocks skittering downslope. His raw breaths whistled. His kneecaps squealed and popped. His beleaguered heart struggled to keep blood everywhere it needed to be.

The outfit wasn't helping. It was a homemade sniper's ghillie suit – volleyball netting tied with layers of dyed jute threads and desert underbrush for camouflage – but it was like wearing a goddamn greenhouse. Crouching was awkward, running was difficult, and taking a piss had been disastrous the one time he'd tried.

He reached the summit under a hard blue sky, dropped his rucksack (Cheetos, Swedish Fish, a six-pack of grape-flavored energy drinks), and gathered his equipment. From here the view was striking; a vivid panorama of Nevada scrublands and violet mountains that could have scored a Pulitzer. Tapp didn't notice.

He slipped the ghillie hood over his face, felt the prickle of dead grass on his lips, and like a descending shadow, morphed into the prairie.

Now William Tapp looked like nothing at all.

* * *

"Look out!"

James Eversman stomped the brakes and the Rav4 lurched like a cigarette boat dropping anchor. For a second, the world uncoupled. His seatbelt yanked him and he tasted a hot splash of copper. He couldn't tell if he'd banged his mouth on the steering wheel or just bitten his tongue.

His wife Elle fared better, as her reflexes were sharpened by three coffees a day. She caught herself on the dashboard with her palms, her chocolate-brown hair covering her face, and hissed something that sounded to James like "crap-ass." Sometimes her profanity didn't quite come out right.

It wasn't a crash but it felt like one. The parked cop car – a brown and white Ford with dusty windows – had materialized in the middle of the road on the last bend of a 70 mph S-curve. The highway was carved into the earth here and granite walls crowded the single-lane road like blinders. Had James been a heartbeat slower on the brake pedal, or distracted, or speeding, or . . . He pushed those thoughts out of his mind because they were unproductive. He knew what highway collisions looked like from EMT Basic, wherein a colleague had once described the human body as 'curiously tomato-like.' As the blood returned to his head and the acrid odor of burnt brake pads came sweeping in, James stared at the parked Paiute County patrol car not six paces from his front bumper and allowed himself to quietly marvel: *Wow.*

"Huh." Elle flipped her hair from her eyes. "That almost sucked."

"Indeed."

"Why'd he stop in the middle of the road?"

"I don't . . ." James' throat dried up. "Well, here he comes."

He was a compact little sheriff's deputy approaching at a trot with his sidearm wobbling on his hip and one hand raised to steady a comically oversized campaign hat. It was almost a sombrero. He was coming from the road's beveled gravel shoulder on the right, where James noticed a second vehicle pulled up and parked snugly against the oxidized walls. A newish white truck. It didn't appear damaged, just empty. James had time to wonder: *Where's the driver?*

"I . . ." Elle held in a laugh. "I think Smokey Bear wants his hat back."

"Don't stare."

"*Only you* can prevent car accidents."

"Elle, please don't stare." He thumbed the power window and it felt like depressurizing an airlock. Thick air poured inside and his voice disappeared under mouthfuls of swallowed heat and alkali dust.

The deputy's footsteps sounded sticky, like the blacktop was melting under the sun. James took a weak breath and tried not to cough it out – he was nervous and he hated himself for it. Admittedly, this was a new experience. He had never even been pulled over before, which he had always attributed to his remarkably unremarkable driving. Elle had once compared him to one of those little circular vacuuming robots rich people buy. What were they called again?

"Oh, Christ." The cop caught his breath and rested one palm on the door. "I should've had my lightbar on."

"It's okay," James said without really meaning it. He was startled by how young the deputy was. This guy was fresh out of high school, small-framed, acne-encrusted, and apparently trying to grow a mustache. It was going poorly.

"I was just . . . this road gets three cars a day, tops. Shoot. Sorry." The kid sniffed, straightened, and pointed to the white truck on the roadside. "There's a . . . this truck is abandoned all the way out here. Doors unlocked. Engine running. Forty bucks in a money clip in the center console. Like some guy stepped out to take a leak and never came back. Just sitting here, abandoned on the shoulder."

"Parked on the *shoulder*?" Elle cocked her head. "Maybe he was on to something."

James inflated his fake smile.

Deputy Doogie Howser didn't notice. He had a strange way of speaking; he over-inflected the first word of every sentence to deliver every idea like a PowerPoint bullet. Almost like he was hiding an accent. He apologized again (and again) and asked if they had seen anyone hitchhiking or walking along the roadside. Of course, they hadn't. The nearest town was Mosby, a shit-splat silver mine burg the deputy estimated to be "eleven clicks" east (*Why go by kilometers?* James wondered), so leaving a functioning vehicle behind out here in this Mars-like world of rock and sky was fairly strange. And possibly dangerous.

The deputy said another thing that bothered James: "You a cop?"

"No." The question hit him between the eyes. "Why?"

"Fire? Rescue? Security?" The kid squinted under the brim of that stupid hat with the solemn importance of a gypsy. "I swear, I can pick out an emergency guy from the regular civvies. It's in the eyes. You have busy eyes."

James shrugged politely. "Nope."

"He took a few medic classes," Elle said. "A long time ago."

"Nah." The deputy sighed. "That doesn't count."

Says the cop in the sombrero, James thought. He imagined Elle was thinking something wittier but hoped she would keep it to herself. He let the awkward moment pass and asked as sincerely as he could, "How can I help?"

Deputy Doogie Howser's eyes thinned. "You see anyone walkin' alone out here, on the side of the road, elderly, confused, whatever, you call me. This desert eats people. It's a big county and we're a small department."

"How small?"

"You're talkin' to fifty percent of it."

Then with a polite farewell nod, the cop turned and paced back to his patrol car, his size-eight boots slurping on the molten blacktop.

"And he's like, thirty percent hat," Elle whispered.

James nodded absently, watching.

This desert eats people.

The door thumped like a gunshot. Brake lights lit up as the deputy squeezed his car off the road and motioned them through with a circular wave. James rolled up his window and raced on past, again sneaking a sidelong glance at that mysterious white truck. Nothing special about it. Its windows blazed with reflected sunlight, rendering the interior unknown. He caught a flash of a bumper sticker – MPR, stenciled in all caps – and in another flash the truck was behind them, going, going, and gone forever. For a while he idly wondered what MPR stood for – *Mexican Public Radio?*

As the highway curved through more bends, the granite grew sharper and poked through the earth like bone tearing skin. James made a point to check every shadow and scan every stretch of plains for a humanoid walking figure, just in case. He wasn't a paramedic – not even close – but he knew just enough to be useful in a crisis, and to wish he hadn't been a salesman instead.

Elle exhaled. "Good thing you drive like a Roomba, honey."

He nodded. *Roomba. That's what they're called.*

Uncomfortable silence descended, and the tedium of the road took over again. In another few minutes they would revert to the unhappy people they had been before this little distraction, sharing cold pauses under the hum of tires on pavement. That little jolt of adrenaline had been nice, he realized, and he wished for a little more of it today, if only to appease the elephant in the car awhile longer.

"You want to talk about it?" he asked.

She shook her head.

Good. He didn't want to talk about *it*, either.

* * *

It was a long drive to Tulsa and it wasn't half over.

James and Elle Eversman stopped for gas six miles later at the Mojave Fuel-N-Food – a quiet little place with seventies-era fuel pumps and a roller grill of seventies-era hotdogs. Over a pair of concrete picnic tables and a parked jeep, a bone-white signboard welcomed them to Mosby's city limits (population: 88) and underneath, in blocky motel font: ALIENS CRASHED IN ROSWELL TRYING TO FIND MOSBY!!!!!

Five exclamation points, James observed. *Four wasn't enough.*

He was too easygoing to be a Grammar Nazi but he had the eye for it. Back in California he represented eleven local radio stations as an account executive, although his soft hands made the handshakes awkward. No one trusts a man who doesn't work with his hands. More than once before a big client meeting, he'd considered callousing his palms with steel wool.

"You think he's watching us?" Elle asked him furtively as he cranked the gas release and stepped out under the shade of the fueling lane. The heat was more manageable here, but the air was still as thick as gelatin.

"Who?"

"The guy in the jeep." She pointed with her head. "Black jeep, over there."

James peered an inch over the Rav4's roof. It was a lifted rig, powdered with dust, pulled parallel to the Fuel-N-Food with a calm disregard for the chalk parking lines. Sunlight on tinted glass painted silhouettes of two headrests and a bulging, asymmetrical head staring directly at them. It was so oddly misshapen (would a hat even fit on it?) that it took two glances to cross the uncanny valley and register it as human. It didn't move or breathe.

James shivered.

"I can feel his eyes on the back of my head." She thumbed the door lock and blocked her face with an elbow. "Crawling up and down. I hate being stared at."

"Two minutes. Then we're gone."

"No wonder they tested A-bombs here. This state blows."

He nodded. "I have no idea why Mexico wanted it back."

He put the gas on credit. The old-fashioned fueling nozzle was canted and stuck. As he tugged it free he caught motion in his far periphery – the Black Jeep Man's head was bobbing behind the sunlit glass now, and the asymmetrical part of the silhouette revealed itself to be a walkie-talkie receiver clamped to his ear with cigar fingers. He lowered the radio and swung his driver door open with a metallic squeal.

Elle sank in her seat.

James pumped gas and tried to look nonchalant. It wasn't working.

Out climbed a bearlike man draped in a trail duster that swished a curtain of oilcloth with each step. He could have been the Marlboro man, except there was also something oddly foreign about him; he looked like the kind of asshole James Bond would garrote on his way into a secret Soviet base. His hair was knotted into a black ponytail and his six-

7

inch beard was streaked with pewter. He kicked his door shut and paced to the Fuel-N-Food, carrying a silver coffee thermos with a bright circular marking on it, too far away for James to discern.

"Hello Kitty," Elle whispered.

"What?"

"It's a Hello Kitty sticker. On his thermos."

"Oh." James' gut squirmed. "Oh, *good*."

The Soviet Cowboy passed the building's double doors without entering and instead took a seat at a concrete table under the Mosby signpost, facing them directly. He was less than twenty feet away now with the barren land canvassed behind him, quietly sipping his stupid thermos. His eyes were locked on Elle again.

She peered over the dashboard and sighed.

The fuel pump ticked like a metronome. Something rattled brokenly inside it, so James checked the gray digital screen – only a gallon had gone in. He jostled the pump impatiently. He was waiting for Elle to say something, something like: *Don't try to confront him, James. Just let it go. Don't be a hero. It'll only escalate things.* He waited a few long seconds with his hand on the pump before realizing it wasn't coming. She knew that he was a pacifist. He couldn't even ask a waitress to take a burnt steak back to the kitchen without blushing. He hoped she would say it anyway, to be sweet, as she sometimes did.

"I've decided," she said.

He did a double take. She sat on her hands in the passenger seat, eyes down, lips pursed. He knew the topic had boomeranged back to *it* again, and this time there was no avoiding it. "Decided what?" he asked her with one eye on the Soviet.

"I don't want to get pregnant again."

"You're sure?"

"Yes."

James felt his lip burst warmth in his mouth. It hadn't been bleeding much before, but suddenly it reminded him of those candies that squirted fruit juice when you chewed them. The metallic taste turned his stomach, but he welcomed the distraction because anything was better than this conversation, right now, about *it*. Hell, he'd punch the Soviet Cowboy in the mouth right now just to buy another few minutes.

"I'm sorry, James." Her jaw quivered. "I can't do it anymore."

He spat in the dirt. Bright red.

The Soviet took a swig from his Hello Kitty thermos, threw open his duster, and slapped a sheet of yellowed paper on the table. He carefully spaced three stubby pencils, feathered a hand over each, and selected the middle one.

"What's he doing?" Elle asked.

"Doesn't matter." He leaned inside to face her with his palms on the Rav4's hot roof. "We're almost back on the road."

A scratching sound underscored his voice. Like snakes coiling in dry brush. It was charcoal on paper, a Morse code rap of long and short scrapes. The Soviet was sketching in big strokes, with his veined tongue hanging over his beard. *He's drawing a picture of us,* James realized. *Or maybe just Elle.*

"It's the hope that's killing me," she said quietly. "I think."

"How?"

She sighed.

"How, Elle?"

"I dread seeing the test come up positive. I *loathe* those two pink lines. Because to be devastated, you have to be happy first, and all I see is another miscarriage in three months. And unlike you, James, I'm having a hell of a hard time seeing every one of them as a human soul."

He ran his hands through his sandy hair, already dulling as his thirties approached. He had made a point of naming every one of their children and he could recite their names, starting three Januaries ago after they married – first Darby, then Jason, then Adelaide (who almost finished the second trimester and poisoned Elle with hope), then Carrie, then Ross, then . . . well, they'd named *almost* all of them. The last one, six weeks ago, seemed to be the final straw. That was when an exhausted Elle had decided she wanted to start reusing names, which offended James. It felt unconscionably cold. If there's even an outside chance of a human life existing, the least you can do is give it a name. And not reuse it.

"We'll make it happen," he said.

"You don't know that."

He imitated her doctor's Swahili accent: "Eet's not impossible. Eet's just unlikely."

"Yes. Having a baby is unlikely." She rolled her eyes but managed a small smile. "*Unlikely* is our car transforming into a talking robot. Even though it's a Japanese car, I'm not holding my breath for that."

"No. That's *impossible*," James said. "*Unlikely* is winning the lottery."

"Not holding my breath for that, either."

"People win all the time."

"Then prove it. Buy a million tickets."

"Sure." James paused. "Are we talking about the lottery or sex?"

She didn't laugh. The joke hung in the air unacknowledged. Her face was downturned so he kissed her forehead and smelled green apple from whatever bargain bin shampoo she had used back at the motel in Fairview. He saw constellations of freckles by her eyes, and tears perched on her eyelashes like little raindrops.

The fuel pump ticked – ten gallons.

The Soviet switched pencils, twirled one across his knuckles, and his strokes became shorter. He must have been on the fine details now. Every few seconds he paused to rub delicate shadows with the pad of his thumb. Then he looked up at James with a dark glower, as if to say: *Get out of the way.*

James dug his feet in and spat a glob of syrupy blood. He wanted badly now to confront the man, stupid idea as it was, because it would at least be something. Maybe if he dealt with a small problem here at the gas station, the huge one would feel smaller. He'd once heard that the crisis of modern masculinity was that so many problems existed today which couldn't be solved with a punch to the face. As punching faces wasn't James' strong suit, he had figured this made him well adapted to the modern world. He was sensitive, intelligent, and a terrific listener – but none of this helped Elle or their dead unborn children. Right now, he just wanted to punch a face.

He heard his father's words, utterly dark and alien even inside his own head: *Be polite, be courteous, but have a plan to kill everyone you meet.*

The fuel pump clicked. All done.

Elle's smile evaporated. "Do you really believe all the optimistic crap you say?"

"I do," he lied.

He crumpled the receipt and slammed the door hard enough to rattle the glass. She wiped her eyes with her palm. He gunned his soccer mom Toyota, skidded back onto the highway and floored it. Then he rolled down his window ("James, what are you doing?") tooted the horn, and flipped the Soviet Cowboy a cheery one-finger salute.

"Yep," he said with a lump in his throat. "I just did that."

She gasped. "Please drive fast now."

With a stomach full of swallowed blood, he watched the man shrink into a stick figure in the rearview mirror.

11

He had swiveled around on his seat to watch them leave. The mysterious walkie-talkie (*shit*, James had forgotten about the radio) was back out in his hand. It was too far to read an expression, but James imagined a smug grin on that weathered face, and he hoped he hadn't just made the biggest mistake of his life, in a county with a police force of two.

Why did I do that?

"Honey . . ."

He saw the speedometer pushing a hundred and tapped the brakes. "And . . . that's the story of how I got us murdered."

"If he follows us," she said, "I'm going to punch you."

The Soviet Cowboy didn't, which was somehow worse. They had blown Mosby's outer limits and were two miles into the badlands when the Toyota's radio, which had caught only electronic slush for the last forty miles, registered a crackle-snap of writhing static. And under it, a human voice.

2

William Tapp's radio hissed, signaling a connection.

He was eating Cheetos, lifting them to his mouth with a pair of medical forceps to avoid contaminating his fingers with orange dust. This one was number eighteen (he couldn't help but count things, by force of habit). Usually the bags contained somewhere in the ballpark of one hundred and thirty Cheetos, but lately the average had dropped to around one hundred and fifteen, and even one hundred and four in one bag last year. He chalked it up to the tough economy.

A verdict on the California couple in the yellow Toyota?

He hadn't decided yet.

Before answering his headset, he let a nineteenth Cheeto sit on his tongue un-chewed, where it would soak and swell into a mushy glob to be swallowed whole.

* * *

James and Elle heard only two fragments of conversation, mid-sentence and stilted, like channel-scanning an old analog television. The first sounded like "four hours left."

The second was "black eye," spoken as one word. Then the garble reached a sharp peak and the anomaly passed like blue-sky lightning, leaving them in stunned silence.

Elle twirled the volume dial. "Was that . . . ?"

"No." James was certain the voice didn't belong to the Soviet. It was wrong. It was thin, weedy, produced by scarred vocal chords and a compact chest. The speaker also seemed to have something in his mouth, occupying his tongue, like a piece of candy. He remembered once hearing that Abraham Lincoln had a raspy little voice famously at odds with his grand persona, and for some reason this was exactly what the radio voice sounded like. Yep, Abraham Lincoln. The ghost of history's favorite Republican just came on 92.7 FM and scared the hell out of them.

"Could be talk radio," James said weakly.

"Four hours left," Elle said. "Until what?"

"I don't know."

"Where will we be in four hours?"

"Arizona." He checked the GPS unit cradled on the dash. "It'll be getting dark by then. We're just a half hour from the interstate and from there it will be a straight shot over the Rockies. We'll leave this nightmare factory of a place far, far behind. Deal?"

She nodded with colorless cheeks.

He accelerated. "You okay?"

"Who . . . who just leaves a functioning vehicle out here?" Her voice was dull, zombie-like. "With forty bucks in a money clip, ten miles out of town, when it's a hundred degrees out?"

James had forgotten about that lovely episode. There were plenty of possible explanations, but all of them were only possible and not particularly convincing. He focused on the road instead, which rose and fell in lazy humps. The terrain became rough, like crumpled paper, as they approached the foothills, with odd pillows of plateaued earth jammed together to form stair steps. The only reminders they weren't on Mars came from the yucca trees dotting the landscape like hunched scarecrows. If you watched them long enough, you'd swear you saw a few walking.

Elle watched the scenery pass. She had slipped into one of her trances; into what he had once called her photographer's thousand-yard stare. The Sacramento Journal had once named her number two on a list of twenty local artists to watch. James had hung that framed page in the dining room back in California, and it was now brown-boxed with everything else they owned, in the back seats, gently rattling. It had been published four years ago. She had since dumped her cameras on Craigslist.

"Don't worry," James said. "I've seen a lot of horror movies. Nothing bad ever happens in deserts."

She chuckled.

He thumbed the radio dial and made sure it was all the way off. Usually when you get a signal bleed, it's a local television affiliate. Maybe that was it. Part of him wanted to keep scanning for more, just in case there were more tantalizing clues, but really it was just a distraction. What mattered now was driving, moving forward, and not stopping until they reached Flagstaff, Arizona as per schedule. They would be there by now, he realized grimly, if they hadn't veered a hundred miles into the nuclear wasteland for Elle's stupid tourist trap Gore Museum.

"Oh, hell," she said.

He saw it, too. A red roadblock appeared at the end of a half mile straightaway, shimmering behind curtains of air and boiling puddles of sky. In another thirty seconds the mirages dissolved and the largest signboard turned legible, flanked by highway barrels: ROCKSLIDE DETOUR. He almost punched the steering wheel but stopped himself; he needed to at least appear calm for Elle's sake. He had put her through enough today.

"It's official." She crossed her arms. "I hate this place."

"At least there's a detour road," he said. "So we don't have to turn around and drive past the guy I just gave the finger."

"Dare you to."

"I'll do you one better." He whined the brakes and approached the rockslide barricade. "Every town we pass, I'll find the scariest person there and flip them off. By the time we get to our new house, we'll have a conga line of murderers following us."

"Our new house," she said with a flickering smile. "Honest to God, nothing sounds better."

He touched her hand.

The house wasn't theirs yet. Neither were the jobs.

He twirled the wheel and skidded right onto the detour. After hours of buttery asphalt, hitting a dirt road was a teeth-chattering shock. The route itself seemed fine enough – just a winding access road walled off by sandstone faces and scree piles – but he knew he'd feel different if the Toyota broke down all the way out here. Obviously the rockslide on the pass gave them no choice, but he still felt like a character in the first act of a horror movie, pelted with popcorn by an exasperated audience: *Don't go in there, you idiots!*

He stomped the gas and accelerated.

Elle craned her head to watch the rearview mirror, as if expecting that black jeep to materialize behind them. "Four hours left," she whispered cryptically, like a fortune-teller. "Black eye."

He drove faster.

* * *

After ten minutes of serpentine bends, the landscape opened up again and the sightlines suddenly stretched forever. They were on the rim of it – a mile-wide fishbowl of descending plains and oxidizing rock forming a walled

16

horizon on all sides. It looked like a matte painting of an ancient caldera. Their detour road shot straight in and down like a hairline fracture, bisecting the valley and crossing a darkened riverbed on the bottom. Then it crawled up the opposite side. *Some detour,* he thought. *We'll be in Mexico by the time it loops back.*

Elle jolted forward as if she had been electrocuted, making stabbing motions with a pointed finger, and James punched the brake. "What?"

"See him?"

"See who?"

"Tell me I'm not crazy. Do you not see him?" Her voice pitched.

He squinted in the white-hot sunlight and followed her index finger straight ahead. He had brought the Rav4 to a complete stop, which made him anxious – the Soviet Cowboy could be pursuing them in his ass-ugly black jeep right now. That was the real concern. That walking shadow of a man could appear behind them at any second, his engine bellowing like a monster truck, unencumbered by witnesses out here.

He sighed. "All I see is desert, hon."

"Just look. You'll see him." Her voice was a whisper under the loping motor. He noticed her finger was trembling. Something about the way she said *him* spooked him, too. Like she was talking about the devil or something. The Toyota's windows creaked and popped around them, shattering the stillness, as if the outside air was depressurizing. That smell was back, too. Over the last hundred miles he had noticed these badlands possessed a unique odor – the gunpowder of cracked rock mixed with the coastal stink of tidewater. He whiffed it again under the recycled air and felt nauseous.

"You need glasses," she said, which wasn't untrue.

"I see him."

17

He or she (or it) was a tiny humanoid figure several hundred yards downhill in the crater, following the road, back turned. Head hunched, arms straitjacketed forward, dwarfed by the open land. A hitchhiker, maybe, although James couldn't fathom how anyone could be stupid enough to walk alone out here. The sun would suck the moisture from your mouth in an hour. In two hours, your eyelids would be sandpaper. In three: waist-deep in dementia and courting death.

He ran his tongue over his sore and swelling lip. *Could this be the truck guy?*

"Shady Slope Road," Elle said.

"What?"

She pointed at a piece of driftwood propped beside the road. The letters had been burnt into the bleached grain with a poker or hot iron. The handwriting was strangely childish, with exaggerated loops and crushed spacing as the wood tapered.

She sniffed. "That's not ominous at all."

"Nope."

Well, he decided, *we sure as hell can't turn around.*

So he hit the gas and continued down the detour path now identified as Shady Slope Road, which was the opposite of shady and barely a road. The man became centered in the windshield and slowly grew as they passed the crater's edge and began their descent. It reminded James of a rollercoaster – that last moment of calm on the summit of the first rise, and then the point of no return. They dropped and the road turned nasty. Broken slogs of earth churned, rocked the suspension, and vibrated the pedal under his foot. Rocks pinged off the chassis. In the back seat, the bookcase settled noisily.

James found himself focusing on the distant man and not the road. Already he could feel his bleeding heart pumping away. What if the guy really needed help? He could be stranded. It would be morally wrong to just drive

18

past him without offering help. Right? He remembered the deputy's words and choked on a nervous laugh: *That's a long way to walk just to take a leak, buddy.*

"Mount St. Helens-esque," Elle said.

He ignored her.

"You didn't laugh," she said. "You always laugh."

Back in Sacramento, they'd had no idea that their neighbor was a meth cook (meth chef?) until they woke to smoke curling under their bedroom door. The lab had detonated in such a convenient way as to send a lateral fireball directly into their living room, which the fire marshal later likened to Washington state's iconic 1980 volcanic eruption. There was actually nothing funny about it – the mustached old man had simply remarked post-investigation that the triggering blast was "Mount St. Helens-esque" – but for some reason James had giggled until his eyes watered. She had, too. Pitch-black belly laughs. They must have looked crazy; two twenty-somethings laughing their asses off over an accident that had destroyed their home and killed their neighbor. Sometimes *awful* and *hilarious* occupy the same weird space.

He let it in and grinned. "The explosion appears . . . Mount St. Helens-esque."

She snorted.

Another pothole banged under them. The engine made a popping noise, like a steel cable snapping. The boxes and furniture in the back seats shifted and creaked. He feathered the brakes and hoped a tire hadn't been punctured. Not out here, not now.

He rolled to twenty yards behind the guy, still pacing with his back turned. He wore jeans and an ashen yellow jacket – and then James saw something else, something stenciled on the man's back in white letters, which turned his blood to ice.

"MPR," Elle said. "What does that stand for?"

He swallowed. "I don't know."

She hadn't noticed the bumper sticker back on the truck earlier today. He didn't like withholding information from her, but couldn't bring himself to tell her.

MPR.

Also strange was that Deputy Doogie Howser's mysterious walking man didn't turn around to acknowledge the car idling behind him. He must have heard them approaching. He must have heard the lope of the motor, those gunshot potholes, the crunch of gravel under rubber, *something.* He just kept pacing alongside Shady Slope Road in his lonely stupor, head low, face obscured, holding a small object forward in a slightly quivering hand. James couldn't see it.

"What's he holding?"

"A cell phone." Her angle from the passenger seat was better. "Looks like he's trying to get a signal." She pulled her own phone from her purse, a battered old Samsung relic, and flipped it open.

"No bars?"

She shook her head.

No 911. Great.

Growing impatient, James gave the horn two short bursts and one long one. When the man still didn't react, he felt his stomach flutter in that weightless way it did during airplane takeoffs.

Elle asserted her mastery of the obvious: "This isn't right."

He drummed his fingers on the steering wheel and exhaled through his teeth. This guy was trying to operate a cell phone but ignoring a car horn? It didn't make sense, but neither did leaving a perfectly functional pickup on the side of the highway, all the way back on the other side of Mosby, Nevada. All he knew was that if he swerved around this walking mystery and sped on past, it could very well be a death sentence to this man. Back in Sacramento he'd heard of old folks dying in their seats on

20

the bus and going unnoticed all day, traveling the same boulevard loop for hours. He wondered if he'd ever sat next to one.

He cranked the Toyota into park.

Elle's jaw dropped. "James—"

"I have to know he's okay."

"*Seriously?*"

He unbuckled his seatbelt. "Seriously."

"I'm glad I married the last idealist left on earth," she muttered.

"There were more idealists like me," he said. "They just all died stopping to help stranded motorists who turned out to be serial killers."

"You're not going to flip him off, right?"

"Got your pepper spray?"

She fished it from her purse – a thin, black canister with a red button.

"Okay, Elle. I'm going to talk to him but I'm going to leave the engine running." He studied the man through the bug-splattered windshield and reminded himself, again, that it would be morally wrong not to check. The guy's safety wasn't even on his mind anymore. It was more selfish than that – stubborn curiosity. Too many little hints had been dropped today, and now he just had to know what was going on out here.

He opened the door. "If . . . if anything happens to me, Elle, don't stay. Just drive."

"Wait," she said.

He stood half-in, half-out. "Yeah?"

"I just have to get this off my chest, in case you die."

"What?"

"James, I have had . . . *so many* affairs . . ."

He closed the door.

He'd heard that one before. That was a sure sign Elle was getting anxious – when she started repeating her jokes.

He started walking, and his footsteps on the packed dirt sounded like breaking eggshells. The air was tiring to breathe. It felt strangely dense, over-pressurized, but he was certain this valley couldn't be far below sea level, if it was below sea level at all. His right eardrum popped juicily, and he felt his wife's eyes on his back. A few paces ahead, the man sensed him and halted on crooked legs.

Silence.

James found it oddly chilling that they were both now aware of each other. This was a milestone. There was no turning back. The man bowed his head, showing bristled gray hair around a bald patch the size of a poker chip, burnt lobster red by the sun. He wobbled as if he was turning around to face James, and then didn't.

He just stood there. Like a department store mannequin facing a wall.

Great idea, James.

He noticed a small bulge on the man's right hip and wondered if it was a holstered firearm. With his luck, it would be. James hated guns. He hated everything about them. The mechanical efficiency of their designs, their springs and pistons and calibrated clicks, snicks, and snaps, even their elegant Porsche curves – he hated it all because guns illustrated better than anything else mankind's myopic genius for engineering death. As he saw it, his father had been killed by a gun and nothing else.

Five feet away, the man exhaled through his mouth.

James had lost all momentum now. He knew he could still turn around, climb back into his car with his loving wife and few remaining possessions, and race on past this mystery to a new life in Tulsa. This would be a distraction, a few lost minutes and nothing more, no worse than that damn pointless Gore Museum that had pulled them off the interstate earlier at Elle's puppy-eyed insistence. That had been . . . well, exactly what the brochure promised. Wax dummies posed in dioramas of medieval agony –

racks, swinging blades, an imaginative way to keep rapist recidivism rates at zero – and Elle had lapped it all up like the self-identified "gore hound" that she was. James had spent most of his time in the lobby, reading an old People magazine and sipping a four-dollar Diet Coke.

He wanted badly now to be a worse person so he could walk away and leave this MPR man alone in the crater. Or a less curious one. Either way, he couldn't.

He took a small step forward. Another eggshell crunch punctured the quiet, as sharp as a slamming door. Then the other ambiences came seeping back – the hot air stirring, low grass tensing and flexing, sand hissing in the wind. Crickets that sounded like flies buzzing over bad meat. Elle said something from the Rav4, but it was muffled by glass and congested air.

The man just stood there. Back turned. James noticed with an uncomfortable jolt that the back of the guy's neck was also cooked by the sun, scorched bright red just like his bald patch. It was bad; bad enough to start peeling off in crispy sheets soon. This old man had been walking in the Mojave for some time and had clearly been unprepared for it. *Why did he leave his truck?*

James cleared his throat, dry as paper. "You okay?"

No response.

"You need water?"

Nothing.

"Hello?"

Nope.

James whistled a sharp note. *Maybe he's deaf.*

Then the man moved suddenly, like a puppet on tangled strings. His head rolled on his shoulders, first one way, then the other. His joints popped like firewood. He let out a sigh and his left hand dropped stiffly to his side, and a red smartphone fell into view – the one that had occupied his attention this entire time. The screen was black.

23

A breeze hit James and felt shockingly, bracingly cold. The sweat on his skin felt like ice.

The old man spoke: "I lost it."

"What?"

"I lost it."

James felt his other eardrum pop like a crushed grape.

I lost it?

"I . . . almost had it. But I lost it." The man drawled his syllables, testing and exploring each one in ponderous monotone. Then finally, he turned around.

James saw his face and tasted raw oysters in the back of his mouth.

* * *

"James!"

She called his name three times as he returned to their car. Her husband said nothing – eyes busy, jaw set, cheeks bloodless. She knew that face. She had only seen it once or twice in nine years, but by God, she remembered it.

He missed a step and stumbled.

"James, what did he say to you?" She looked back at the strange man, who was still standing where her husband had left him down the road. She couldn't tell how much they had actually spoken. The man was still facing away, staring down at his cell phone. He wavered a bit, like a scarecrow nailed to a wobbly post. Then her photographer's eye noticed an . . . an odd darkness, a shadow that wasn't quite correct, peering gremlin-like around the crown of his skull.

The driver door screeched open. Her husband leaned inside with sweat beading on his forehead. "We're getting him to a hospital right now. Start the car."

"What happened?"

"Start the goddamn car."

Wasn't the engine running a minute ago?

She scooted into the driver seat and grabbed the chattering keys, but morbid curiosity seized her and she chanced one more peek over the dashboard, through the windshield streaked with insect guts, and by coincidence, the man turned around and looked at her at the same moment.

At first she didn't know what it was that disturbed her. Her stomach knotted up and her spine chilled at the blatant wrongness of what she was seeing, but she couldn't knuckle down on why, exactly, it was wrong. Then she had it. The silhouette of the man's head was incorrect. A small v-shaped pie slice of his skull was gone, torn away from his temple to just above his right ear. There was surprisingly little blood, just a thin peel of scalp hanging off like a loose flap of wallpaper and underneath it an absence of matter, negative space, shadowed black in the sunlight.

Her mouth opened.

"Don't scream," James whispered.

A strangled squeak escaped her lips.

"Don't stare at it."

The man had a grandfatherly face, doughy J. Edgar Hoover jowls, and a dusting of silver stubble. He reminded her of someone she knew; she couldn't recall whom. He read her bug-eyed face – *He's looking right at me* – and his own eyes narrowed into slits. He glanced over his shoulder, then back to her, and his lips moved, as if to say: "What's wrong?"

Oh, God.

She nodded politely. Faked a smile.

Oh, God, he doesn't know he's hurt.

"We can't let him see his reflection. We need to cover the mirrors." James grabbed her hand, squeezed her fingers, and turned the key. The Rav4 coughed and something twanged loosely under the hood, like a weed-whacker wire slapping a fence. He tried twice more as her

25

slackening fingers slipped from his and the engine made no sound at all, just a dry electric tick.

"Elle," he said blankly. "We have a huge problem."

3

James Eversman could do many things well, and some things exceptionally well. He could speed-read with remarkable recall. He could operate a sailboat tiller. He could roll sushi and had briefly dabbled in beekeeping. He spoke Spanish and had a grasp of German.

He knew exactly nothing about cars.

But he was a quick learner, so he relied on that. He popped the hood release and raced to the front of the Toyota, trying to ignore the heartbeat in his neck. His legs were numb, his knees jellied – he tripped on a rock and hoped Elle hadn't seen.

She rocked in her seat, her legs to her chest. "What happened to him?"

"I don't know."

"He has no idea he's . . ."

"He's not all there." James winced at the awful, accidental pun and opened the hood. He could see immediately that the fan belt was torn and knotted up in gristly strips like discarded snakeskin. Worse, the entire engine, from the radiator to the edge of the dash compartment, was splashed with wetness. Dark wetness, stained with desert dust kicked up through the undercarriage. He touched slimed grit on the belt and recognized oil. "No signal," he said faintly. "Right?"

She checked again. "No bars."

Shit.

"Try 911 anyway," he said. "An emergency tower might ping us." He snapped his hand to flick the oil against the underside of the hood and saw it was already splattered, shotgun-peppered with running droplets. Like the Jackson Pollock painting of bug guts on his windshield. Yellow, orange, green, black, all gummed up with sand. It hadn't just leaked – *leak* was too delicate of a word.

"It's like the engine exploded," he said.

She slammed the driver door and came up on his right, her phone to her ear. "Exploded?"

"Exploded."

"That's impossible." She lowered her cell. "Just dead air."

"Try sending a text message to 911. Less bandwidth." His tone betrayed his lack of optimism. He took a knee by the driver-side tire, winced at a migraine flash of pain, and saw a dark puddle spreading in the red soil. He saw rainbow ribbons curling in the sun and his heart sank hard. "Gasoline. Oil. I think that's coolant over there."

"All leaking at once?"

"Yeah."

"Someone screwed with our car." She rubbed her eyes and mashed keys with her thumb. "The drawing guy, the Hello Kitty man. He did it, so we would be stranded all the way out here with no help and no signal. Maybe we . . . maybe we saw something we weren't supposed to, and . . ."

He held her shoulders. "We never left the car unattended."

28

"He followed us all the way from the Gore Museum, then. He obviously liked what he saw." She looked back at the old man – standing askew at the road's edge, gazing further downhill into the titanic crater with his hands on his hips. From this angle they couldn't see the hole in his head, lending the situation an undeserved calm. "How long can a person survive like that?" she asked.

"I don't know."

"It doesn't seem possible. It's like . . ."

"Stop." He lowered his voice. "Stop talking about him like he's already dead."

She looked back at him uneasily. Words danced on her tongue. He saw traces of her from the Fuel-N-Food, marveling at him sadly like he was some sort of hopeless, emotionally retarded child – *Do you really believe all the optimistic crap you say?*

"We need to make him comfortable," James said. "We need to . . . I don't know. Cover the wound. Give him water. Keep him upright and talking."

She sighed. "I think someone shot him."

He pretended not to hear.

* * *

Elle tilted the Aquafina bottle to the man's cracked lips. At first he refused and warm water dribbled down his chin.

She had been ten when her grandfather stopped recognizing her. He progressed from early-stage to moderate with cruel speed; most of his long-term memory was gone in the two weeks her family spent building school desks in Honduras. Returning to his room, she could tell immediately that he was a different person. The hard drive of his soul had been magnetized. There was something guarded about his eyes, defensive, prickly, to the way he investigated her under the fluorescent lights. It hurt to be forgotten. She hated it. He had become a stranger, and she hated being stared at by strangers. Even thinking about it now made her strangely nauseous – *Stop looking at me. Please.*

The man gagged and the water came back up. So did foamy bile, bright yellow. She turned away and breathed through her mouth.

"It's okay," she lied. She didn't know what else to say, so she said it five or six more times in a cooing voice that she didn't trust. It's tough to sound reassuring when your stomach is a ball of coiling centipedes. She heard the Toyota's rear door slam and James' hurried footsteps.

The old man lowered to a crouch, and the sunlight hit his wound at such an angle that everything was suddenly exposed. She didn't stare. The gore itself didn't disturb her; she'd grown up on slasher flicks. What disturbed Elle was how dirty it all was, how every inch was caked black with windswept grit. It was his brain, his most personal organ, and there were handfuls of sand blown inside it. Something about that made it offensive, *awful*, in a way that a thousand exploding heads in a thousand horror movies couldn't touch. She cringed.

She remembered sitting in the car with her mother. Hospital parking lot. She had been looking away with her cheek pressed against chilled glass, watching the rainwater bead up and bloom the streetlights. She hadn't wanted to talk about it. *People are like machines,* her mother had said. *Machines have parts. Parts get old and wear out and break. Your legs can break. Your stomach can break. Your Grandpa Ellis – his brain is breaking.* So Elle had concluded then, at age eight, that souls don't exist and everything we feel and love is just wet electricity inside tissue. She hit that moment earlier in life than most atheists she knew. She wasn't sure that was a good thing.

The man looked right at her and asked, "Are we real?"

She froze.

"Is this really happening?" he asked.

She blinked away tears and saw that he had something in his hand. A leather billfold, stained a tobacco brown. He flicked it open and she glimpsed a star of some sort, gleaming hot gold in the sun, and recognized it as a badge. Then James cast a sudden shadow as he leaned in to fasten a crumpled white shirt around the man's head.

"No way." Her husband saw the badge, too. "He's a *cop?*"

* * *

"His name is Glen Floyd," he heard Elle say while he wrapped the shirt around the man's head like a sloppy bandana. Over, under, through. He tried not to touch the wound, but when he accidentally brushed an upturned cornflake of bone with his thumb, the old man didn't even seem to notice. "He's . . . okay, he's Fish and Wildlife for Clements County."

"Where's that?"

"His driver's license is . . ." She steadied the wallet in the man's trembling hand. "Montana. Pictures of kids, grandkids . . ."

Montana Park Ranger, James thought suddenly. *MPR.*

"So he's a long way from home." He met both sleeves on Mr. Floyd's forehead, tying a square knot and tugging it tight. The wound outlined itself in the fabric with a thin perimeter of soaking blood. That bone chip raised the cloth like a broken fingernail. He was bothered that there wasn't more blood, aside from a thin trickle behind the man's left ear that stained his collar like spilled coffee. Bad Situations 101: there's always either much less blood than you expect, or much more. Mortal injuries are strange in that way.

God, I wish I was a paramedic.

He tried to tell himself it didn't matter. It was too late already. Glen's head, his exposed cranial vault, was already

31

so packed with foreign matter that the surgeon would need a hand vacuum to get it all out.

"I was driving on the freeway," Glen said abruptly.

James froze. So did Elle.

The old man licked his lips and squinted up at them. "I . . . I see the man next to me. He's in a little Subaru with one window rolled down a little."

A growl of wind passed between them.

"And he's got a comb-over." He smiled, all wrong, like the muscles in his face were operating independently of each other. It reminded James of how small children smile for photographs – all horse teeth, no eyes, like mummies with their skin drawn tight. "And the breeze is tugging his long hair right off his head, and he's too busy driving to notice, and his comb-over . . . it's racing around inside the car with him like a trapped muskrat. Just . . . flapping around in there." He choked on two wheezy laughs and drew a firm point with his finger. "That was the day I decided I'd embrace baldness. Like a man."

"What day was this?" Elle asked, grasping for a lead.

Glen's eyes clouded. "I don't remember."

"But you remember it."

"I have . . . some things," the man said ponderously. "Like . . . friction between colliding thoughts. I don't know whose they are."

Elle's voice broke. "We're going to help you. I promise."

This road gets three cars a day, James remembered grimly. He wondered if they could hike back up the crater slope to the rockslide detour at the highway. It was at least three miles back, up and over rough foothills. And then another six or seven to that Fuel-N-Food in Mosby. On foot, they wouldn't make it until nightfall – not good enough. Maybe they could walk until they caught enough cell reception for a 911 call? His phone had less than a quarter of its battery, but Elle had charged hers last night in the motel.

Still, every option would cost time, and how much of that did Glen have left? How far could he walk before collapsing? James supposed he could take a few bottled waters and run it faster on his own, but he couldn't stand to leave Glen – and especially Elle – alone in this crater. Something was wrong here. Something felt strangely purgatorial about this valley – the fishbowl horizons, the starkness of the open land and sky – and he felt as if just by being here, he was being judged. The sun was a spotlight. He was on stage.

"Grab more water," he said quietly. "Sunscreen. Anything you think we'll need for a few hours. We can't wait here. We're leaving the car, all of us, and walking back to the highway. Then Mosby."

Elle agreed, surprising him. "Anywhere but here."

"Exactly."

It occurred to James that he had never actually seen the landslide behind the roadblock. The road had just curved on beyond the orange highway barrels. It was crazy to think this, downright Zionist-conspiracy-paranoid, but . . . what if there was no actual rockslide on the pass? What if the roadblock was a ruse, to get them out here, with poor Mr. Floyd?

A chill crawled up his spine and lingered between his shoulder blades. If it had been a ruse, it had worked beautifully. These two California liberals were out in the wilderness now. Red rock and prairie under an unsympathetic sun. Spiny plants and animals with fangs and stingers. Salty wind and gunpowder rock. No phones, no weapons, and a two-man local sheriff's department apparently in the business of employing nineteen-year-olds. If anything, anything at all, seeing another car out here would be a bad thing because, to use Deputy Doogie Howser's own math, it would most likely be driven by whoever blew that hole in Glen's head.

33

So in that case, he thought, *thank God we haven't seen anyone.*

She tapped his shoulder. "A car's coming. Fast."

4

He saw it. A red Acura, maybe. Something low and sporty, burning with sunlight and chugging up toward them from the darkened center of the valley. Behind the approaching vehicle rose a rooster tail of dust.

James knew this was either very good – or very, *very* bad. No middle ground existed here.

Glen sat cross-legged with his head limp, staring between his knees. He had fallen into an uneasy trance, neither awake nor asleep. A crimson inkblot about the size of a fist had formed on the makeshift bandage. Worried for a moment that Glen had quietly slipped away, James squeezed his collarbone and the man grunted painfully.

He looked back up at Elle. "Someone did this. Gunshot or not, someone did this."

"And there's no one for miles."

"Except that car." He pulled his multitool from his back pocket – a junky Korean Leatherman clone that had come free with his climbing shoes last year – and retracted the blade between his thumb and finger. It was a slim, two-inch paring knife. It was probably the closest thing to

35

a weapon that James the pacifist had ever owned. He tested the point against his thumb, with increasing pressure, and failed to break the skin. He exhaled, feeling unprepared and useless.

"I thought you were an optimist," she said.

"I am."

She forced a smile. He wanted to kiss her but didn't.

The Acura closed to two hundred yards and hit the slope with everything it had. The engine roared. Fiery sunlight danced on its tinted windshield and James could make out the silhouette of a crowded interior against rising dust. At least two, maybe three, or even four heads. His stomach turned.

"The Soviet Cowboy." Elle brushed her hair for the fiftieth time.

"That's not his car."

"He was on the radio with someone—"

Something snapped beside them, like a towel whipping a tile floor. Elle jumped and gave a yelp. He looked to the low brush beside the road and saw a small, yellow flag quivering on a twelve-inch wire post.

"What's that?" he asked her.

Dumbstruck, she pointed down Shady Slope Road. Every fifty yards or so was marked with a little yellow flag. Some hissed and snapped in updrafts and others hung motionless. Like golf flags. He hadn't noticed them before. Again, he felt like he was on a stage, blinded by God's million-watt key light. The entire world suddenly felt alien to him and he wondered with a squirt of acidic panic – *what the hell did we just drive into?*

She shrugged. "The flags follow the road, both directions, as far as I can see."

"Why?"

She shrugged again.

The Acura pulled up close and growled. The gears changed. Now he could discern three heads, bobbing in soundless conversation. He supposed three was better than four. The brakes whined, the tires stuck and cut ruts in the earth, and the dust cloud caught up and swept past.

"Get behind me," he told her, as if that would make a difference.

She moved behind him and squeezed his hand. "I love you," she whispered behind his ear, as faint as the grass creaking in the breeze.

"I love you, too."

"*So many* affairs, James . . ."

The last rocks crunched as the vehicle came to a full stop in front of them, canted a little east, half-on Shady Slope Road, half-off. The side windows were opaque but the windshield revealed furious movement – the driver was shouting something now, and pointing.

Again James' stomach turned, this time a full somersault. "I think they're fighting about us."

Elle said nothing.

He took another dry breath and his mind fluttered. Maybe these people had killed Glen – shot him in the head – and left him for dead, only to return hours later to find the guy inexplicably up and walking. With a dumbass husband and wife who stopped to help. So now they had two extra witnesses to murder, and they were pissed off and bickering about it. He began to feel personally responsible for all this; he had dragged Elle into a situation he wasn't equipped to handle. He heard his dad's voice again: *Be polite, be kind, but have a plan to kill everyone you—*

The driver door banged open. Thrash metal blared for a half second before the driver punched his CD player. He lurched out and stood, hands at his sides, stringy hair lifting and curling under a frayed LA Lakers cap. He was broad, barrel-chested, with the squinty gaze of a fighter and a black t-shirt that read I PISS EXCELLENCE.

Silence.

"Thanks for stopping." James choked on basalt dust, figuring that if this excellence-pissing stranger were here to kill them he would have started killing them by now. "So we . . . we have a hurt guy here who needs—"

"I didn't stop for you," the driver said.

"What?"

The passenger door screeched open, and a twenty-something girl with ponied hair the color of bottled honey pushed out and staggered to her feet. She slung on her shoulder a purse large enough to hold a car battery. She wasn't wearing much.

"Stay in the fuckin' car," the driver said.

"I need to stretch my legs."

"I said stay in the car with your sister, Saray." The driver wiped his nose and revealed a lion tattoo under his bicep. "We don't know these people—"

"Why'd you stop?" James asked.

The driver reached inside his car and cranked the hood release—

"*Hey.* Why'd you stop?"

"Right when I saw you three—" The driver licked his chapped lips and paced to the Acura's front bumper. He had a way of talking, maybe a country accent – too fast and too slow, at once, like he was trying to channel Clint Eastwood. "Right when I came up the hill and got within a hundred feet of you, I lost steering and ran hot. Like a belt went out." As if on cue, the Acura farted a cloud of white smoke.

Elle looked at James, her eyes wide.

What are the odds?

James looked past her, over her shoulder at their own Rav4, at something he hadn't noticed in the fuss before. Ten minutes ago when he was gawking at the dripping engine he had been standing with his shins to the bumper. Now with a few yards of distance, he could discern two off-color marks on the caged grill. Two dime-sized holes

38

concealed under shadow. And a third skimming the bottom edge of the bumper, peeling the aluminum into cracked ridges. Like three little—

Oh, no.

"We're being shot at," James said. It came out deadpan, like a joke.

The driver blinked.

The girl, Saray, looked like she was about to say something. Then her cheeks chipmunked, and through her teeth she sprayed a mouthful of hot blood.

* * *

Tapp threw the bolt and ejected a golden casing. Up, back, forward, down, driving another bullet into the chamber and sealing the door behind it. It was a smooth action, made smoother by frictionless mechanical perfection and decades of muscle memory. Sometimes he cranked imaginary bolt-actions in his sleep.

He ran his tongue over his molars and rationed himself another breath. Every lungful was catalogued somewhere in the back of his mind while his heart contributed a steady twelve beats per breath. He knew his own clockwork well – between heartbeats, and within his natural respiratory pause, was a golden stillness, and inside those microseconds, the superhuman gift of William Tapp was to will the trigger to break with a power beyond nerve or muscle. To use the words of an awestruck witness at a gravel pit in Wyoming, he simply *made the bullet go.*

He's a demon, this William Tapp.

His rifle was a Finnish design chambered for the internationally acclaimed .338 Lapua Magnum. Olive green composite stock. Black bolt and receiver, cold-forged. Sixty degrees of bolt rotation and a glassy smooth throw. Free-floating chrome barrel. Two-stage trigger, customized for length and vertical pitch. Ten-capacity box magazine brimming with his personal homemade ammunition, cigar-sized and gleaming like missiles in the sun. A bulbous scope towered over all of it; an oily black optic that could belong in a NASA observatory somewhere.

His gear was carefully spaced around him. To his right, a tripod-mounted spotting scope, a handheld ballistic computer and weather meter, and a notepad with a clipped mechanical pencil. To his left, a laser rangefinder, two ribbed magazines loaded and neatly stacked, and six additional boxes of hand-loads stored in skeletal plastic bands. And behind him he kept a half-buried emergency box stashed with a backup optic, a sleek handgun chambered in .17HMR, and various other goodies. And his snacks and energy drinks, of course.

At first, he didn't think he'd hit the girl.

Slut McGee wavered in his scope, rocking on her heels ever-so-slightly as if a sharp burst of wind had disturbed her skirt. She looked one way, then the other, in mute confusion as the others hushed their conversation and turned to face her. To her, the miniature sonic boom might have sounded like a hornet whizzing past and harmlessly plunking into the dirt twenty meters up the road.

I missed.

His heart squeezed. He sagged his head, deflated and let the air hiss through the two gaps in his front teeth. He couldn't blame wind or a change of target velocity. It was a miss, plain as iron sights on a clear day, and an ugly, embarrassing one because she had been standing perfectly still. Most competition-legal x-rings are smaller than this dumb bitch. He should have been able to hit her blindfolded, with just a piece of gravel and a goddamn rubber band. Figures. It was the first easy (by his standards) shot he'd taken today, and he'd biffed it—

Slut McGee toppled, and Tapp sighed with relief.

She hit the ground and tucked into the fetal position. Now she lay in the precise center of the dirt road between the yellow Toyota and the red Acura, and he saw a tongue of darkness creeping out from under her. It was her blood turning the packed earth black. Judging by where she'd clamped her hands – *Why do they always do that?* – he tallied a low stomach hit, a little to the right. Devastating to the internals and circulatory system. One could call it a . . . *gut-wrenching* shot (ha!). Who says puns are the lowest form of humor?

I got her?

He'd got her.

The others stared with gaping horror – soundless panic, numb steps backward, their hands clenched to fists and pressed to their mouths to hold back screams. The intricate mechanisms of the human body ripped inside out and splattered, quivering and dripping and drying up, all over the ground. The usual reactions Tapp counted on, giving him time to prep his next shot.

Four targets. Four and a half, counting the Montana park ranger.

Which one?

He chose the brunette wife from the Toyota and quartered her in his crosshairs. She was standing by her husband with her hand hooked on his elbow, a few paces from the vehicle's engine block, and he figured if he could hit her center-mass he might spray a big red sheet of her all over the Rav4's hood and grill. That was always satisfying. Nothing is better than the bold splash of John F. Kennedy viscera when you shoot a person against a backdrop—

They're running.

No biggie. He swiveled his crosshairs to follow—

No, not just running. Everyone runs. Everyone eventually runs. But not like these people – they scattered with coordination and clarity of purpose. The husband and wife turned and went for the yellow Toyota, the wife vaulting the hood like a runner clearing a hurdle, then pivoting and disappearing behind it. They were both covered now, tucked tight against the car under a billow of cream-colored dust. Tapp swung left and saw the Lakers fan had already reached the nose of his Acura and was now staggering and pulling the second uninjured girl, who was already climbing from the back seat, around the driver door and out of view.

All four survivors were now hidden, crouched behind their two vehicles.

The dust thinned.

They know where I'm shooting from. He blinked and his eyelashes scraped the scope's rubber eyecup. He felt another surge of shame but consoled himself. He had done everything right, after all. One of them had simply paid enough attention to Slut McGee's entry and exit wounds to deduce the direction his shots were coming from. Not an impressive trick. Anyone could do it.

I'm okay?

He was okay. Better keep shooting.

I'm doing great, he told himself. *It's been a good day. Good shots.*

He curled his tongue back and probed the far reaches of his tonsils, where bitter globs of old food sometimes accumulated in tasty crystals. Today's special was the morning's peppered omelet, rounded out with Cheetos leftovers. The first time he'd discovered these little treats the bacterial taste had been shockingly foul, but if you do anything enough, you develop a taste for it, and eventually, a hunger.

He dug back into his firing stance, found that sacred golden stillness befitting a marksman of his *caliber* (ha!), and like a breath exhaled from the earth, plunked a second .338 into the Acura's engine block. Just to be sure.

Yessir, I'm doing great.

He would kill them all.

5

James heard a metallic ping. "There. That's how he does it. He just shot the car again."

"I didn't hear a gunshot," Elle whispered beside him.

"No gunshots." Words stuck in his throat. "There's no bang because . . . I don't know."

"A silencer?"

"Stay down."

"Could he have a silencer?"

"I don't know."

"There's nothing for the shooter to hide behind." She scooted back against the rear tire and gravel crackled under her like popcorn. "Just miles and miles of open desert."

"So he's very, very far away."

"How far?"

"Very far." He squinted. "Far enough that we can't hear the gunshot."

"That's impossible."

He shrugged coldly.

"So . . . he's that way." She pointed over the Toyota's hood, about thirty degrees to the right of Shady Slope

Road. That angle, combined with the slight leftward pivot James had parked at, afforded them nearly the entire car-length of the Rav4 for visual cover. "And we know he's shooting from that direction."

"Yeah."

"Great." She swallowed. "What happens when he moves?"

He sighed. Of course, she was right. A million percent right. Yes, they were protected from the shooter's firing angle, but he could be flanking in either direction, right now, this very second, and they wouldn't know about it until someone else literally dropped dead.

"Saray!" the driver screamed. "Saray, how bad is it?"

He heard Saray breathing fast and shallow. She coughed and it sounded wet.

Elle paled. "She's still alive?"

James dropped to his belly, pressed his cheek to the heated dirt and looked under the Rav4. The girl lay sideways in the center of the road, facing away from them. She had both hands clenched tightly to her abdomen, right at her kidney. Her white tee was now bright red, her skirt glossy black, and he could see more blood pooling beneath her and darkening the sand. Like oil on a beach. She kicked and dug ruts in the soil. She cried out, all vowels.

"Oh, God." Elle covered her mouth with her hands. "Crap-fuck-ass-*shit*."

James remembered something. "Where's Glen?"

She didn't hear.

"Where's Glen?"

"I . . . I don't know."

Then James saw the old man – his brown boots, pacing crookedly downhill past the Acura. The angle was too flat to see any higher than his waist. He could see Glen's denim-clad legs moving slowly, calmly, oblivious to the dying girl behind him. He turned and walked back uphill, then turned around again. And so on. Like a broken toy, he had defaulted back to his hitchhiker routine.

"Saray," the uninjured girl – her sister? – cried from behind the Acura. "Saray, crawl to me and Roy. Crawl toward us."

Saray rolled on her belly. Her back was dark with clods of bloodied dirt. Then the exit wound above her left hip rose into view – a ragged flower of torn flesh the size of a palm, crossed by a pale strip of skin drained of blood, punching through the front legs of what looked like a unicorn tattoo just above her skirt.

"Oh . . ." Elle looked away.

"You're gonna be okay." The driver – Roy – sniffed and his voice broke. He was a bad liar, and he couldn't even see the exit wound from his angle. "I love you. You're going to be fine. Crawl toward me."

The girl flopped and splayed her legs on the road. She had ten, maybe fifteen feet to crawl to that Acura. James could see up her short skirt and looked away, embarrassed for her. "I can't," the girl whimpered through tears and snot. "I can't."

Elle gagged behind him. He heard a warm splash.

"I . . . hang in there, baby." Roy's voice changed pitch, like he was rising to a crouch. "I'm going to help you."

She's bait, James realized. *The killer is using her as bait.* They were all behind cover now. They had concealed themselves and created a stalemate; so logically, the killer was doing one of two things. He was either relocating to fire again from a better angle, or he was staying put and watching them through curved glass with his finger on the trigger, waiting for someone to expose themselves. Maybe he'd shot to wound Saray for that very purpose – to lure her family and friends out of hiding with the sound of her screams. The viciousness of it shocked him.

Why would someone do this?

He couldn't think about that. It was unproductive right now. Saray's bleeding needed to stop. The human body holds almost six liters of blood and at least two of hers had soaked into Shady Slope Road already. She had to be losing another liter every minute through that gaping hole in her side. He was taken aback by how huge the cavity was – in EMT Basic, he had seen the case photographs from a patrolman peppered with AK-47 fire in a 1994 shooting. The exit wound in his shoulder had been about the size of a golf ball. Saray's was . . . Jesus, it was at least twice that.

What kind of weapon are we being shot at with?

Again, he stopped his thoughts. Unproductive.

"Saray. Put your right hand on your right hip," James said. "Your left on your left. Hold both wounds, keep hard pressure on them."

She did. Her chest rose and fell.

Roy was moving now. A boot scuffed dirt. A hand squealed on the Acura's hood. "I'm going to run for her," he said. "I'm going to carry her back—"

"Don't do it," James said.

"What?"

"He's waiting for you to do that. We have to think about this—"

"Fuck you. She's my fiancée—"

"He's *using her*," James shouted louder than he'd intended, and his voice boomed in the congested air. "He's using her, like he used Glen to get to us. He can't shoot us right now, so he's using your fiancée to lure us out into the open. He's smart. We know he's smart, because we're all right in the middle of his trap. If you run for her, you will die."

Silence.

Roy chuffed. "What are you, a marine?"

"I . . . sell radio ads."

"For the marines?"

"No."

"Why should I listen to you?"

"You can do exactly what he expects — and die." James exhaled, dug his fingers into the red dirt, and calmed his chattering teeth. "Or we can make a plan. A diversion. Something."

"Like what?"

"Maybe . . . maybe someone can stand up real fast."

"Great. I volunteer you."

Saray was looking at James now. He wished she wouldn't. Her eyes brimmed with tears. Her lips opened and shut like a goldfish out of water, blowing blood bubbles. He was relieved to see that she had a good grip on both wounds, although a thin line trickled between her fingers. She would certainly stay conscious for a few more minutes – long enough to think of a way to get to her, or get her to them.

Then what?

James didn't want to think that far ahead. "Stay where you are," he told her. "I'll help you. I promise I'll help you."

She nodded and a heavy glop of blood rolled down her cheek. "If I go . . ." She spat a mouthful and it hung off her mouth in dark strings. "I can't go because that would make all the things I said to my mom our last words. I can't make it final. I called her . . . I called her horrible things."

James wished he hadn't promised. "Before we do anything else . . ." His throat lumped and he raised his voice for everyone to hear. He wasn't a public speaker. He hated being listened to. He was uncomfortable with the way his voice rang in the open air. Everyone was waiting for him to speak and fill the silence. He wished there was someone else there, someone smarter and tougher and steadier, who could make the calls instead. A lot of things had already terrified him today, and being in charge of this little survival team was definitely in the top three.

No one spoke.

A low gust of wind came and went.

He exhaled and went for it. "Before we do anything else, we need to figure out where the shooter is. And how far away he is."

Elle wiped her mouth and looked up at him.

Roy spat loudly. "How?"

* * *

Tapp saw a hand swoop over the Toyota's hood and bash the driver side mirror with a tile of rock. Two soundless hits bent it and dumped a glittering shower, and then the hand disappeared.

Mirror shards. To peek over the car. Tapp ran his tongue over his bristled upper lip and tasted Cheetos.

That's just adorable.

He was locked into his spotting scope; a tripod-mounted telescope dialed in to 100x magnification and capable of reading a newspaper at a hundred meters. Incredible image, just incredible. Right now he could *feel* the dusty hood of the Toyota, warmed stove-hot by the sun, and the porous texture of volcanic rock. He could smell the panic-sweat, the coppery odor of dribbling and drying blood, and he could hear all the gasping profanities, the sobbing, the futile arguing, fussing, and dick-measuring. With this powerful optic he was inside it all, holding his breath and dunking his head and immersing himself in every tiny detail. Like a video game, the entire experience waited obediently on Tapp and his input. Inside his glass world, where things were carefully posed and arranged for his pleasure, William Tapp was God. He sucked a seventy-fourth Cheeto from the bag with just his lips.

And God (crunch, crunch) *needs to shoot something again.*

So he rolled back to his rifle, poured himself around it, wrapped his right hand around the cozy polymer and squeezed a fist underneath with his left, and swiveled his needle-thin crosshairs to the Montana park ranger. The man was still up, still somehow half lucid after taking a glancing .338 to the skull, pacing a drunken figure-eight several meters north of the two dead cars. A walking ghost.

Years ago, Tapp had shot a transient from Portland in the temple with a jacketed 5.56 NATO. The hobo's driver's license had read Malton Chango or some such bullshit (generally, the weirder a person's name, the weirder their death throes) and damn if that wasn't in full effect. The man died – by one definition of the term – more or less instantly but his nervous system exploded into overdrive. He ran a few paces backward and somersaulted twice before collapsing in the brush, kicking up a storm of prairie dust, flopping like a retard for fifteen full minutes. The Funky Chicken, performed by a corpse. In the hot shock of the moment, Tapp had laughed giddily until his throat knotted up and he was choking out piggish little schoolgirl squeals. But in retrospect the sight had disturbed him. He didn't know why. It was like he had crossed some line he wasn't aware of.

This undead park ranger also made him uncomfortable. *Why?*

He didn't know. Sometimes a shot just turned icky and that was that. The human body was, after all, an endless supply of anecdotes to be crushed, splattered, inverted, or vaporized. Not all of them sat well.

Did you hear about the guy whose left side was blown off?
Yeah. He's all right now.

He ran the pad of his index finger over the curve of the trigger, a motion he had performed perhaps a hundred million times in his fifty-six years on this earth. Trigger control, basically smooth rearward pressure, is the foundation upon which all marksmanship is built. Doesn't matter who you ask. Squeeze the trigger – don't you dare pull it. Apply your squeeze so gradually, in fact, that the shot actually *surprises* you when it comes out. Otherwise your body will anticipate the kick and unconsciously flinch, and in those crucial microseconds while the projectile races down the bore at thousands of feet per second, even the slightest twanged muscle in your forearm will blow a shot to hell. The marksman understood that a properly executed shot should strike like lightning from a clear sky, surprising the target and the shooter alike.

I do it for my shooting, not their pain.

I don't enjoy their pain.

Their pain is just necessary for my shooting.

Nothing more. As Tapp settled into his millpond stillness and applied his trigger squeeze, he realized that in his dialogue of faraway violence, this mercy shot on Mr. Floyd was possibly the most sincere gesture of goodwill he could offer another human being. It made him feel good.

The trigger broke cleanly, and that felt even better.

* * *

Elle heard a wet slap, like a beef flank slamming against a tile wall, and saw Glen Floyd's jacket quiver just above his tailbone. Then he folded to the earth as if invisible scissors had snipped his spinal cord. No blood, no apparent pain, very little sound, only merciful relief from this waking nightmare. His troubles were finally over, and she envied him a little for that.

She sat on her hands with her back to the Rav4's rear panel and her feet tucked inside the vehicle's safe shadow. She was thirsty. Her contacts burned with sand that stuck under her eyelids and scratched with every blink. Her throat was raw from inhaling the baked air, as if she had been leaning into a wood stove and breathing heavily. Her stomach still hadn't settled and the odor of vomit lingered in the still air. It smelled like salty Chinese food.

Glen sighed.

It sounded childish, frustrated. It reminded her of James exhaling after losing an argument. The familiarity of the sound made it comforting for a split-second, until she realized it was the sound of air leaving Glen's dying lungs.

One-one-thousand.

She counted. She didn't know why.

Two-one-thousand.

Then she knew. She counted because she wasn't here anymore. She wasn't on this godless stretch of burnt earth, pinned to rock and metal by unseen eyes. She wasn't in the Mojave. She wasn't even in this shitty year.

She was on the roof of the stucco Whimsical Pig apartments – the first place she and James had lived together – under a violent night sky. The summer electrical storms in southern Cali were vivid but rainless, so they had scaled the cracked drainage pipe by their kitchen window and lain together on the red tile roof, wearing only a blanket, watching the sky split open.

Three-one-thousand.

Each flash meant to start counting the seconds. Some came and went in blinks and others took their time, slithering from one horizon to the other in crackling wires. Some traced ornate patterns like tangled Christmas lights. Others were so close and so powerful that she flinched into James' arms.

"I did this when I was a kid," he'd said. "After the flash, you keep counting the seconds until you hear thunder."

"Okay."

He shifted, his leg brushed her thigh in a way that was still awkward, and he accidentally elbowed her sugary bitch-brew. The bottle skimmed the gutter and broke on the tennis court three stories down.

"It's okay," she giggled. "It was watermelon."

Four-one-thousand.

"Then after the thunder comes, you divide the total seconds by five." He interlocked his fingers with hers as another flash turned the sky purple. "Because the lightning was instantaneous, but the sound takes five seconds to travel one mile. Then the number you get – that's how far away the lightning struck."

"That works out to three hundred yards a second," she said.

"Give or take."

"Really? Three football fields."

"Yeah."

"Hard to believe sound travels that slow."

He smiled. "Still can't outrun a fart."

She smacked him.

Five-one-thousand.

Back in the Mojave, on this bloody day, Elle Eversman heard thunder. Hollow and supernatural, it rolled through the crater like a wave, breaking and splashing on the rocks and brush and hood of the Toyota, then sweeping back out. It could have been a high-altitude passenger jet chopping the clouds, or a boulder stirring, or a gust of air thumping against distant cliffs. No one else noticed the weak and warped gunshot.

Five seconds.

One mile.

* * *

"He's a mile away?"

"Yeah."

"You're sure?" James held the largest shard of side view mirror he had recovered – a triangular splinter three inches across – daintily between his thumb and finger. Then slowly, like ice crawling down a mountain, he inched the little fragment up and over the Rav4's hood. Rolling his head back against the top of the tire, he adjusted it until he found the craggy crater ridge in his fingers. An improvised periscope.

"I heard the gunshot," she said. "Five seconds after he killed Glen."

"He killed Glen?"

She pointed uphill. James saw the body twenty yards up the road, facedown. He wiped dust from his eyes and waited for an emotion to wash over him — fear, shock, rage, sadness — but nothing came. Nothing changed and he felt exactly nothing. Glen was dead. They weren't yet. That was all. He tried to remember Glen's driver's license, the color of his eyes, his weird comb-over-in-the-car story, anything solid, but couldn't and was worried to discover he didn't much care.

Elle gritted her teeth. "Rest in peace, Glen."

He nodded. "The sooner . . . the sooner we find out where the shooter is, the sooner we know our options." He steadied the northern ridgeline in the mirror piece. "If he's going to relocate and shoot at us from a different angle, maybe we can read the land and guess which way he'll go."

The opposite end of this hellish valley — he would need to study it in cubic segments. He rotated the glimmering blade between his fingers — slowly, slowly — to pan east and then west. He would need to take a few seconds to study each spot, because somewhere out there, in all that bleached rock and bruised earth, among the talus piles and erosion gullies, somewhere in all that formless seismic violence, was an eye and a scope and a horrifically powerful firearm, staring back.

"A mile," Elle said.

"I know."

"That's *sixteen* football fields."

"Maybe you counted to five wrong." He steadied his palm. His head throbbed with sinus pressure, pushing in

53

from behind his eyes. It was too damn bright. He felt strangely hung over. He forced himself to study details, to scrutinize every cluster of shadows and creeping patch of brush, but his mind wandered. He could faintly discern dark smudges speckling the skyline and knew they were those creepy walking spirits of the desert – yucca palms. From Mosby he knew those gnarled giants were over twice the height of a standing man, but he could barely keep track of them amid all the smearing earth tones. Was it possible to see a standing, six-foot human figure a mile away? Even under ideal conditions?

He realized it was a waste of time. Of course, the killer wouldn't be standing. He would be sitting, or lying on his belly.

A mile away.

1,760 yards.

5,280 feet.

A . . . lot of inches.

It's like playing 'Where's Waldo.' Only Waldo has a gun.

His thoughts fell out of his brain. His eyes ached and refused to align. He knew heatstroke was setting in – having been spoiled by the Toyota's silent blessing of air conditioning, he hadn't drunk anything since that morning. And even that had been a Diet Coke from the Reagan-era vending machine at the Gore Museum. Artificial sweeteners and sodium.

"Water," he said. His tongue stuck to the roof of his mouth. "How are we on water?"

"I'll check."

He heard her move to the back of the Rav4 where they kept a Costco forty-eight pack of bottled water. Hopefully it was accessible under the storage bins; he couldn't remember exactly how he'd stacked them. He had loaded the rear bay on Saturday evening, under a sky of puffy red clouds, but it felt like weeks ago.

He heard rocks skitter under Elle's knees and flinched. "Keep low. Below window-level, or he'll see you."

"I know."

"And don't lean out at all. He's at about a thirty-degree angle to the road—"

"The potholes."

"What?"

"Those potholes." She opened the Rav4's rear door and it double-creaked in that familiar way. "When we were driving up to Glen, those noises we heard. That was the sniper shooting our engine."

"Yeah. I think you're right." He wished she wasn't. He thumbed the glass another millimeter left and saw a small manmade structure nestled in the low end of the cliff. Bone-white. It looked like a single-room building. He couldn't make out doors or windows. He squinted hard, turning the world into an oil painting, but discerned nothing else. "I see a house." The glass nearly squirted between his sweaty fingers. "Or a shed, or something. Maybe he's shooting from inside it."

"That's it?"

"It's a piece of mirror. Not the Hubble Telescope." He heard her thumping and banging around the back of the Rav4 for the water bottles – *Jesus, please keep your head down* – and he heard the bookcase settle uncomfortably. The vehicle rocked a little on its shocks, which he felt against his shoulder. He cringed at all the careless noise.

"I might have something better," she said.

"What?"

She froze, not speaking.

"What do you have that will work better?"

"The Costco pack is empty." She rustled loose plastic.

He sighed. He remembered the three Aquafinas in the console, minus the one they'd given Glen. "So we have two bottles," he said quietly. "For four – no, five of us."

"How long will that—"

55

Something smacked into the Rav4. It sounded like a suspension bridge cable stretched to its limit and released. As bracing as a gunshot, but strangely hollow, like a bamboo whip. The suddenness and strangeness of it turned his blood to ice water. His wife screamed.

"Elle!"

He heard crunchy bits of plastic pinging around the interior of the car. The driver side window fell out of its frame and rained gummy bits on his scalp and shoulders. He pushed forward, his hands crunching safety glass into the dirt, and saw Elle wrestle her way out of the Toyota's rear door, hair tangled, eyes wide, mouth agape, but unharmed. She hit the ground on her back and crawled to him.

"What was that?" she gasped.

James noticed a shard of blue polymer stuck on his collar. He recognized where it came from.

Oh, shit.

"What?"

"That was my GPS," he said quietly.

"He shot our GPS?"

"Yeah."

She ran her hands through her hair. "Why?"

"Because . . ." Something big, impossibly huge, occurred to him and he rolled his head back against the hot door and stared at the sky. Glass fell from his hair. The world wobbled.

"*Why*, James?"

He crunched a shard in half between his fingers. "Because the GPS had a satellite emergency SOS function. This whole time."

6

Sometime around then, twenty-two-year-old Saray lost consciousness and died.

Don't think about her.

Her passing had no drama, no pomp or spectacle. She took an otherwise unremarkable breath, and then there were no more after. Whatever awful things she had called her mother the other day quietly cemented into history. That was that.

There's nothing you can do for her now.

James estimated it had already been an hour since Saray had taken the bullet. His tongue stuck to the roof of his mouth and unpeeled with a Velcro crackle. His neck and face were fiery hot to the touch and a morbid part of his mind imagined he could feel his flesh slowly cracking and blistering in the sun. Like old paint peeling off a house. The more rational part of him knew that every drop of sweat, wrung from every inch of exposed skin, was a drop he would never get back. The sun would go down in a few hours but it would return. The sniper was out there, a mile away, presumably sitting atop a mountain of food, water, and ammunition, fully equipped to outlast them. After a day or two in these badlands, he realized, catching a bullet would be the easy way out.

That answered his question – the killer hadn't relocated because there was no need to. Eventually, as the sun set and rose, they would either wither from the creeping death of dehydration or choose to break cover and make a futile run back up the northern wall of the crater. And then the bastard would enjoy hundreds and hundreds of yards of luxurious open ground to pick them off, one by one.

James couldn't decide which death was better. Maybe, he decided, they were past better and worse, and the new yardstick was *shitty* and *less shitty*. As he considered this, Elle stirred, moved to his lap and lay with her hands around his shoulders and her face buried in his dusty white shirt. She sniffed once and squeezed the back of his neck. He knew she shouldn't be here. Her life was hard enough. Miscarriages and a nonstarter career and her two beloved pets gone forever. He had to get her out of here, at any cost. He rallied himself and tried to pare the enormity of this nightmare into something smaller, simpler, more bite-sized and manageable.

Think of it like a puzzle.

He'd loved puzzles as a kid. He'd had books of them – little one-off situational riddles less than a page or two long. They'd give you a location, list the objects at your disposal, set a few ground rules, and then it was up to you to engineer a solution. Many involved escaping inescapable concrete rooms or solving unsolvable murders. He loved them. He was great at them. He never had a sibling and he built only shallow friendships, but James Eversman always had his puzzles. Even – no, especially – after his dad died.

You're crouched behind a car, he thought grimly. *A sniper, a mile away on the opposite ridge of the valley, has you in his scope. You're thirsty and tired. It's a hundred degrees, and you only have two bottles of water for four people. You have no cell phone signal.*

You're surrounded by hundreds of yards of open prairie, in all directions, with nothing to hide behind. Every inch is no man's land. Any mistake, any exposure, is instant death.

He sighed. *And the asshole shot your GPS.*

He wanted to do something he had never allowed himself to do – flip to the back of the book and read the solution. It was always reassuring to know that a solution existed (however cheap or poorly constructed) and that was comfort he sorely missed here. There might be no humanly possible way to overcome this situation, and if that was the case, what then?

"You said you'd think of something." It was Saray's sister – tall, waifish, dyed blue hair. Ash? He hadn't gotten a good look at her when she was inside Roy's Acura. Her voice was hoarse, and he knew she'd been crying, watching her sister bleed out.

"I'm sorry," he said.

She sniffed and said something unclear, choked with tears.

He knew his words were hollow. There were no words worthy of the moment. It came to him then, a crushing wave of guilt – why hadn't he thought of something? A distraction? Anything? Sure, he'd intervened, but he might have actually made things worse. Failing any breakthroughs, he should have at least given Roy the go-ahead to try and save her, if he'd really wanted to risk it. He was certain the sniper would have shot Roy. Right?

Did I save a life? Or let one go?

He would have done it for Elle, he realized. In a heartbeat. He would have grabbed her and hauled her dying ass back behind the car. He wouldn't have even thought about it. And Elle would have done it for him, too.

I told him not to save her.

He felt sick now; his stomach coiled and heaved. Elle's teeth chattered against his shoulder and she sniffed again, wetly. She was crying but fighting to hide it. She didn't like anyone to see her cry. Not even him.

"You're an asshole, James." It was Roy now. His voice shivered with rage. "You told me you were thinking of something. So I waited. I waited for you to think of something and *now she's dead.*"

"I'm sorry."

Elle stirred and put her lips to his ear. "Don't listen to him."

"You don't . . ." Roy spat in the dirt. "You don't tell people you'll help them if you can't. Your optimistic shit . . . You're lying to them. You told me, so I waited. That's on you, you piece of shit."

"You did everything you could," Elle whispered.

James closed his eyes and ignored Roy. He knew his wife was lying and that he had already screwed up terribly, but he appreciated it. He needed a new project now. He needed to busy himself, to do something, to keep his thoughts in motion. He couldn't allow himself to lose momentum and dwell on his mistakes, on that poor girl he'd failed, because if he allowed himself to step into that quicksand he would never claw himself out.

"Don't hate yourself," Elle said. "Just keep thinking."

Goose bumps crawled up his arm. She could read his mind sometimes.

Water, he decided. *Drinking water for the survivors will be my project.* He rolled over, grabbed the two Aquafinas and held one in each hand, swollen with hot liquid. One for him and Elle. One for Roy and Ash.

"She was right there." Roy coughed. "She was ten feet away—"

James arched his back and two vertebrae popped like gunshots. He kneed his way to the rear of the Toyota and peered around the taillight to see Roy, huddled on his knees by the Acura's grill, holding Ash by her shoulders. The vehicle sagged, something internal drip-drip-dripping a steady beat, forcing them to hunch even lower to stay out of the killer's view. It was eerie seeing such a big man bent under the hood of the sporty car, shoulders sloped, spirit crushed. He couldn't see Ash's face, just a waterfall of blue hair in the indecisive wind.

"Water," he said hoarsely.

Neither of them looked up.

He tossed the bottle – too hard. He watched in horror as it twirled over Saray's dead legs, tumbled past both Roy and Ash before they could lunge for it, and – oh, *thank God* – wedged under the Acura's front tire with a puff of dust. A few inches from Ash's sandaled toes, gleaming hot in the sunlight.

"It's all we have," James sighed. "Make it last."

Neither of them reached for it. Fair enough.

James broke the seal on his own bottle and took a half sip. He swished it through his teeth and tried to enjoy it, but there was nothing to enjoy. It tasted like boiled plastic and burned the roof of his mouth. Reluctantly he swallowed and let it disappear forever. The Aquafina bottle held twelve fluid ounces – how much was that sip? A quarter-ounce? He dealt in advertising market shares and percentages at work, so his brain immediately jumped there and estimated that miserable little sip had cost them two percent.

He passed it to Elle and she took a big gulp. Ten percent.

He didn't want to argue. What difference would it make?

When you're trapped in an ambush . . . you charge your enemy.

A military thing he'd heard from his father while watching a fuzzy Audie Murphy movie on the brown living room carpet. He was only seven – he didn't know if it was true or even tactically sound. What had it mattered then? His father only spoke to him when there was another entity in the room, like a chattering radio or television, to fill the quiet spaces. In another year, his father would be slumped against the dishwasher, one eye shut, slain by the walnut-colored squirrel rifle he kept loaded by the front door.

The idea being, if you're in an ambush, you're already exactly where the enemy wants you to be. They built this engagement. If you stay where you are, and try to fight on their terms, you will die.

He spoke in circles sometimes, but James listened patiently because his father was undeniably fascinating. He would work his jaw in circular, wolfish motions mid-sentence, like he was trying to yawn but not quite pulling it off. He made violent gestures with his hands, stabbing the air emphatically through curls of smoke. He touched his beard – not a stroke, not an adjustment – just a touch, as if checking on it. Sometimes his friends would come over, ragged men with long hair and loud laughter. Camouflage pants, mullets, and dirty fingernails. The Anti-Weathermen, they called themselves, with sarcasm or pride or maybe a mix of both. His mother would hide James in the bedroom, and the tiny house would rattle with voices and stink of skunk marijuana. James would sleep watching the cracks of light around the door, hearing only fragments. Something about a coming war. A great war. The Tip-over, they called it.

So you charge your enemy. You charge the fucker, close-quarters, and surprise them, and most importantly, you relocate yourself out of their kill zone. And maybe, if you're lucky, you can swing your odds back to fifty-fifty.

Charge your enemy.

When the Tip-over happens, James, you remember that.

Now James had a crazy-stupid idea. If he could kick the Toyota into neutral, and he and Elle ducked low in the seats, they could roll the car down the sloped road and crash it somewhere in the darkened riverbed at the center of the crater, a half mile away. Anywhere but here. Maybe, just maybe, the arroyo would be defiladed from the sniper's scope, if they survived the crash. He knew it was a desperate idea (moving *toward* the armed killer?) and it chilled him to realize that yes, he was indeed this desperate. The situation was that bad. Then he remembered the Rav4's shift lock release was useless without the keys, which had been jingling in his fingers when Saray took the bullet. In the ensuring blur, he had no idea where he'd dropped them. And Elle's set, of course, had been lost in the house fire.

She capped the water bottle, set it between her knees and looked at him purposefully. Her tears had smeared her eyeliner, giving her raccoon eyes.

"What?" he asked her.

"I lied."

"When?"

"I lied when I told you I sold my cameras on Craigslist." She brushed a flyaway bang from her eyes and grinned, half-embarrassed. "I couldn't do it. I have both of them still, in a black case under the clothes, under the crib."

"Really?"

"Really."

He kissed her forehead, scorching hot. "I told you not to sell them."

"I did it so . . . so I could prove a point to myself. So if I ever came back to it, it would mean something." Her voice lowered, as if divulging a secret: "The Nikon has a telephoto zoom."

"How far?"

"Far."

"Far enough to see him?"

She smiled cautiously. "I think so—"

A hollow *snap* interrupted her, and a pillar of dust billowed from Roy's Acura and scattered into the prairie. The hiss of falling sand came and went. A few clods of dirt

63

pattered down. James tensed his back against the driver door and shouted to the other car: "Hey! What was that?"

Silence.

"Roy, Ash, you still alive?"

"Bullshit." It was Roy's voice.

"What happened?"

"Asshole just shot the water bottle."

* * *

Tapp clacked the bolt and the ejected brass pinged off limestone to his right, ringing like a little bell. He couldn't hear his victims but he liked to imagine their shocked reactions to his power:

Oh my God.

Did he really?

How is that even possible?

It was an incredible shot. A small bottle swollen with warm water, sideways on the gravel, 1,545 meters away, and behind two sporadic crosswinds. It was barely a dot in his hyper-magnified optic. It could have been a speck of windblown sand on the lens, or an opaque cell inside Tapp's own eye. It was a minor miracle that every intuition and rounded decimal point had guided his hand-loaded projectile to exactly where he wanted it to go. No other marksman alive, in any army or competition, could hit a target that size, at that range, with any degree of certainty. Simpler men might find the supernatural in Tapp's work, and he could think of at least one who did.

Just like how he shot our GPS.

Could he be military? Ex-Special Forces?

He has to be.

He hoped they understood how difficult shooting was. Movies fostered grotesque misconceptions about marksmanship. It's not point-and-click, even at the shortest ranges. The human body was the shooter's greatest enemy – a furiously pumping machine full of spasms, aches, and softness. To plot a bullet's trajectory every environmental force had to be calculated. The parabolic tug of gravity, the elevation and angle, the air pressure, the air temperature, the round's ballistic coefficient, the rotation of the earth, and of course, the devastating, unpredictable wind.

Isn't it windy today? Doesn't that make it even harder?

Meanwhile you got these asshole CSI agents on television diving over backwards in slow motion and still shooting the bad guy, like a gunfight is some kind of fucking bullet ballet. Or shooting with a pistol in each hand – who decided that made the faintest lick of sense? It was bullshit. Preposterous. It made Tapp angry. He couldn't think about it now.

He must be the best sniper in the world.

Tapp cracked open his second energy drink (grape-flavored, of course) and replayed the last few seconds in his mind. It wasn't a headshot but it was close enough to send a rush of pleasure down his favorite neural pathways. After the rifle's kick, first came the 'swirl' in his scope – the bullet's vapor trail, more visible on a hot day like today. By reading it, he could watch the shot go low and left to burrow under the wind shear, exactly how he'd planned. Then the impact – magnified in his 100x spotting scope because during the projectile's flight he had time to comfortably lean forward and switch optics – he saw the fountain of mist and dirt. The water itself was vaporized, blown into a fine curtain of fog that blossomed and swept sideways in the low wind. He envisioned this, the lovely payoff, again and again until he was exhausted and felt only the creeping hunger to hit more.

More, please.

This was becoming his longest shoot ever. Typically they were thirty-minute affairs; heavenly little bursts of excitement after months of work and buildup. He would kill one, two, three, a runner here, a crawler there, and then he would shed his ghillie suit, grab his target pistol, hike a mile across the crater, and study the stiffening bodies where they lay. He would close his eyes and reconstruct the shoot as a play-by-play, imagining each second from their ground-level viewpoints, sketching mental lines suspended in the air like lasers to mark each move, counter-move, and kill shot.

This shoot was different. These four were intelligent enough to immediately take cover behind their cars at a perfectly observed angle. No one had lost it. No one had hit the dirt like the sissified modern human is trained to. No one had chanced a run for the hills (yet). As it stood, this engagement was becoming a stalemate, which Tapp did not want. Not this late into the afternoon with dwindling sunlight. No, sir. No thanks.

"Move their cars for me," he said into his headset radio. "Now."

As he spoke he spotted a flash of movement under the Toyota's front bumper. The wife – it appeared – was doing something there. Her shadow bobbed against wiry grass, then shortened and lengthened. Something small and silver scooted slowly into view under the bumper, feathered by mere fingertips.

He blinked and his eyelashes scraped the lens.

What's this?

* * *

Elle steadied her Nikon digital camera on the soft earth. She gently swiveled it to face downhill across the crater and then another thirty degrees to the right as James had instructed. The reflex viewfinder allowed her to see the image without exposing her head. She hoped. At this obtuse angle beside the Toyota's front tire, she wasn't sure how far, exactly, was too far to lean out.

She could hear the girl – Ash? – sobbing by the other car. What an awful thing. She couldn't imagine losing her own sister, let alone in such a graphic way, in full view and unflinching sunlight. She had to say something.

"Hey. Hey, your name is Ash, right?" she shouted. "Like Ashley?"

Silence.

"Yeah," the girl said.

"I'm Elle."

No response.

She could barely see the viewfinder at this angle. The aperture was still set for indoors and let in far too much sunlight, registering a blizzard whiteout. Carefully exposing one finger at a time (she doubted the sniper, for all his godlike powers, could possibly target individual fingers, right?) she dialed the f-stops back to four, then eight, then eleven. Finally the horizon traced itself on the screen.

"How . . . how old are you, Ash?" She licked her lips and lowered the camera, dipping the two center hash marks below the craggy skyline.

"Eighteen," the girl sniffed.

"Tell me about yourself. What do you like to do?"

"I . . . I don't know."

To see the viewfinder, Elle contorted her back into an s-curve — shoulders forward, head twisted back. She couldn't possibly know where the invisible line between life and death was, but she imagined her cheeks were just touching it, her eyelashes fluttering against it, her heaving breaths and arched spine holding her back and upright and just barely out of the killer's scope. Maybe she was teasing him.

"Why is your hair blue?" she asked. Stupid question.

Ash huffed. "Why not?"

Swing and a miss, she thought. She thumbed the optical zoom and watched the far valley wall slowly enlarge and darken. Good Lord, she loved that telephoto lens. She loved the compressing effect it had on buildings, how entire city blocks of steel, glass, and brick would flatten into a single wall of crushed depth. Downtown had always been an amazing place for her, full of verticality. Some of her favorite shots were on the roof of the Quigley building looking down on the rooftops of Wallace, with those parapets and utility boxes and gargoyles suffering Big Apple envy. She had a hell of an eye for compositions, but she quickly learned that talent doesn't pay the rent.

She tried again. "You going to school for anything?"

"September. I start vet school in Reno."

"That's good. I love pets."

"Yeah?" Ash sniffed. "You seem like a dog person."

Silence.

James looked at his wife and stifled a laugh.

Elle smiled bashfully. "No. Snakes."

"*Snakes?*"

"Yeah. Two snakes and—"

"Snakes are disgusting," Ash said. "Not even God likes snakes."

"I do. They're neat pets." Elle tried not to sound like she had delivered this speech before. "They're not slimy, although that's a popular misconception because of the reflective sheen on their scales. They feel . . . cool and dry to the touch, kind of like leather. And lots of species are really docile and never bite, like ball pythons, or corn snakes, or green racers. I think you'd really—"

James squeezed her shoulder, as if to say *easy there*.

Elle bumped the f-stops to let in more light and saw that the image, quivering with her heartbeats, was now magnified to its maximum. Five times. She was zoomed in somewhere on the far wall and saw darkened hillside, glacial talus flows, flash-flood gullies and jutting rock teeth, smudged yuccas and clusters of tangled brush, all drawing tall shadows and hued an unnatural Sesame Street orange. A small, anal-retentive part of her wanted to white-balance the Nikon to correct that.

"See him?" he whispered into her hair.

"No."

"Anything?"

"Just desert. An overabundance of desert."

"Okay." Ash sighed. She sounded like she was finally smiling over there. "Okay, Elle, if we get out of here, maybe I'll touch one of your snakes. But I'm warning you, if it bites me, I'm tying it in a knot."

Elle felt a dagger in her gut and exhaled sadly. "I . . . don't have them."

"Why not?"

Then she saw something in the Nikon viewfinder. A pinprick of white light.

* * *

"Oh my God," James heard her say.

"What?"

Then the camera exploded under her hand, into her face, a smoky firecracker of slicing shrapnel. She screamed, thrashed her arm, and twisted hard like a yanked rag doll. The snap of displaced air raced over the desert floor and suddenly she was motionless, low in the dirt, her face covered by her ponytail. He blinked – he had grit in his eyes – and saw dark drops in the dirt, arced in a blotted stream, and it registered late that it was blood.

"Elle!"

He couldn't see her right hand. Just blood. More blood, dribbling in the sand. She clutched it with her left and hissed a mouthful of hot air. His stomach fluttered as he threw himself toward her, tugging her shoulders back against the driver door, trying to pull her vise-tight fingers away so he could see the injury, his mind racing with awful possibilities. Chunks of her Nikon click-clacked around them like hail.

"Tell me I'm okay," she gasped.

"You're okay."

Her ponytail hit his face and she pulled her right hand up into view, clasped between white fingers. She peeled them away one by one to reveal the damage – a thin strip of skin had been peeled from the pad of her thumb, as if it had been caught on the blade of a cheese grater. Maybe she'd partially lost a fingerprint, but that was it. Thank God.

He kissed the back of her neck. "No more of that."

"I loved that camera," she said blankly, rocking back into a sitting position against the door. Her cheeks were gray, her words clipped, and she was trying to act nonchalant but he saw right through it. She held up trembling fingers: "Three paychecks at the reptile store. *Three.*"

"Elle!" Ash screamed from the other car. "Elle, are you okay?"

"Yeah."

"What happened?"

"I . . ." She shrugged with chattering teeth. "Nothing much. What's up with you?"

"I'm glad you're okay," Ash said. "I'm starting to like you."

Elle smiled – a real smile – showing white teeth.

James held her shoulders. For as long as he had known her, his wife had maintained a particular uneasiness with people. She might pretend to be in her element, but she wasn't really. She had a deep grab bag of rehearsed smiles, tension-breaking jokes, fake compliments, and all the other calculated niceties of social interaction. She only had two friends – one was her sister Eowen, and the other had moved back to Boston two years ago. Sometimes he worried for her, because he felt like he was one of only three people on earth who could make her genuinely smile. Four, maybe, counting eighteen-year-old Ash.

"What did you see?" he asked his wife.

"A flash."

"Like a gun flash?"

"Yeah," she said. "Like a kernel of light, in the middle of the hillside—"

"How much time passed?"

"What?"

"Between the flash and impact?"

She squeezed her bleeding thumb. "Felt like a second."

"One second." He stared into the badlands, letting the syllables drop off his swollen tongue. "It takes his bullet one entire second to get from his gun to us."

His mind jumped to a ninth grade science fact; that it took light from the sun eight full minutes to reach the earth. The distance was that unfathomably vast. Something about it had always disturbed him and conjured a mental image of the earth as a lonely grapefruit floating in a Pacific Ocean of nothingness. Nothing out there for us beyond a universe of indifferent stars. He could hear his teacher's voice now: *How humbling it is, to know our smallness.*

Elle was looking at him, waiting for it.

"We can use that," he said.

"What do you mean?"

He leaned closer and grinned mischievously. "When he's aiming at us, and he shoots, he's not shooting to hit us. He's shooting to hit where he estimates we'll be. In one second."

"That's it?"

"We own that second. Not him."

"That's . . . extremely optimistic." She opened her hand and studied the way the blood filled the cracks in her skin. "What can we possibly do with one second?"

"We'll think of something."

"Christ!" It was Roy again, sharp and hoarse. "Why is anyone listening to him? One second. One goddamn second. *Really?* This is like being trapped on a desert island with goddamn Ned Flanders."

"Please," Ash whispered. "Please stop."

"So . . ." Elle sighed and looked at her husband. "We have one hypothetical second of borrowed time. He still has a sniper rifle."

"I'm thinking," James said.

She kicked a chunk of blue GPS plastic and looked at him sideways. "Honey, just once, can you please drop the optimism and admit that we're so far up shit creek, we're actually two miles up shit mountain?"

"Hey!" Roy shouted, suddenly dead serious. "Hey, hey. Car coming."

Elle froze, her eyes turning to wax.

James leaned forward and peered around the Rav4's left headlight, down Shady Slope Road's plunging valley. It was the black jeep. A hundred yards down the road, lifted tires jostling, flanked on both sides by a plume of swirling dust. Coming at them fast. The Soviet Cowboy with his Hello Kitty thermos.

Elle huffed. "Not him again."

"We need to warn him," Ash said. "We need to signal him to stop, and turn around, and get help—"

"No," James said. "We don't."

"Why?"

"He's . . . he's part of it."

Roy punched something that banged like a drum. "Even though . . . Christ. I got a speeding ticket two hours ago for going seventy-four in a seventy. So this county is apparently swarming with murderers, but at least the traffic enforcement is fucking *immaculate*."

James wasn't listening. He stared down the road and imagined the inside of the Soviet's jeep, the rotten trail duster pressed warm and clammy to his slashed leather seats, his coffee burbling in the console, his charcoal pencils and yellow paper pressed against his sweaty back, and the man himself, or itself – a bleak silhouette, a human shadow against a scorched world, racing toward them.

"Hey, Elle!" Ash shouted.

"Yeah?"

"What were your two snakes named?"

His wife forced a smile. "Gray and Iris."

The girl sighed airily. "I like their names."

7

"Weapons," James said. "What do we have?"

"Same as before."

Pepper spray and a crappy multitool.

The black jeep skidded into a handbrake turn and an abrupt halt twenty yards down the road, throwing a wave of rocks and passing out of James' view. He groaned with frustration. He couldn't lean any further around the Toyota's headlight without exposing himself. He heard the jeep's driver door open with a velociraptor scream that echoed to the distant cliffs and back.

"Your pepper spray."

She plucked it from her purse and tossed it to him.

The jeep's door slammed shut and the echo cracked on the prairie. Then, crunching footsteps. Elle, lying prone by the rear tire, could see the Soviet – or at least his legs and feet. James, kneeling to her left, could not. The canister slipped in his sweaty hands. He snapped off the protective cap. "Which way is he walking?"

"He's circling to the back of his jeep." She exhaled, creating a puff of copper dust. "He's . . . he's doing something with the back end."

A rhythmic squeal. Faint at first, but growing in shrillness and intensity like rigging cables drawn tight. Hot friction. Metal on metal. James shuddered.

"What's he doing?" Roy yelled.

"I can't see," Elle shouted back.

James held the pepper spray with both hands and squinted to read the fine print. His eyes weren't focusing. He saw shadowed doubles and blinked – *Blink, damn it* – until they slipped together and he could read: 10% OLEORESIN CAPSICUM. A standard lachrymatory agent. Tears, snot, coughing, itching, burning, the usual good stuff. But his heart sank hard when he read the directions for use.

"What?" Elle asked.

"Effective range of six feet." He squeezed it. "I can piss farther than that."

"You bought it for me."

He pulled the Leatherman knockoff from his back pocket, retracted the two-inch paring knife, and locked the blade into place with a crisp click. "So our arsenal is . . . eye irritant and a butter knife."

Elle nodded tiredly.

"When he's close, you get his eyes." He passed the pepper spray back to her and closed her fingers around it. "And I'll use the knife."

"He'll need to be *really* close."

"I know. Hopefully he's made of warm butter, too." James tucked the blade underhand and flattened the handle against his right thumb. He remembered once seeing on TV that there was a proper and an improper way to wield a fighting knife. He recalled something called a Filipino grip and a handful of cutting stances to avoid because they branded you as an amateur, which of course he was. He wished he'd paid attention. He couldn't imagine stabbing another person with it anyway. With a tiny blade like this one, where the hell did you even stab? Two inches wouldn't penetrate the stomach or chest far enough for immediate results. The throat or the windpipe, definitely. Maybe the forehead. Or the eyes.

The eyes?

From the Soviet's jeep came a final snap of tortured metal, and then brisk footsteps.

"He's walking again." He tapped Elle's shoulder. "Which way?"

"He turned around," she whispered. She scooted beside the tire on her elbows, craning her neck to follow the man. Her shoe scraped gravel. "He's . . . he's walking to Roy and Ash's car."

James hit his belly beside her. He saw black trail boots and recognized them from the gas station, caked with dust and creaking as they paced up the road toward the Acura's rear. Every calm step was somehow mechanically identical – the same stride, the same height, the same heel-first stomp on the crumbling dirt road.

"Ash! Roy!" Elle shouted, her voice quivering with fear. "He's coming to you."

"No shit," Roy called back.

James pressed his chin to the road but couldn't improve his viewing angle. "Is he . . . can you see a gun in his hands?"

"No," she said.

"No gun?"

"No, I can't see his hands."

He watched the Soviet's dark legs and swishing duster vanish behind the Acura's rear quarter panel. With dawning panic, he remembered what had happened at the Fuel-N-Food and wondered if the Soviet was here for Elle, looking for her to take her away and—

"He stopped." Her voice jumped. "By the . . . behind the trunk of their car. He's looking at them. They're looking at him. Oh, God, I think he's *gonna kill them*—"

Another metallic shriek.

It rotated, deepened, and found new dimensions of awfulness like a screwdriver digging into a chalkboard. It turned into a blackened creature that crawled down James' spine, and for some reason his mind jumped now to the stagey horrors of the morning's Wax Gore Museum, to all that mechanical ingenuity used for the sole purpose of causing pain. Humanity hadn't yet discovered penicillin but knew exactly how to pull a man apart while keeping him conscious for maximum agony. James could feel the hammer-pounded iron, the weathered oak, the drum-tight metal twine, all slick with Karo syrup to approximate blood. They even got the blood right, glazing the fresh splatters bright red and the older stains a dull brown.

Pacing in the lobby, he had asked Elle: How is this entertaining? It's not. She had smiled grimly. It's life-affirming.

The Soviet took a knee behind the Acura and his duster skimmed the ground like a theatre curtain. He reached under the bumper – James still couldn't see his face – and coiled in big loops in his hand was a spool of metal cable. Winching cable, attached to his jeep.

Elle grabbed his wrist. "Is he . . ."

James nodded. "He's towing their car away."

* * *

Tapp squeezed a fist under his right hand and settled into his cheek rest. As he logged his heartbeats and breaths he slid out of this world and into another one, a better one, where nothing could touch him. Snipers called it their *bubble*. Every physical distraction bled away. He no longer felt the volcanic gravel crunching under his belly, the beads of sweat on the bridge of his nose, even the wet rhythm of his heart as it fired off blasts of color inside his retinas—

A voice jolted him.

"Okay . . . Okay, each of you, Roy and Ash, run to our car—"

The caffeine in his veins turned to frigid panic. Tapp spilled his energy drink, bucked his rifle off-target and whirled to look over his shoulder before realizing – with a rush of embarrassment – that the voice was artificial, electronic, trickling from his own headset. He recognized the tinny distortion of Svatomir's radio and remembered that the TALK button on that particular receiver was dirty and occasionally stuck while jostling in his pocket.

That was it. That was what was happening now.

Tapp let a breath curl through his teeth and forced himself to relax. His beverage leaked sideways in the dirt beside him – *bloop, bloop, bloop* – while he listened for more from Svatomir's radio. He heard only static and the sandpaper scrape of oilcloth. Then footsteps, as his spotter returned to his jeep.

That voice, though. Tapp already knew that voice. It was the husband. The thinker. The one who'd told the others which sides of their vehicles to crouch behind. The one who'd broken the side view mirror and used the shards to—

The husband said something else, inaudible.

What?

Tapp freed his left hand and thumbed the headset into his earlobe, suddenly engaged and eager for more. The white noise intensified until he could feel it vibrating in his molars.

Come on.

He checked his scope (magnified by forty) and saw Svatomir pacing back along the length of the glimmering winch cable, running his fat fingers against it as he returned to his jeep. He didn't seem to realize his radio was on and listening, flopping against his belt as he walked.

Say something else.

78

Tapp pressed with his thumbnail until his eardrum rang, and then:

"We can't wait for the car to start moving. We need to surprise the sniper," the husband said. His voice grew smaller, more distant, as Svatomir walked. Tapp closed his eyes and strained to hear the voice as it shrank under deepening waves of electronic garble: "Both of you. Choose a different side of our car to run toward. So he has to split his attention between you. Zigzag. Change directions. Don't let him predict your path."

Tapp felt it approaching, teasing, the pink mist of a fatal .338 hit . . .

"Three . . ." the husband said.

He saw Roy and Ash's shadows ducking and digging their heels into the road. He wished he could switch back to the 100x spotting scope to savor the smaller details, like the updrafts of kicked dust, the coiled nervous energy in their shoulders, the way their palms were flattened to the cooked earth. This was it. This *was it*. These huge moments happened so quickly that trying to appreciate all of it was like catching rain in a cup. A tiny distracted corner of his mind replayed the words of Svatomir's young cousin, Sergei Koal: *You know fast? You know slow-is-smooth, smooth-is-fast? This guy here is beyond fast. This guy is so far beyond fast that he reacts to you before you've acted—*

"Two . . ."

William Tapp was ready. His eye melted into scope. His lungs held half a breath. His index finger held the trigger locked at three ounces. Every stray thought in his mind crystallized into a single focus. Find, anticipate, fire.

He's a demon. He's supernatural. He's the speed of light, an African freakin' swallow, a greased-up cheetah racing down a goddamn laundry chute—

"One."

* * *

Roy swung around the Rav4 with his hand on the bumper, kicking rocks in James' face as he slid in on his ass. "Her leg. Her leg is gone," he gasped.

Ash had fallen just a few feet from the front of the Toyota. James couldn't see all of her behind the passenger side tire; only her heaving shoulders and a black shadow thrashing on the dirt. Then he heard her cry, an awful teary wail, like a little girl skinning her knee on the playground and seeing her own blood for the first time. It made him weak.

"Her leg." Roy clenched a fist to his mouth. "It's hanging by a *little string*."

Her cry reached a horrible peak.

"I'll grab her." James bellied down and slid under the Rav4's engine. "She's close enough that I can pull her to us—"

The sniper split Ash's head and silenced her. James didn't see all of it, just a splash of blue hair from behind the tire and then a puff of misted blood. Her shadow slackened. The rifle's distant bark, from the first shot, thumped against the badlands.

Silence.

Then the second gunshot came, thinner than the first.

Twenty yards away, the Soviet kicked his jeep into gear. The motor snarled, the tires dug deep, and the winching cable lifted off the road with a piercing twang. The Acura's bumper groaned and the vehicle moved on locked tires, digging tracks. James crawled beside the Toyota's driver door and watched the Soviet depart downhill, trailing that cable, a pillar of dust, and finally, the surrendered Acura. Under a flash of reflected sunlight, he could suddenly discern a crowd of silhouettes in the jeep's back seats. He saw broad edges and jutting right angles, and with a sigh of realization and creeping shame, he recognized the red ROCKSLIDE DETOUR signage from hours earlier.

It was a fake.

And it worked.

He was sickened with himself. There were a lot of things he wished he'd done differently now. He should have done more to help Glen in his confused final minutes. He should have immediately noticed the two dime-sized holes in the Rav4's grill and realized the engine hadn't just sprung a dozen leaks; it had been *shot* by two silent, fragmenting bullets. He should have thought to activate the GPS's emergency roadside assistance function before the sniper had noticed it and destroyed it. He shouldn't have discouraged Roy from saving his fiancée while she bled out in plain view. All of these failures came back like the tide, and he felt them all at once.

"I'm so sorry, Elle," he whispered.

She wasn't listening. She sat trance-like with her shoulders sloped and her fingers interlaced around her knees. She didn't move while he scooted beside her and put an arm over her shoulder. Her eyes glimmered in the sun. "Ash . . . Ash spent the last five minutes of her life listening to me talk about snakes," she said quietly.

"That's good," James said.

"No, it's not. I talk about snakes to everyone."

"She had just watched her sister die. And in all of this, you gave her someone to talk to and something better to think about."

"Yeah. Snakes."

James sighed. He didn't know how to reach her. She had turned to glass before his eyes. She looked like she had two years ago, after the first miscarriage, when he came home from the radio station and found her sitting on the stairs with her arms folded. Only her lower lip had moved, only a tiny bit. All it takes to break glass is a single fracture, and that had been just the beginning.

Here lies Elle Eversman . . .

He heard her voice in his mind, singsong and drunk as he'd dragged her out of her Subaru, engine loping inside the garage at 2 AM on a Thursday: *Here lies Elle Eversman — only cold-blooded children for her and her arsenic womb.* It wasn't a suicide attempt (she had started out with a clear objective, apparently, which was to drunk-drive to the gas station on Wellesley for a burrito) but it wasn't quite *not* a suicide attempt, either. He had been so furious with her. His hands were shaking as he carried her into the living room and propped her on the couch. She had thrown up down her shirt. She was barely coherent, reeking of exhaust, babbling in a way that legitimately frightened him, as if she was possessed: *No babies for Elle because her uterus is like the surface of Venus. Showers of acid rain and poisonous air and volcanoes of sulfur . . .* He went back to the stuffy garage (her voice called out to him over his footsteps, echoing, strangely lyrical: *Volcanoes of molten sulfur and an atmosphere made of mouthfuls of quiet death . . .*) and he shut off the engine and lifted the garage door, and by the time he had returned inside with his eyes watering, she had fallen asleep on the couch.

If that seemed like the sort of thing you'd discuss in the morning, you'd be damn right — but James hadn't brought it up. He'd waited for her to mention it, which of course never happened. A few days buried it, then a month, then three, and then the meth lab exploded next door and the world changed. In the peaks and valleys of their life together, the Subaru incident had just been one more valley. James thanked God that there were no guns in their household or that night could have ended very differently.

Only cold-blooded children for Elle.

Only snakes.

"I know . . . I know how we can escape the sniper," she said now, in that same dreamy tone that turned James' spine to ice.

He looked at her. "How?"

She looked down at her Converse, as if embarrassed. "I'm not saying . . . we do it. I'm just saying that if nothing gets better, it's an *option*."

"Just say it."

"We stand up. Both of us." A tear rolled down her cheek.

"No."

"We'll hold hands. Like this." She wiped dried blood from her wrist. "And we'll think of a memory. You know what mine is?"

"Shut up, Elle." He didn't have the energy for this. Not now.

"My mom . . . so we're at the hospice and she's still coherent. And she's telling me in that rock-steady voice that if there's life after death she'll find a way to communicate it to me. Like knocking on the walls, or dumping a book off a shelf and opening it to a certain page, or blowing up a light bulb. Something to tell me that she's still real somewhere, and that there's . . . you know, a point."

He pressed his forehead against hers and felt her breath on his cheeks. Something about the way she said *a point* profoundly depressed him.

"And of course nothing happened." Her voice broke. "I never expected to see anything paranormal, but it was just . . . you know. A nice thing for her to say. Her last gift to me, I guess, to make it easier."

James knew where this was going. He wasn't proud of it, but *of course* he had intervened. He hadn't even given the ghost of Rachel De Silva much time to send a real message. A week after she'd quietly succumbed to bone cancer, he had met with one of the engineers at work and learned a practical, safe method of making light bulbs explode when you turn them on. Shockingly practical, in fact. All you needed to do was plug in a significantly lower-voltage bulb (the cheaper, the better) and wait for the show. He did exactly this with the overhead light in the living room – but when Elle sat down to pick photographs for the funeral slideshow the next morning, it lit up just fine. Over the next few weeks, James had secretly installed several more low-voltage bulbs – the kitchen light, the bathroom light, the oblong light beside the couch – all with zero results. By then the grief was receding. Elle had started smiling and making her little jokes again, so he decided to just let it be and forgot about his little plot.

Until two weeks later, when a minor power surge slithered through the city's electrical grid. Elle had been pulling a bowl of soup out of the microwave when all seven bulbs, in three rooms, went off like firecrackers. James had been outside checking the mailbox when he'd heard them exploding like champagne corks behind the front door. He raced inside to find Elle hunched under the dinner table – the floor littered with crunchy glass, the air curling with smoke, her noodles splattered all over the sink and fridge door – and she was rocking back and forth and hugging her knees like a PTSD victim. She was half-crying, half-laughing, and even though she somehow knew it was one of James' schemes, and he knew she knew, and she knew he knew she knew, it had been a weird moment he wouldn't let himself forget, sitting under the table together in the darkness with burnt filaments stinking up the air like gun smoke.

Even out here in the Mojave, if he shut his eyes he was almost back there.

"And you made a poltergeist for me," Elle said with a scratchy smile.

"Yep."

"I never thanked you for it. But . . . thank you."

"How'd you know it was me?"

She looked up at him with suddenly vacant eyes, and the dream was over, and the crappy world took hold again. "Because there's no life after death, James."

He never understood how she could be so certain. It broke his heart.

"He's going to come back," she said coldly. "He's going to drop off that car somewhere, and then he's going to come back to tow ours. And then we'll have nothing to hide behind and nothing to run to. And we'll die."

He nodded.

"We have a few minutes. At most."

He nodded again, emptily. Tires spun in his mind.

Burnt filaments.

What?

Burnt filaments.

What about them?

Burnt filaments stinking up the air like—

Then an idea slipped into his head and stayed there, at once stunningly brilliant and stunningly obvious. He held a half breath in his lungs and sat rigid, as if the slightest motion, even a sigh, would shatter this fragile realization. It was too perfect to be real. It couldn't be real. It was a half-gone dream, turning to mist.

He turned to face Elle and said, "You're not going to die here."

"James, please." She traced random patterns in the dirt with her finger. "For everything you are, and everything I love about you, there's nothing you can do to save us from an impossible situation. I've accepted that. That's the hardest thing we have to do today, and I've done it."

"We're going to Tulsa."

"You can't save any of us in the next twenty minutes." A ghost of a smile flickered over her face. "And I forgive you for it."

He stroked her cheek with a dusty hand. And he smiled too, fragile at first, but gaining strength and conviction, curling into a boyish grin. "I have an idea. It's not impossible." He imitated the doctor's Swahili accent. "*Eet's just . . . unlikely.*"

She looked at him.
Then something struck his jaw.

8

Elle screamed.

Roy was bigger than James and knew it. It was a knuckle-to-teeth, brain-jarring hit from a man who had delivered a few in his life. James saw a Windex-blue sky, caught himself with an outstretched palm, and felt warmth race down his nose and chin. He blinked but saw only white sunlight, couldn't find Roy, and raised his hands to guard against the next hit, whenever it came, but it didn't.

Elle screamed something else. Louder.

He saw him. Roy was . . . he was crying. He cut a sad silhouette, falling on his ass against sun and sky, cheeks slick, pulling his own wrists up in a trembling fighting stance. He wanted to fight. He needed to, but James wouldn't give it to him. The man – kid, really – whispered something through ragged gasps, rocking back and forth, his fingers tightening as he repeated it again and again, each time with more awful truth: "I didn't save her, I didn't save her, I didn't save her . . ."

Saray.

James pulled himself up to the Rav4's driver door and squeezed his nose. Pain flared between his eyes. It ached but probably wasn't broken. Even if it was, it was the least of his worries right now. He tipped his head forward to keep the blood from running down his throat but kept his eyes cautiously fixed on Roy.

"I'm . . ." Roy looked up at him, suddenly ashamed. "I'm sorry."

James spat red for possibly the hundredth time today. "It's okay."

"I'm so sorry, man—"

"Asshole." Elle scooted out from behind James, knees scraping, throwing her ponied hair back. He grabbed her by both shoulders and held her.

"Let him be." He crossed his arms over her chest. "Let him have this."

"He hits you again, I castrate him."

"I believe you."

Roy punched the Toyota's back door. The bamboo crack of bone on aluminum made James flinch. The guy's shoulders sagged and he fell against the car with glimmering eyes, and then he slugged the door again, and again, and again. The last hit burst his knuckle and left a butterfly print of red on the yellow paint. He cried out, but not in pain. It was a long note of larynx-shattering rage.

Elle buried her face.

James pinched his nose and his nostrils stuck together with a double-clicking sound, like a computer mouse. He wasn't angry with Roy. He should have been – he could have been pushed into the sniper's crosshairs, or knocked unconscious, for God's sake – but he wasn't. Not even a little. James Eversman was never angry with people. He pitied them and empathized with them, even when their pain spilled out and struck him on the jaw. It was a simple truth he had understood for years: people hurt others when they are hurt, and hurting them back won't make a

Eyeshot

damn difference. He had always been ashamed of this sensitivity because it felt like a personal weakness, but Elle had told him once, on a drunken walk home under amber streetlights, with her lips to his ear as they passed iron gates, that it was a secret sort of strength and she loved him for it.

"Roy," he said.

The guy sniffed, his face to the door.

"Roy." He placed a light hand on his shoulder. "Listen to me—"

"Saray was bleeding. And I didn't help her—"

"Roy."

"I let her die. And I—"

"Roy, *shut up*," James said. "Blame me."

He blinked. "What?"

"I told you not to go to her." James swallowed a mouthful of metallic-tasting blood. "And I told her not to move. So blame me. Because I own it. I screwed up and got your fiancée killed. That's on me, not you."

An uncomfortable silence descended.

Am I lying? James honestly didn't know.

Finally, Roy shrugged. "We're dead anyway. When that jeep comes back and winches your car, it's open season on us. So what does it matter?"

"Because . . ." James couldn't suppress his crooked grin and stopped trying. "Because I think Glen Floyd had a gun on him."

Elle gasped.

"I saw it in the way he walked," James said. "I saw the bulge on his hip."

Roy's face didn't change. "You're sure?"

"No. It's a hunch."

"So how do you know?"

"I don't. That's what a *hunch* is."

"When I was sixteen, I was at a cabin party that got rolled by park rangers," Elle said with dawning hope. "They carried guns."

"We're going to get Glen's gun," James said. "And when the Soviet comes back to tow our car, we'll give him the biggest surprise of his life. We'll steal his jeep and we'll drive out of this godforsaken place and we won't stop."

Roy narrowed his eyes. "What if he doesn't actually have a gun?"

"Then we'll be no more screwed than we are right now."

"Problem." Elle threw her head back at stared at Glen's crumpled body, thirty feet up the road where he'd taken that fatal bullet. "He might as well be on the moon."

James smiled. "One second."

"What?"

"One second. Remember what we learned with your camera? The shooter has to think one second ahead of us. Plus however long it takes for him to find his target and zero in on it. So maybe . . . maybe two seconds."

"Two seconds," she said, unimpressed.

"Still have your older camera?"

She pulled it from the back seat, encased in bubble wrap and brown tape, and started tearing at it with her fingernails. "You know the Sony doesn't have much image magnification. Right?"

"*He* doesn't know that." James pointed across the valley. "We'll scoot the Sony out, under the bumper, just like you did with the other one."

"He'll shoot it again."

"Yes. That means he'll be watching the shot." He glanced back at Glen's body. "That gives us our first second. Immediately, instantly, the microsecond that camera explodes, I will run for Glen."

"How fast can you get there?"

"A second and a half."

Elle crinkled her nose.

"Fine. Two seconds," he said. "It still works."

"He'll be targeting you by then. He might have already pulled the trigger."

"Maybe." James opened and closed his hand, rehearsing the motion. "I'll stop at Glen's body and take another second to throw his jacket open, unlatch his holster, and grab the gun."

"He'll shoot you."

"I won't take more than a second over Glen's body. So if he shoots at me, he'll miss."

"Right." Roy leaned forward like a football player in a huddle and spoke with surprising clarity and focus. Almost like he'd done this sort of thing before. "But what if you take more than a second to grab the gun? Or he predicts that you'll stop at the old man's body and shoots before you get there?"

"He'll . . ." James swallowed. He knew that was the biggest flaw in this plan. "He'll have very little time to predict that."

"What if he does?"

"My run back will take another two seconds," he said. He couldn't afford to start thinking critically about this batshit idea because scrutiny would only expose more holes. "I'll start to run for the back of the car, and then change direction halfway to throw him off. That'll give me one final second. Five seconds, four changes of movement."

"Ash zig-zagged," Roy said. "He still got her."

"The shooter's good. He can't be perfect."

"Neither is this retarded idea—"

"The math works," James hissed. "It adds up. In theory, it's possible. You can doubt my running. My zig-zagging abilities. But you can't doubt me when I tell you that one plus one, plus one, plus one, equals four."

Roy shrugged. "If it equals five, you're dead."

"If it's stupid and it works, it's not stupid."

"It has to *work* before you say that."

"James, honey, you're making a lot of assumptions." Elle tore the last piece of tape away and pressed the Sony into his hands. It was bigger than the Nikon, heftier, with an analog VCR feel to it and a silver chip where James had dropped it on a marina dock five years ago. "One mistake, one little unexpected detail, and you lose your one-second lead. What if . . . how fast can you even open a gun holster?"

His stomach plunged. "I'll find out."

"Not good enough." Roy rubbed his eyes. "My stepdad carries. I used to play with the holster when I was a kid. A couple different kinds, depending on whether it was the Colt or not. There was one where the gun just rested on it and could be, you know, pulled right out. And another was sheriff-style, a button strap on a little latch—"

"What are you saying?"

"I'm saying if you've never handled a holster, you'll dick it up. You'll take longer than a second. It'll be a new motion for you and it needs to be instinct. I have some muscle memory. Not a lot, but maybe enough."

"You're volunteering?"

Roy nodded weakly.

"Your exact words were *retarded idea*," James said.

"I stand by it."

"What changed?"

"Nothing. And nothing will change if we don't try something." Roy leaned forward, gravely serious in his I PISS EXCELLENCE t-shirt. "I haven't been entirely honest with you. I have my reasons, my important reasons, to not catch a bullet out here. So yes, James, I'll do it. I'll do it on one condition."

"Shoot."

"That's it, actually." Roy bit his lip hungrily. "When that bastard comes back to tow your car, I want to be the one to shoot him in the face."

* * *

William Tapp lay still and listened to the wind change.

He understood, as any decent mind could tell you, that such stillness was illusory. Everything was always moving. He imagined he could feel tectonic plates groan and crack under his belly like sleeping dinosaurs. The earth whirled on its axis with such violence that the planet bulged at the equator. Even the solar system, one of a million shards of an expanding universe, hurtled through space like a handful of thrown gravel. For this reason, shooting at long range ceases to be shooting and becomes something else entirely. For every hundred meters of added distance, a new dimension of subtlety and instinct enters the equation. Even a little guesswork. At a mile and beyond, Tapp finds himself acting as something of a coordinator or an organizer, arranging appointments between target and projectile – two moving objects on a moving world – and ensuring they both arrive at precisely the same place and time. Down to the centimeter and millisecond.

I'm running out of time.

No, he wasn't.

Yes, I am. Two hours left.

He felt the temperature drop and whiffed the salty stink of coastal air pushed hundreds of miles inland. A low-pressure system brimmed over the western hills, ready to pour, while a billowing wave of cumulus clouds and the anvil shadow of a thunderhead took up positions on the horizon. One by one, his yellow flags quivered. The air churned and thinned. Every constant would need to be reassessed.

"Hurry up," he told Svatomir.

Two hours of usable daylight left. The storm wasn't a concern because it would arrive well after nightfall. By then he would be sitting at his reloading bench under the sulfurous glow of his shop light while Svatomir stripped the Acura and Toyota for parts and burned the bodies in a crispy stack. Tapp hated that part, which is why he always delegated it. He never truly felt guilt for the wasted life but he did always feel a strange sort of fatigue afterward. Maybe it was overstimulation, maybe it was the comedown after the high, but he had always compared it to overeating – like he had gorged on a greasy buffet and now had to pop antacids, unbutton his pants, and lie down. Burning flesh always *reeked*, too. It was a persistent foulness that would cling to your sleeves and gum up in your hair, like fatty beef sizzling in a frying pan. Or maybe severely burnt lamb or pork. Different people produced different flavors, none of them good.

Svatomir's cousin Sergei would sometimes come to watch the bodies crackle. He was a ratty little teenage mouth-breather who dabbled, via email, in some semi-serious Satanist groups in Wyoming. A fire-and-brimstone organization calling itself the Order of the Black Flame but having a Hotmail account struck Tapp as pretty contradictory, but there you go. Svatomir's little cousin would scrutinize the flames for hours until only glowing coals and bones remained.

Tapp once asked him what he saw.

Mankind purifying itself, Sergei had said without an ounce of irony.

Ah, Tapp had said.

God wants us to be weak and subservient, the little bastard whispered. He's the king and He likes the status quo. How do you bring down a king? You go after the peasants, the foundation He's built on. It's a ground game, and not one of these bubbling faces was strong enough to survive it. This is how we fight our war with God. Through you.

You're mulching His foot soldiers into paste, bringing mankind closer to His level.

A woman's blackened arm shifted and loosed a flurry of embers.

Sergei smiled. *And rightfully, that terrifies Him.*

Tapp had smiled too, through the blue shop towel he held clamped to his mouth, and quietly wished he could see things with such vividness. Although that might require brain damage.

Why? Sergei asked. *What do you see?*

Tapp shrugged. *Just firewood with unhappy faces.*

You're a demon, the kid said. You just don't know it yet.

That last remark had hung in the air with the rancid smoke. Tapp was never entirely certain how it made him feel. Some days it was inspiring that people could look at him and see such timeless grandeur, demons, and God; all that purple bullshit. Other days it just hung over him like a musty dog blanket; a title he didn't believe in or want. What is evil, after all? What is being a self-appointed servant of God or Satan? As meaningless as being a Red Sox fan, that's what.

Movement!

Behind the Toyota.

He leaned into his spotting scope and recognized a second camera scraping timidly forward under the vehicle's front bumper. It was a little chunkier than the first one, black, an older model perhaps. He clucked his tongue and wondered why these survivors would try the same thing twice. Obviously he would just shoot it again. How many damn cameras did they have back there? Were they testing him? Were they probing his shooting for weakness or inconsistency? This raised the stakes, he realized.

I can't miss now.

That would be embarrassing.

As sure as the changing wind, somehow this engagement wasn't on Tapp's terms anymore. It was on *theirs*. In some small way, he had lost control. While he considered the ramifications of this, he popped the tab on a second energy drink and took a warm, grape-flavored slurp.

It was definitely a . . . *long shot*.

* * *

"What's he waiting for?"

"This better work," Elle said. "Last camera."

James feathered the Sony with his fingertips and figured this must be what it's like to dangle a hand over a screaming meat grinder. He turned away to protect himself from catching an eyeful of shrapnel, but not being able to see his hand made it somehow worse. He had no idea when the shot would come, or where it would hit, or if it was even coming at all. He was starting to wish he had insisted on running for Glen's gun instead. To his left, Roy dropped to his knees with his palms flat on the baked road in a shaky runner's crouch. He raised his head and locked his eyes on the old man's body. His calves bulged spring-tight.

"You're sure you want to do this?" James asked.

Roy nodded and slipped off his Lakers cap. "After this, after I shoot the bearded guy, how do we get to his jeep? It'll be twenty feet away, at least, if he parks like he did last time. He has a lot of cable."

"My husband doesn't think that far ahead," Elle said.

"Seriously?"

"Seriously." James gritted his teeth and switched hands on the camera. The odd angle was cramping his wrist and more importantly, if he *must* lose a hand in the next few seconds, he didn't want it to be his dominant one. "We'll make it up as we go. But right here, right now, seconds literally count and we need that gun."

"If it exists."

"It does."

"If I get all the way out there and it's just a candy bar, I'll come back and punch you again."

James shrugged. "If my plan's as retarded as you say, you won't make it back."

Roy smiled. "Asshole."

James swiveled the Sony another inch to the right to keep the act authentic. This camera didn't even have an LCD viewfinder like the Nikon – just a rubber movie-camera eyecup, impossible to see through without putting your face behind it. He hoped the sniper wasn't tech-savvy enough to notice. There was something strangely personal to this, he realized. This long distance bluff had upped the stakes by introducing the human element, and like that eggshell silence when he first approached Glen Floyd, there was no coming back from it.

"If he was going to shoot the camera, he would have done it by now." Roy rested on his left knee, and James smelled stale chew on his breath. "It's been what, how many minutes now?"

"He'll shoot it."

"Four." Elle clacked her phone shut. "Almost five minutes."

"Five minutes and he hasn't shot it yet." Roy rubbed his eyes with his thumbs. "I think he's onto us, James. I think he's going to call it. So this was Plan A. Do we have a Plan B?"

"Die," James said.

Elle nodded. "Let's try to stick to Plan A."

"Die," Roy said thoughtfully, rolling his tongue over it. "I . . . I lied when I said Saray was my fiancée. If I'm going to die, it feels wrong to take that with me. So . . . Saray wasn't my fiancée."

"What do you mean?"

"I told her we'd get married eventually. But I have a wife right now. And a daughter, named Emma, out in Prim. She's two. She's . . . the sweetest little mistake ever." His throat clogged and he forced a laugh. "She's not supposed to exist, she shouldn't be, but we had her, and now that's . . . wonderful. Right?"

"Right."

"So I drive a lot. I pick a direction and I just go. And I pretend that I can keep driving and I don't ever have to turn around. The desert is great for that. Infinity in all directions. Simplifies things. Makes you feel small, and I like feeling small, and feeling like what I do to people doesn't matter, because of the sheer bigness of the world." He exhaled, motored his lips and looked up at James tiredly. "I lie to people. I lied to Saray and her sister. We went to the amphitheater. It was a fun night. Ash threw up in someone's hair, I think. And now I'm here. And I think about Emma and I wonder if God is punishing me. Like I deserve this."

Noticing the rainclouds stacking on the horizon, James decided *what the hell* and offered him a sip of water. "Nobody deserves this."

Roy refused. "Maybe I do."

"You don't."

"What was your life before this?"

James shrugged. He was having trouble keeping a serious conversation going with a man in an I PISS EXCELLENCE shirt.

"I work on cars," Roy said. "You said you sold stuff?"

He nodded but said nothing. It's strange how you can go to work every day for five years and lose everything only five days after quitting. He retained the memories but they felt second-hand, like they belonged to someone else. He had already forgotten what the coffee machines sounded like. He tried to picture his office and remember if his scanner was parallel to the cabinet or beside it.

Between spells of productivity he used to stare up at the radio group logo on the wall – *Your Advertising Dollars at Just Under the Speed of Light!* – and try to fathom how anyone with a business degree could think up something so asinine. He'd made some good friends there. Most left to work in television, web startups, or retire. A good one, Keith, had been killed by a drunk driver on Christmas Eve. James remembered being one of the last people to see him alive as he left the holiday party, and couldn't even remember what final things they'd talked about. Did it matter?

In that life, in that city, he and Elle had discovered a fate worse than misery. Comfortable mediocrity. Things were never truly bad, but they were never truly good, either. Every miscarriage seemed to pull Elle closer to an unknown precipice. Some days they felt like sad shadows of themselves, sleeping like siblings in a shared bed. He could recall entire days where they didn't speak, and didn't care to. Just incompatible strangers sharing a house; an insufferable optimist and an insufferable pessimist. The fire was just an excuse, really. James and Elle had decided to reshuffle the deck, head to Tulsa, and take a mulligan on life.

They could have stayed, of course. Even after the fire. They could have found another home in Sacramento, maybe up on the fancier East Ridge (known to the locals as Douchebag Ridge) since his client list had bumped him up an income bracket. He could have continued to play kiss-ass with media buyers and sell invisible, weightless airtime to pawn shops, assisted living facilities, and car lots. She could sell reptiles at the pet store by day and do contract work by night – a wedding here, a brochure there, maybe an independent film credit or two. They'd keep the same restaurants, the same traffic escape routes, the same tired faces and fallbacks.

That life wasn't theirs anymore, he realized. Even if he and Elle somehow survived today, that comfortably mediocre life in Sacramento was gone forever.

He noticed tears in his wife's eyes.

"Elle?"

"I deserve this," she said.

"Why?"

"I had an abortion. When I was sixteen."

He held her arm and squeezed. "I . . . I know."

"James, I've never told you that before."

He nodded. "You told me when you were drunk. Once."

"That wasn't official." She smiled bashfully and a spurt of wind caught her ponytail. "Now it's official because we're both sober. And because of that, because of that one stupid choice I made forever ago, I wonder if something changed and it's my fault."

The wind drew silent.

"Now . . ." Her voice broke. "I wonder if it's my fault we can't have kids."

James exhaled. He tried to find something comforting to say but he was too exhausted, his nerves drawn too tight.

WRACK!

The Sony exploded beneath his fingers and he felt a bite on his knuckle. He kicked backwards, clutching his hand, hoping everything was still there and intact, and he screamed hoarsely at Roy beside him. Now was his moment. *The* moment. Everything hinged on what happened in the next few seconds.

"*Roy, go!*"

Roy didn't go.

* * *

A mile away, Tapp threw the bolt sixty degrees and ejected a golden .338 brass casing. He was relieved to see such a decisive hit. The streak continued! Nothing ruined a day like a single blown shot – much like shooting paper targets, you wing a hole at ten o'clock and it's there forever. You can't unshoot it. But if this day was to be dashed by such a failure, it hadn't happened yet.

Not yet.

I'm still good.

Like butter, I'm on a roll—

Mid-throw with his eye half on scope, he caught a rabbit-dart of motion in his curved glass world. He snapped back in, bruising his cheekbone, pounding the rifle's action forward with the palm of his hand and locking a fresh round in the chamber. Through the magnification he drew on a figure breaking into a dead sprint from the rear of the Toyota Rav4. Dashing north, directly away from Tapp and directly up the road, in a perfect straight vector that almost eliminated the need for any lateral holdover at all.

The wife.

9

"Elle!"

She heard her husband screaming somewhere far behind her but there was no time to listen. She exploded into the open ground, flattened her hands into blades and dug her feet deep into powdery earth, every muscle in her body focused forward. Only forward. The microsecond she broke free of the Rav4's safe shadow she felt an overwhelming vulnerability, a nakedness, as if treading the surface of Mars without a spacesuit. She punched through the fresh air, so frigidly cold by comparison, so hard and so fast that her hair tugged and her ears whooshed.

One second elapsed.

Glen's body came up fast. Three yards. Close enough that she needed to slow down, to lose momentum, or she would tumble over and past him. She dropped both shoulders, kicked up the toes of her Converse and skidded hard, hitting the road on her back with her left elbow scraping gravel in a flash of searing pain. Her feet, turned sideways, threw dust and jangling rocks.

Two seconds.

She landed on her ass beside Glen. Perfect. She rolled once, sucking in a hard breath, and was on top of the body. Straddling the man's stomach. The scope was on her now. She felt a gathering tingle on her spine and knew it was the killer's crosshairs hungrily forming a crucifix. She threw open Glen's MPR jacket with her left hand, slashing her mouth on the corner. With her right hand she searched, grasped for the holster above his hip, under his belt, behind his clammy back. She found nothing. Nothing at all.

Three seconds.

Cold panic. Her stomach sank and her heartbeats thumped like machinegun fire. The gun, the holster, was on Glen's left side. James had said so. His left? Or hers? She pivoted, hurled open the jacket's other side with a crackle of hardened blood, and her fingers hit treated leather. Milled metal. Something solid and heavy.

Four seconds.

Too late . . . already too late . . .

She found the wooden butt of the gun and a thin strap. She thumbed it and felt a button click free like a single popcorn kernel. She pulled the gun but it stayed. Didn't budge an inch. Was there a second strap? Somewhere lower, maybe, deeper inside, where she couldn't see? She brought in her left hand, fumbled, couldn't find it under his tucked shirt.

Five seconds.

The air drained away and turned cold. She tried again to pull the whole thing with brute force, the entire damn holster with the gun, but it was firmly attached to Glen's belt, and her fingers were too slimy with sweat to grip it – then a blast of pressurized air exploded in her face. Her eyes stung, her sunburnt cheeks felt slapped, and she heard the buzz louder in her right ear. Not unlike a jacket zipper, only much harder and faster. She fell backward, sprawling on her shoulders, hitting the back of her head on the road hard enough to spark flashbulbs, and all she saw was blue sky and a shower of gritty earth sprinkling back down around her.

"*Elle!*" her husband screamed, louder and sharper.

She watched the last bits of rock settle and realized some of it was sticky and wet. Like hot raindrops, Amazon showers, pattering loudly to the ground. Blood. She felt another surge of animal panic. Was it Glen's blood? Or hers? She hurled her head to the right and saw a red trench sliced up Glen's thigh, opening him up like meat. That's where it hit. The sniper's bullet had passed right over her elbow, or just below her armpit perhaps, and missed her by an eyelash.

"I'm okay," she gasped.

"Come back!" Roy shouted.

Run, she urged herself. *Now*. Forget the stupid gun. Get back to the car. Had she already spent a full second on the ground? Probably. She kicked, heaved sideways—

"Don't move!" James shouted.

She froze.

"Don't move," he said again, his voice small and distant. "He thinks he hit you."

She needed to move. Badly. She inched her right hand forward, tarantula-crawled her fingers over the road and miraculously found the revolver beside her. Yes! She must have yanked the little weapon free of whatever was snagging it when she tumbled backwards, somehow. She clasped her thumb and index finger around what she hoped was the safe end. How embarrassing would it be to accidentally shoot herself, here and now? *Here lies Elle Eversman: Shot at by a homicidal sniper. Shot herself to save him the trouble.*

"I have it," she said. "Glen's gun."

"Don't even talk," James said. "He might see your lips move."

Her chest was rising and falling with adrenalized breath – if the killer could see her lips move he could damn well see that, too. She felt her heartbeat again, swelling in her neck. She was starting to hate herself. She had no idea why she'd done this. What recklessness! And for what? She hadn't admitted it to James, but she'd never really believed that Glen had a gun on him. Even in her hand, she somehow doubted its existence. Like God, like an afterlife with wings and clouds and harps, it just felt too *easy* to be real.

Why had she run for it, then?

A warm wind passed over her, raising drifts of sand and peppering her dry eyes. Her contacts burned. She desperately wanted to rub them but knew it would be a dead giveaway. But what did it matter? The sniper might have already fired his next shot anyway. The supersonic bullet might already be racing toward her, right now, and she wouldn't know until it hit her.

"Don't breathe," James said.

She blinked once, twice, wincing from the sudden pain and digging her fingers into the road. Her elbow felt hot and damp where she'd scraped it. Somehow she sensed the crosshairs were back on her, if they'd ever left her at all, and she felt *his* eyes, silent patient eyes, moving up and down her body with piggish amusement, just like the Soviet Cowboy at the Fuel-N-Food. God, she hated being stared at.

"What do we do, James?"

"I'm thinking."

* * *

Tapp was thinking, too.

The wife had crumpled in that weightless, soundless way that bodies always did inside his scope. Part ragdoll, part muscle spasm. She had landed on her back beside the park ranger's corpse, arms flat at her sides. He saw a jetting

105

fog of pink but he couldn't ascertain an exact point of impact, so he leaned into his 100x spotting scope and scanned her nice little body for a wound. She was hyperventilating but struggling to control it. He saw the fingers of her left hand clawing and holding fistfuls of chalky dirt. He couldn't see what the right was doing.

Tapp figured he should shoot her again, in the head. To be humane.

The visceral pleasure of the shot – the impossible, wind-curving, against-all-odds shot – was unmatched, but watching the victim succumb to the damage was the uncomfortable and necessary evil that came with it. Yet another shooting myth nurtured by movies is the pleasant fantasy that a gunshot to the torso equals instant death. It doesn't, unless the heart is pulverized on impact, and even then the victim still has ten to twenty seconds of miserable awareness while their circulatory system depressurizes. Shot anywhere else in the torso, the human body takes its sweet time.

That was Tapp's first kill in a nutshell, back in the dewy Oregon field where he'd watched a nineteen-year-old hitchhiker in a brown Nirvana shirt choke to death on his own ribs. His breathing had sounded like fluorescent light rods crackling. His fingers had crunched into vulture claws. Mouthfuls of blood rising like tidewater. Tapp had turned away. He couldn't watch. He couldn't be near that awful fireworks display of human misery. Until you've actually killed a person, nothing can prepare you for how bad it will be.

Stay with me, Nirvana Shirt had said.

Tapp had been hunched over a fence, power-puking into the nettles. At first he'd thought he'd only imagined the hitchhiker's voice, or maybe he'd just hoped he had, but the second time was unmistakable: *Stay with me. Please.*

Nirvana Shirt hadn't even seemed upset. Certainly not angry. He was shivering, teeth clicking, and his face was graying out. He looked like he'd spent an hour in a walk-in freezer. So Tapp took a knee and awkwardly held the boy's hand. It had been excruciatingly uncomfortable, like square dancing, where you sometimes had to hold a guy's hand. And the damn false alarms! He'd kept looking like he was going to die – this is it, here comes the final breath – then he would swallow and stoically wheeze on.

Don't go, he gurgled.

I won't, Tapp said. *I'll stay with you.*

Another light rod fractured in his chest. *Thank you.*

What?

Thank you.

Certain this was a misunderstanding, Tapp said: *I did this to you.*

I know, Nirvana Shirt said peacefully.

That made Tapp angry. Or something – a white-hot flash of something stirred snake-like in his gut. He wasn't sure what reaction he had been hoping for (he still wasn't) but this quiet forgiveness sure wasn't it.

I did this to you, he told Nirvana Shirt again with more of a snarl: *I saw you crossing the field and I knew there was no one for miles, so I pulled over and grabbed my .270 and sat on the tailgate and shot you. On a lark. Like a split-second decision to pull off at a gas station for Cheetos, I ended your life. I did this to you, I destroyed your entire world, and it means almost nothing to me.*

I know, Nirvana Shirt said again with Christ-like peace. Then he had quietly died, somehow winning the argument forever.

Tapp would never be fully okay with killing. He had accepted that. Hadn't that guy on the news (the one in Reno, who cut up his aunt and uncle and baby twin sisters with a paper-cutter blade) said that he would have killed more if he hadn't been caught? He had grinned through his trial like a fat Cheshire cat with yellow teeth. That guy was a monster, a genuine piece of human garbage. He deserved the chair and got it last spring. Tapp knew he was something else, something better.

Yes. This woman has suffered enough.

Let's punch her ticket. Shall we?

Dust curled around the wife's body in smoky wisps. Her breathing had stilled and her hands had stopped moving. She stared straight up at the sky, her shoulders flat to the road, anguished but unmistakably alive.

Not for long. Like the blue-haired girl, Tapp would excuse her from a slow death of blood loss by splitting her head like a squashed melon. This, again, was the kindest gesture he could offer another—

Wait.

What's this?

* * *

James stood up.

Elle rolled onto her stomach, kicked up another swirl of dust, and looked at him with gaping horror. He saw the gun – *Oh my God, it exists* – a tiny black thing, clenched in her right hand. She tucked it in her back pocket.

"Run!" he screamed.

She hunched her legs, raised her heels, and launched into a dead sprint. She shouted something but he couldn't make it out. He felt like he was underwater. One ear rang, then the other.

Keep standing . . .

He turned to face the sniper. 'Feeling exposed' didn't do it justice. He felt like he might plunge off the surface of the earth at any moment and keep falling. The world was a colossal fishbowl, the horizon stretching in all directions and lazily curving to meet the infinite sky. A small, selfish part of his body urged him to sit back down – *That's enough, she'll make it* – but he swallowed it. His mind darted to memories of rock climbing, to the part where you'd scaled the artificial wall and now you had to let go. You fall into your belay rope so your partner can winch you back down. The fall of faith. It always looked easy from fifty feet below, until you're the idiot clinging to concrete and fiberglass by your fingers and toes. You had to ignore millions of years of evolved self-preservation instinct inside yourself, will your mind over your body, and just do it. That had been over two years ago and there sure as hell wasn't anything resembling a belay line here.

Keep standing . . .

I'm not afraid of you, he thought, which was a lie. He was terrified.

He heard Elle's footsteps racing back behind him, kicking a wake of hissing dust. She was close, almost back to safety. He couldn't turn around. He kept his eyes locked on that distant cliff rippling with heated air, on that invisible killer a mile away, who was certainly staring back at him now. He hoped he was making history here. He hoped that if the sniper did cut him down, he would never forget the one man who stood up and stared back.

Keep standing.

The wind tugged his shirt and hair, surprisingly cool. A sweat stain on the back of his shirt had turned freezing cold. The ringing in his ears became an ambulance siren. He knew enough time had passed now, at least two or three seconds, and that the sniper had to have pulled the trigger. He was certain that a mile across the crater, the end of his life was racing toward him at thousands of feet per second—

"James!"

She'd made it.

He threw himself to the road, back to earth and shadow. Sure enough, he felt the shot slice the air above him, buzzing like a hornet and snapping a concussive blast in his left ear, and he flinched only a little because he already knew he was alive and had literally just dodged a bullet. When he hit the ground beside the Rav4 she was already there. He wanted to tell her how stupid she was, how furious he was at her for risking everything, but words were weak and small and not enough. He grabbed the back of her neck, mashed her forward and kissed her, every inch of her goddamn stupid face. Her hands clasped the sides of his head, bracing hard, fingers squeezing. The report of the sniper shot came and went, but they didn't care.

He pressed his forehead to hers. She was laughing now – she tried to hold it in but blew a nasal snort – and shuddered with giddy chuckles, her hot breath on his face, a buoyant hymn of *holyshitthatworked*. He kissed her again and held her while the world bled away, and he whispered something in her ear almost beyond words, half-formed syllables floating in a sea of gasping breath, that only they understood.

I'm lost without you.

"Get the gun?" Roy asked.

She flashed a goofy smile and cradled the weapon in both hands. It was a revolver, blued steel and checkered wood battered with scrapes and dings. She pressed it toward James. He took it and was surprised that the weapon felt at once heavy and light. Maybe just dense. Or maybe its power made it feel heavier. Suddenly it all seemed within reach, the situation still fluid, the world still alive and thumping with possibility.

James looked at Roy's shirt. "Did you piss some excellence in your pants?"

"I . . . can't believe I did that."

"It still worked."

"I once jumped a thirty-foot creek on an Enduro bike." Roy's lip curled and he stared at the road between his knees. "I've never . . . I don't know, frozen like that before."

James immediately felt bad. "I'm sorry—"

110

"No." Roy beamed a signboard grin and forced a laugh. "It makes sense. I'm not afraid of hurting or dying, but I finally found something that truly scares me. I had to go all the way out here, in this asshole's personal shooting range to find it. Liza and I won't work, I've accepted that, but I can still be a dad to Emma. That's still on the table. And I want so badly to fix it. And I can't, because I'm stuck here, and if I die, it's all erased."

James touched his shoulder.

"I'm not afraid of dying," Roy said. "I'm afraid of dying an asshole."

"You won't. Alright?"

"Alright."

"We'll get out of here."

"Man," he sniffed. "Your wife has *balls*."

James hesitated. "That's . . . please word that differently."

Roy laughed uncomfortably.

"Here." James handed him the revolver and gladly let the burden shift. "I hate guns."

Roy grabbed it with his finger on the trigger and aimed up the road, scrunching one eye and sticking out his tongue as he aligned the stubby little sights. Then he lowered it and thumbed a button on the left (guns have their own language, and the initiated seem to be able to pick up any model and intuit its operation) and the central cylinder rotated a few inches out. In it, he saw five golden bullets seated in a circle, gleaming in the sun. Five?

Roy made a sour face.

"Don't they usually hold six?" James asked.

"I wish that was our problem."

"What's our problem?"

Roy huffed and threw the gun back.

James caught it with both hands. "What?"

"You tell me."

Uncomfortable with it in his possession again, he studied the five brass circles. He noted the smooth twirl of the cylinder, the .38 SPECIAL stamped on the perimeter of each bullet, and . . . *Oh, no.* A tiny metallic ping impressed in the center of each one.

"See?"

James nodded numbly.

One of his earliest memories was of a party in his parents' farmhouse. He had crawled on a blotted carpet through a forest of legs, searching for his mother. He couldn't have been more than six, but he knew that when his father was with his friends that he'd be ignored. That was the way it was. The Anti-Weathermen were serious business. The Tip-over was coming, ready or not.

There was one man in particular at this gathering – tall, skeletal shoulders, dark as ebony, with a polished head – that all the others, even James' father, seemed frightened of. Everyone watched and hushed when the Tall Man was near because something about him, or something he had recently done, made him dangerous and toxic. When he walked through the crowded living room, Diet Coke in hand, the others parted like water breaking off the bow of a ship. And he was walking toward James.

At that age he didn't like to look adults in the eye, but the Tall Man took a knee to his level. The crowd spread in a circle around them, voices lowered to a murmur. The man gently took James' hand with knuckled fingers and opened it, palm up. Then with a smile of piano-white teeth, he produced a single brass bullet casing and placed it upright in his hand. The Tall Man said something too quiet to hear, closed James' tiny fingers around it, and then he was gone. James had studied the tiny ping in the center of the shell for a long time before his father noticed and snatched it away without a word. He never learned the story behind it. By the time he was old enough to ask meaningful questions, his father had been dead for years, and the Tip-over had never happened anyway.

What did it matter? You can't rationalize evil. Like the Tall Man, or the Soviet Cowboy, it just *is*.

"Is it—"

Roy nodded.

Five spent cartridges. Elle had risked her life for an empty gun.

"Oh, no." He stared at the weapon. "Elle, we—"

He noticed something on the heel of the gun's grip, a sidelong brushstroke of blood, and immediately knew it wasn't Glen's. The old man's blood had long ago browned and cracked under the sun. This was fresh, oxygenated, pulsing with bright red life, and had only been spilled in the last minute.

He turned to Elle.

She had fallen silent. He realized that she hadn't spoken at all for the last few moments. She held both hands out as she had when she presented the revolver to him, and stared mystified at them. There was suddenly much more blood, a thin stream running down her wrist and beading between her fingers. He followed it up her arm to her chest, to just below her armpit, where her shirt was clinging and soaked.

The sniper hadn't missed her after all.

She sighed and it sounded wet and thick, like water running down a plugged sink drain. "Well, this sucks."

10

Tapp stacked his .338 casings in a tidy, single-file row, toppled one, and realized his fingers were trembling.

How had they learned so much, so fast? They knew the bullet's flight time. They knew where he was. They knew how fast he could fire. And they had used all of these factors against him and misdirected his attention twice. He had been humiliated by three strangers cowering behind a disabled car. Nothing would undo that. Like shooting paper targets, that hole was there forever.

He strained to replay Sergei Koal's awed words about him being a demon but didn't feel any better because, of course, there were no gods or demons. There was only this charming little accident that is the universe, expanding to its heat death. Life existed only here on this rock, only by chance, not for long (atheism: the ultimate non-prophet organization). And on this godless little rock, William Tapp had just screwed up.

Are they laughing at me?

Laugh all you want. You're still going to die.

His naked eye saw Svatomir's jeep as a tiny dot following the hairline Shady Slope Road, chugging up the valley wall to the survivors. He tried to muster some shivery excitement – he'd tow the Toyota away and then they'd all be his, three easy little squeezes, gouts of red, joints flopping unnaturally, bodies pirouetting under spurts of gravel – but realized this simply wasn't fun anymore. Somehow it had become work. It was worse than work, he decided, because now his emotions were tangled up in it and he had something to lose.

They're not laughing. They're too frightened.

Probably.

He wished he could just enjoy this without brutalizing himself in pursuit of the perfect day of shooting. It was ridiculous, he knew, to flagellate himself over every minor error. Mistakes happened, winds kicked up, decimals rounded off funny. It was the nature of the craft. This was supposed to be fun. Why else would he be doing it?

This is fun. Right?

Yes. You could say I'm having . . . a blast.

He crunched his energy drink empty and chucked it downhill. He would need to urinate soon, but first he had to take three more lives.

* * *

"He's coming back," Roy said.

James leaned his wife on her back against his shoulder. She was breathing fast, gulping down greedy mouthfuls of air. "I can't breathe," she said, and her voice sounded wrong. Somehow it was too small, squished, like someone was standing on her chest. He tugged her clawed fingers but they were clamped vise-tight.

"I said the jeep is coming back!" Roy pointed furiously. "He's maybe two minutes down the road—"

115

"Then we have a hundred and twenty seconds to decide how we're going to kill him." James fought her hands and finally found the wound. "This is *right now.*"

It was a small hole, just below her armpit and above the curve of her tank top. Maybe the size of a dime – the entrance wound? – flanked with a growing halo of frothy blood. It was much smaller than either hole in Saray's stomach. He had been certain the killer's bullet had missed Elle. Maybe it had?

"I think it's a fragment," he said. "From when the bullet hit the ground under her, it exploded into pieces and—"

"Are you a fucking doctor now?" Roy said.

No, but I have a hundred and ten seconds to learn.

"Can't breathe," she said again and grabbed his collarbone and squeezed. Her other hand closed into a fist and pounded her chest hard. Hard enough to crack ribs. With every breath she took, he heard a persistent, reptilian hiss. Like air escaping a wet balloon. And then a low gurgle, like the sound a toilet makes after flushing. She arched her back, kicked clattering rocks against the Toyota, and fought his grasp.

"Elle!"

She thrashed like she was trapped in a straitjacket, eyes wide with animal panic, and he saw her chest visibly tense as her lungs compressed further. She was in her own version of Hell. He knew this was her ultimate nightmare because she had described it to him once – that she was trapped under a capsized canoe and the chest strap of her lifejacket was tangled in deadwood and she was sucking in cold mouthfuls of green water. Here she was, drowning in the Mojave.

"Elle. Stop moving—"

She threw her shoulders back, he lost his hold on the wound, and he saw now that the blood was different. It was frothy and pink as cotton candy, bubbling like sea

116

foam or hand soap. A big glop of it slid free and stained her shirt. She exhaled, the foamy blood sucked back into the wound, and the term – the sloppy layman's term, because that was all he had – flashed through James' mind.

A sucking chest wound.

The vacuum of her chest cavity was punctured. Simple physics. Her lungs couldn't inflate because outside air was inside her, and every time her lungs exhaled, more crept in to fill the space. Every breath she took would be a little shallower until she suffocated inside her own body. If James had been a paramedic, he would have had a gadget called a flutter valve – a one-way valve that affixed to the wound and let air out but not in. James was not a paramedic. Not even close.

"James." She threw her head back, her hair splashed across soil, and her eyes searched for his. He wouldn't look at her. He couldn't. He was deep in thought. She pulled his face to hers, both of her bloody hands sticky on his cheeks. Who wanted to die alone? He wanted to look at her but he couldn't. He needed to be mechanical, to reach deep inside his skull and *think*.

Flutter valve: noun. A one-way valve allowing air out, but not in.

"Roy?" he whispered.

"Yeah?"

"In the back of the car, by the black bag, there's a roll of duct tape. And there are old sandwich bags under the front seats." He was shocked by how calm he sounded, like he was ordering lunch. "I need both of them."

"What are you doing?"

"I haven't thought that far ahead yet."

"Are you serious?"

"Do it."

Roy crawled for the Toyota's rear door. James turned to his wife and saw her looking up at him with a strange gleam in her eyes. She had something important to say.

117

"Don't talk," he told her. "Save it."

She shook her head.

Behind him, Roy opened the Rav4's rear door and it made that familiar double-creak that it had made ever since he'd first opened it on the dealership lot. For some reason it hit him now, that this was really happening and that tomorrow, if there was a tomorrow, would still exist in this world. This corrupted version of the world, where Elle had caught a bullet fragment and suffocated to death inside her own body. Worse than being only real, this was permanent. Nothing would undo this.

She opened her mouth again like she was about to speak and instead made a thin, wheezy gasp, like a zombie. It didn't sound real. It was so B-movie cheesy it should have been a joke. Why couldn't this all just be a joke?

Her eyes widened, as if she was also horrified by the sound.

"Don't talk," he repeated, and his eyes clouded. "It's a waste, because you're just going to tell me something I already know. I love you, too. It's redundant."

She smiled dumbly. Her eyes were looking up at him but also beyond him, through him. All the fear she'd had a moment ago was now gone, replaced by a strange, insidious calm that he didn't trust. She was almost smiling, which terrified James: *You don't smile when you're holding on. You smile when you're letting go.*

"I can't find the tape," Roy said. "I can't—"

"Under the cover."

Elle parted her lips and found her voice again. It was only a shadow of the real thing, made by a few mouthfuls of scrounged air. Like a pneumonia death rattle: "I . . . I miss my snakes."

He smiled. "Not the snakes, Elle."

"I miss them so much," she said. "I miss them."

"Not . . ." He forced a scratchy laugh. "Not the damn *snakes.*"

"My babies."

She'd had two. Gray was an eight-foot Colombian Redtail Boa her mother had bought for her when she was sixteen. He was a gentle giant, all mass and muscle, with a smooth dryness to his scales and an inquisitive tongue that felt like dry grass on your fingertips. Elle had sat on the patio with a horror novel in her lap and that huge-ass snake draped over her shoulders like a nightmarish scarf. He ate rabbits. Elle purchased them at her reptile store humanely pre-killed and frozen in neatly labeled plastic bags, complete with nutritional facts. He remembered laughing with her for the entire drive home after finding a fine print disclaimer underneath: NOT FOR HUMAN CONSUMPTION.

Her other one, Iris, was a corn snake. Much smaller, shorter, leaner; a shelter rescue after the previous owner left her unsupervised with a feeder mouse. *We will never feed ours live prey,* Elle had insisted. *Almost all snakes can be trained to eat pre-killed. Mashing two animals together in a box to fight is disrespectful to both predator and prey.* Ironically, in the case of Iris, it was the prey that had gained the upper hand. The mouse had chewed nasty gashes along Iris's vertebrae that never regrew scales. They just became pale scars, like wax to the touch. She was a timid little pink snake, head-shy, terrified of being hurt again, and prone to whipping her tiny face under her coils when frightened. Elle took a special liking to Iris.

Eight months ago, she'd sold both Gray and Iris after the doctor had suggested her miscarriages were due to toxicity levels from reptile bacteria. It hadn't helped.

"You hated my snakes," she said sleepily.

"No." He brushed her hair from her cheek and lied to her. "I didn't."

"You never held them. Why?"

"Gray snapped at me."

"He thought your hand was a rabbit."

119

"*That's* why."

"I think I'm dying," she said flatly.

"You're not."

"I feel dead already. It's weird."

"You're not." He knew his words weren't enough anymore.

She smiled grimly and her next sentence took two breaths. "Do you really believe all the optimistic crap you say?"

Yes, he wanted to say, but he didn't. He couldn't. He was all out of bullshit for today. In a rare moment of naked honesty, he shook his head.

"Me neither," she said.

It hurt. He had always known it, but hearing it hurt.

Her eyes lost focus. It was shocking how abruptly it happened. It was like a switch had flipped and her brain unplugged. She was there – Eileen Lynne Eversman, the girl who loved gory movies and hated cilantro and couldn't quite grasp why everyone loved the Batman remakes so much – and then she sank back into her skull and suddenly wasn't. He leaned back, the sunlight hit her face, and only then did he realize how gray she had become. The blue pallor of suffocation made her look like she was underwater and sinking fast.

"Roy!" he shouted. "Where the *fuck* are you?"

The guy kneeled down hard behind him and pressed duct tape and a single crumpled sandwich bag into his fingers. James didn't know what he was expecting – he should have expected exactly this and nothing better – but his heart sank when these little objects jittered in his hands. They told him nothing new. He snapped the clear plastic taut and shook off breadcrumbs from the day before, back when the world made sense, and whispered to himself: "One-way valve. Air goes out. Not in."

"The jeep," Roy said. "He's almost here."

Please work.

"You're okay, honey." One side at a time, he folded the plastic into an approximate square and pressed it to the foamy wound. Then he pulled one, two, three short strips of duct tape, tearing each one with his teeth, and slapped one on the left side of the square, the right side, and finally the bottom, just above her blood-soaked tank top. His fingers were numb, barely responsive, like he was wearing gloves. He pressed each one airtight against her soft skin, but importantly, he left the top edge of the square open (very important, *most* important). Three sides sealed and one open.

"What are you doing?" Roy asked.

"Quiet."

"You forgot a side—"

"Shut up." His teeth chattered. He needed to hear it work.

Please, God, let it work.

He watched her, sleeping serenely with her head lolled against the door, and waited for her to breathe. When she did, he could watch the plastic and check his work. Only problem was, she wasn't breathing.

Oh, no.

No, no, no.

He watched her lying doll-still. She looked used, spent, hollow. For some reason, James' next thought wasn't about his wife at all. He just wanted to stand up. He wanted to stand up like she had suggested, to just get up and walk like poor Glen and wait for the bullet. He couldn't spend another second in a world without Elle.

Suicide suddenly sounded reasonable. It hadn't, that awful time he'd found her drunk in the Subaru. He had been so furious at her then, but maybe he'd just never understood how much she hurt. He had grieved for their kids too, of course, but only as possibilities and vacant names. She had actually felt the life growing inside her, and then felt it die on a cellular level, every time. Maybe he understood now.

Then Elle breathed.

She inhaled and air squeezed through the top edge with a fluttering whistle. Air going out. Then she exhaled, her lungs relaxed, and the plastic snapped tight to the wound to form suction. No air going in. James felt a hot bubble of breath in his throat and quietly watched this timid little miracle happen again, and again, and again. If he tore his eyes away, he feared it might stop.

A one-way valve. With duct tape and a plastic bag.

Roy chewed his lip. "Did it work?"

"I hope so."

"They say duct tape has a million uses, but I think that's a new one."

James was numbly aware of the drone of an engine and the chirp of tightening brakes as the Soviet parked his jeep just a few yards down the road. He ignored it. It would only be a problem thirty seconds from now. He watched Elle, only Elle, the most important thing in his world, and waited.

"Hey, James." Roy rose to a crouch. "Blackbeard. He's here."

"I know."

"We have to think of a way to fight him."

"Give me a minute."

"We don't have a minute." Roy stared at the revolver between them and made a disgusted face. "And who the hell carries an empty gun?"

James ignored him. It didn't matter how right Roy was, that it didn't make sense at all. Five spent cartridges, all inside Glen's revolver, carefully tucked back inside his holster. Why would an off-duty Montana park ranger carry a weapon like that? And what was he doing in Nevada? Then he realized Elle's eyes were open, darting and alive, scanning the bright sky and finding him.

James forgot everything and just stared back.

She grinned goofily, without the slightest trace of self-consciousness, like she had just pounded four Lemon Drops and was beginning a slow slide off her bar stool. He grabbed her hands, squeezed, and couldn't help but laugh, too. Huge, fake-sounding belly laughs, like a sitcom studio audience. Even though they were trapped in this hellish valley and there was an armed man twenty feet away, preparing to tow away the only thing keeping them alive – one victory at a time, right? And this was one hell of a victory. He kissed her forehead.

"I dreamt you saved us," she said.

"Not yet." He smiled shyly. "Working on it."

"Are we real?"

He held her, brushed her hair from her eyes and kissed the bridge of her nose, feeling her eyelashes flutter, and knowing that this incredible person had almost been deleted from the world by something as careless as a dumb-luck ricochet. "Yeah," he told her. "We're real."

Down the road, the Soviet kicked his door open.

11

His heart a marching band, Tapp inserted a fresh magazine and savored the way it glided in and locked. Ten double-stacked .338 handloads on deck, golden and eager. Plus an eleventh already chambered, snug to the micrometer, waiting only for his permission and the surgical strike of the firing pin. As he watched Svatomir step out his jeep under a billow of pale dust, he unshackled his mind and allowed it to wander a few paces. He returned to some of his greatest hits; little freeze-dried memories which still offered a jolt of pleasure.

I shouldn't.

It's sort of wrong—

One, many years back, had been a running headshot at 1,100 meters. He spoke in numbers but for his life he couldn't recall the angle, the crosswinds, the elevation – he only remembered the way he'd felt when he saw her head burst like a popped zit. Intense, chocolate delight. You could say it was . . . *mind-blowing.* Somehow the fact that she had been attractive (about an eight out of ten) made destroying her face even more gratifying. Why was that?

No more.

Focus.

Another good one had been a college student with the mop of black hair and a trunk full of social studies textbooks. Bound for law school, maybe? The kill itself had been one of those happy accidents, where a standard center-mass shot took an odd curve and instead double-jointed the kid's arm halfway from the elbow (walk like an Egyptian!). Gnarly. Tapp had done the right thing and finished him quick.

That's enough.

But the best one was—

Enough.

But the best shot of all had a bitter taste to it, because it had been a ten-year-old girl. It had happened last year. Svatomir's reconnaissance had missed her because she was curled up in the backseat under a Navajo blanket while her parents drove. She woke to her father's head splitting and then the Volvo rolled twice in a curtain of gravel and glass. The mother climbed out through the windshield and Tapp broke her spine. That left the girl, a fifth-grader maybe, staggering from the car and running up the hill with tears in her eyes and chunks of hamburger in her hair. She wasn't even following Shady Slope Road. She was running just to run. Everyone runs. Even children, apparently.

Meanwhile Tapp had screamed, cried, punched rock, ground his teeth until a filling broke. Svatomir babbled excuses in his useless half-English until Tapp tore off his headset off and threw it. He'd tasted a sea tide of stomach acid climbing his throat as that little girl fled further and further into his glass world, and he was dragged violently toward that moment.

I don't kill kids.

Why not, though? Why hold anything sacred in a meaningless universe full of dead stars? We're all dust. It was a relic of a younger, dumber Tapp who held dying hitchhikers' hands. He had no reason to value the life of a child over any other life. They haven't been alive as long. Why should that entitle them to anything?

Doesn't matter. I don't kill kids.

But this one was getting away. Christ, she must have run cross-country or something. Already she was over two kilometers from Tapp, further than he had ever engaged a human target. She was well past the rim of the crater and was now at the point where scrubland becomes scabland. Where wiregrass and yuccas gives way to exposed rocks and bald mountains. Another thirty seconds and she would be lost in the churning land with one hell of a head start. Dumb luck or not, from there she had a chance of finding the highway. That was when it stopped being a choice.

I don't kill kids—

He did. He blew her lungs out at 2,106 meters. His longest kill ever.

I hated it.

He had loved it. Remembered now, it still felt undeniably good. The feedback, the messy feedback that tells the animal part of your brain before your thoughts can even assemble – ding, ding, ding, hit! Even though the impact was soundless he swore he was there inside it. He could taste the metallic blood and feel the bone fragments crackle between his molars. He was ashamed of how good it felt.

Tapp lived for this, his special brand of wet violence, and as clouds gathered in the western sky he decided that was okay. He could stop whenever he wanted. He only did this once or twice a year. He chose his scenarios and victims carefully, like a vampire living in plain sight. That demonstrated real control, unlike the paper cutter killer from Reno or Svatomir's idiot cousin.

"Let's do it," he said firmly. "Tow the car."

Svatomir nodded in his scope.

Tapp's mind rubber-banded back to the wife, bolting to the ranger's body and returning. Her hands had been empty. He had only seen flattened fingers in a slicing runner's form. She had recovered nothing from the old man. But obviously she had wanted to grab something.

What if she has the ranger's gun?

She doesn't.

But what if she does?

It's not loaded.

What if it is?

* * *

"Kill him," Elle whispered sleepily. "Kill him."

James nodded.

"Maybe . . ." Roy tensed. "When he gets close I can take him."

"I'll back you up," James said in his best bar-fight voice.

"Okay."

Roy was a big guy. Not as tall or as WWF barrel-chested as the Soviet, but James was glad the kid was on his side. If nothing else, his swelling jaw told him that Roy knew how to deliver a punch. That was something.

"He'll be close," James whispered. "When he hooks the cable."

Roy nodded.

"That's when. No sooner, no later."

"Okay."

James didn't like making the calls. He didn't even know how the hell it had happened. He, the soft-handed salesman who'd once considered scrubbing his palms with steel wool, was now in charge of a bloody coup against two psychotic killers. And Roy, the burly alpha male from this neck of the woods, was listening and obeying. When had that started happening? And more importantly, when would it stop happening?

The Soviet approached. His shadow crept past the Toyota's front bumper and grew taller, darker, with sharper edges. James heard the man's crunching footsteps, the metallic creak of unspooling cable, and the gentle hiss of cowhide packed around a sweaty body and expanding and contracting with every breath. Another sound, too – like skeleton hands clapping. Working his jaw, maybe.

"Wait," Roy hissed. "We can surprise him with the gun—"

The shadow froze mid-step.

James raised a trembling index finger – *For the sake of everything, shut the hell up!* He could see the top of the Soviet's head through the Rav4's pierced windshield, bisected by two jagged cracks. The man stood ten feet away. His eyes were down and something was inching through his reptilian brain. He was replaying and processing what he'd heard, or thought he'd heard. He hunched a bit, bobbed out of view like a shark slipping underwater, and let out a sticky black cough.

Roy looked at James with panic in his eyes.

It was becoming clear that this empty gun was a massive liability and nothing more. It was a situation escalator. The microsecond the Soviet saw it he would open fire and they, all three of them, would be mulched to bloody ribbons against the Toyota. All done. Roll credits. Audience rises, demands money back.

James grimly decided that they needed to grab him when he attached the winching cable and then pull him down behind the car. And keep him there, out of the sniper's view, while they (hopefully) overpowered the big man. It might have seemed plausible sixty seconds ago but not anymore. He held the pepper spray in his right hand. Crappy Korean multitool blade in his left. Then he sank to his knees, heels arched, coiled to lunge. Time was moving strangely now, at once too fast and too slow. The Soviet would either walk into the trap or he wouldn't. It was all out of his hands now, out of Roy's hands, what that hesitant shadow would decide to do.

Come on.

The shadow stood still.

Come on, you asshole.

The right arm raised with a leathery creak, fingers opened spiderlike on the road, and the winching cable dropped. The hook clattered.

What?

Roy looked at James.

"I don't know," he mouthed. "I think—"

Footsteps approaching.

The Soviet paced a wide circle around the Toyota and the shadow grew taller, taller, moving away . . . until they finally saw the man, all of nearly seven feet of him, a walking silhouette under the fiery sun. He watched them over his shoulder as he closed the loop and halted maybe ten, twelve feet up the road. Hanging loose in his right hand was a stubby machine pistol with a stick magazine, all right angles and cheaply stamped aluminum, scarred with oily discoloration and razor-thin scratches. It looked illegal. Untouchable in the sunlight, the Soviet fixed his eyes on them and slowly lowered to a crouch on the gravel. His other hand disappeared inside his duster, eyes forward, striking an oddly balletic pose of predatory focus.

Ten feet away. Too far to pepper spray.

He knows we have a gun, James thought coldly.

"I can feel his eyes on me," Elle whispered in dreamy singsong.

James tightened his hands into fists behind his back, feeling that sense of powerlessness reach a frustrating new peak. The pepper spray and multitool were concealed for now. Not that it made a difference – the Soviet had a machine gun. Maybe he could arc the pepper spray a bit, aim high and rain it into the man's eyes? Wishful thinking.

"What's he doing?" his wife whispered.

"I don't know."

The Soviet pulled a yellowed notebook from an inner pocket of his duster. It was crinkled and ragged. It was the notebook from the Fuel-N-Food on the outskirts of Mosby, forever ago. He tucked the machine pistol under his elbow, thumbed the pages, and chewed a pencil that had materialized in his hand from nowhere. He spat a glob of charcoal on the road and James realized his eyes were on Elle again, only Elle, as if she was the last woman on earth.

"I hate being watched," she said softly.

"I know." James desperately wished he had bought her the damn ten-foot pepper spray last Christmas. "Trust me. Just trust me."

She buried her face in his shoulder.

"Third best," the Soviet said abruptly.

Silence.

James stared blankly.

"Third best," the Soviet said again. His voice was toneless, uninflected, like a teenager dryly reciting literature he didn't care for. He didn't seem to hear his own words. He layered them with no emotion or subtext. He meant exactly what he said and nothing more.

James realized that the Soviet was holding his notebook up and out, and he didn't remember seeing it open. Under the man's black fingernails, flapping just a little in the breeze, hung another drawing. There was an inherent beauty in charcoal art; James had always admired the contrast of dagger-sharp lines meeting the watercolor blur of thumbed shadows, and there was plenty of that to appreciate here. It was too far away to discern, even if he squinted, but it looked like a car, a sedan, hurled on its side with bruised doors and messy divots in the ground where it had tumbled.

"Too far away," James said, but the Soviet ignored him. He was staring at Elle.

She didn't speak. Had she passed out again?

"Second best." The man licked his lips, quickly flipped pages and showed a new one. Again, too far away to tell. It looked like a black and white rendition of . . . a city skyline, maybe? Steep angles and corners shaded in deep darkness, with lots of negative space.

No one spoke.

The big man exhaled with frustration, tilted the notepad back toward himself, and scanned crackling pages forward and back for a long minute before deciding on another and revealing it with a showman's flourish. "First best," he said with a grin. Like a child presenting a glowing report card.

James narrowed his eyes but couldn't make it out at twelve feet. He didn't even have the energy to imagine what it might be. It looked like a mushy inkblot test of confused shapes.

"Just tow the car," Roy said. "Please."

The Soviet slapped his notebook shut and stuffed the mess back inside his duster. His eyes looked hurt now, and James felt a strange twinge of sympathy. Even psychos felt the sting of a mediocre review. Hell, maybe psychos felt it worse.

"I like that one," Elle said.

He looked up at her.

She hesitated. "I . . . it's good."

He canted his head, skeptical but also, like all artists, eternally hopeful.

She raised a hand, palm out, and lowered her voice: "Bring it closer."

12

It went beautifully at first.

At the last moment, the Soviet Cowboy stuffed his machine pistol into his duster so he could present the drawing to Elle on his outstretched hand. James memorized that spot. Then Roy, from the left, grabbed the man's wrist and tugged him off-balance. James came up from the right with the pepper spray. The red button depressed easily with a visceral clack, and a jet of grey liquid sprayed across the Soviet's left shoulder, slapping and splashing off oilcloth – James found his aim as he found his footing – and then arced it up at the man's beard, pressure-washing his front teeth, shooting up his nose, blowing back a tangle of hair. The Soviet slapped a hand to his face, way too late to stop any of it.

Elle screamed something.

Suddenly pepper spray was everywhere. Everywhere. It was like opening Pandora's Box, and the box was full of goddamn pepper spray. It filled the air, turned it solid, and James was instantly engulfed. He felt crystalline grains under his eyelids, digging into the soft whites of his eyes.

Hot tears on his cheeks. He tasted habanero peppers, wheelbarrows full of habanero peppers, stuffing his mouth and ramming spicy flakes up his nostrils and deep into his sinuses. Head down, world spinning, he heard Roy beside him, somehow fighting through the chemical burn, still going strong, beating the hell out of the Soviet with the soft slap of knuckles pounding flesh, bone, teeth.

James forced his eyes open and saw only silhouettes behind falling water.

The Soviet head-butted Roy with a wet crack, threw his shoulders back, his wrist slipped free of Roy's grip – "He's getting away!" – and he staggered out of the Toyota's safe shadow, grunting and huffing globs of snot and drool, right out into the untouchable open air.

James went after him.

Kill him.

He followed him, multitool in hand, riding a surge of adrenaline, no time to think. He didn't play contact sports – he hadn't tackled anyone since grade school – but dammit, he tackled the Soviet at the shoulders and brought him down sideways. It felt thunderous, brain-jarring. Next second they were both on the packed dirt, rolling and kicking, James on top, blinking back waves of incendiary tears. The man's notepad had burst open. Papers fluttered and scattered around them in a whirlwind.

Stab him.

He fumbled for the blade and it nearly twirled free while the Soviet thrashed under him with clawed hands to his face. His wrists covered his neck, most of his face was protected, but his fingers were pulling his eyelids sideways in a forced squint. His eyes were exposed. The multitool was suddenly so sharp, gleaming with hungry sunlight. It would pierce an eyeball like jelly. It would tunnel right in. It had to happen. It needed to happen. The Soviet would die quickly. It would be easier for both of them. So why hadn't James done it yet?

The sniper was watching. Crosshairs tingled on the back of his neck.

Stab him in the eye.

But something in him wouldn't allow it. He couldn't. Eyes were special to James. Always had been. It didn't matter who owned them or what evil resided behind them. He flinched and gagged at the thought of hurting them, puncturing their gently distended surfaces with unsympathetic metal, bursting them like grapes between teeth. Eyes were our link to the world. Windows to the soul. The Soviet struggled harder, and a blind swipe jangled his teeth. Windswept yellow papers swirled around them.

Out of time.

He stabbed the Soviet in the stomach. It slid in easily. The man squirmed, kicked, and clamped both hands to the multitool handle flopping in his gut like a gross little flagpole. He made very little noise; just an eerie hiss through crooked teeth.

I did it, he realized. *Oh my God, I did it.*

More than a second had passed. A bullet could be coming—

Stab him again.

The last of the loose papers fluttered to the road, revealing a cold silence and that pitiful wounded hiss. Time smeared. James tried to focus, tried to cut through the sweaty panic and think—

Pull the multitool out and stab him again.

He fought for the tool's handle but the Soviet's knuckles were fastened around it now. The man lay tense, impossibly tense, spine arched, all muscles tightened, quietly biting down on his tongue until red bubbled through his teeth. No anguished cuss or cry of pain. Only that damn inhuman hiss, like the Dumeril ground boa at the reptile store where Elle had once worked – a current of air rushing from cold-blooded lungs. There was fear in it, but that only made it more menacing. The tiny knife had penetrated maybe two inches into his flabby stomach. It wouldn't kill him; it would only infuriate him. Never wound what you can't kill.

"James!" Roy shouted. Then something else.

He heard whooshing air as he went for the Soviet's gun. He had to. He had no choice now. It was kill or die. He threw open the man's duster, drawing the oilcloth tight to the multitool handle and ripping it out of the man's gut. It made a sound like smacking lips and skipped across the gravel, dark with blood. James searched for that gun, feathered his fingertips over something metal, or at least hard polymer, buried in—

The Soviet punched him in the neck.

White flared behind his eyes. His windpipe stung with a gasp of air rushing down a vacuum – having the wind knocked out of you was even more painful in an arid atmosphere – and suddenly he was on the ground, on his ass, staring dumbly at Windex-blue sky and Elle was screaming behind him. *Everything's okay,* he would have consoled her if he'd had the air to speak, *I have his gun.* He had the Soviet's machine pistol in his hand. He knew it. It was heavy, dense, block-like.

How many seconds had it been?

"James!" Elle screamed. Terror in her voice. "Come back!"

He threw himself back and somersaulted into the Rav4's safe shadow, slamming into the driver door, and he sucked in a second helping of bone-dry air, whirled around, and wrenched the stolen weapon forward with two knuckled hands to aim it at the Soviet. The shape immediately registered wrong – rectangular. He realized it was a radio. He was holding a radio.

Really?

A radio. The man's trail duster was probably bulging with guns and James had reached in and grabbed the one goddamn walkie-talkie in it.

The Soviet Cowboy was doubled over on his knees now. He held his right hand stiffly to his flank, high under his left arm, where his gun actually was. His watery eyes slid open and fixed on the three of them. James wondered why he hadn't shot them to hell yet. Shouldn't they all be dead by now? Then he recognized something he had never expected to find in the man's eyes, not in a million years – the frozen fear of an animal facing danger and recalculating its options.

The Soviet wasn't even looking at James. He was looking behind James.

"Alright," Elle said, calmer now. "I have him."

He turned and saw her sitting with her white fingers wrapped around Glen's stubby revolver, her eyes set, her teeth bared.

James realized no one had told her the gun was empty.

13

Elle didn't want to shoot him but feared she would have to.

She aligned the blocky sights, mating the u-shaped rear to the squared front just as her sister had taught her. Although this was a wheel gun and not one of Eowen's smooth automatics, the fundamentals seemed to be the same. The sights snapped together like Legos and she pulled the interlocking steel up and over the man's face to obscure all but his glistening forehead. She was still half-out, a little dizzy, and desperately willed her body and mind to pull together.

Her wrist trembled a little. Only a little. She had it under control.

The trick, Eowen had told her over a skunkish porter homebrewed in a giant glass carboy, *is to allow your target to blur. Let your eyes just . . . fall out of focus on the target, and the rear sight as well, while your front sight remains absolutely clear, hard as quartz.*

She did that now.

"Elle," James whispered beside her. "Don't shoot him."

She blinked sunlight from her eyes, saw the reds of her eyelids, and steadied her aim with a second hand. She made sure not to do the movie hold – the *cup and saucer hold*, Eowen had called it with a crinkled nose, wherein the actor clearly has no firearm experience and is merely cradling the weapon like a teacup. She squeezed the thing too, because that's what you're supposed to do – squeeze it until your palms are checkered white. Her fingers were strangely dry, as if coated in chalk dust or that stuff James used to put on his hands while rock climbing. Back on the gun range in Oklahoma, her hands had dripped with nervous sweat. Her sister had teased her for that, too – *I'm sorry. Is this offending your liberal Californian sensibilities?*

That had always been a gulf in their relationship. Eowen didn't *not* like James – or at least, she never fessed up to it – but whatever playful criticisms she had for Elle's blue state life had always seemed to come back to her husband. His embarrassingly well-paying office job, his unassertive presence, his self-deprecating jokes. As if she expected Elle to marry a cowboy? The last time they had visited her in the wheat field outskirts of Tulsa, Eowen's on-again, off-again boyfriend had tried to talk cars with James. When that hadn't worked, he'd tried baseball. Finally, they'd discussed beer, of which James drank only Bud Light. Worst guy-talk ever. It had been excruciating.

"Elle," James said again with a strange desperation rising in his voice. "Elle, don't."

She felt another wave of disorientation. She shook her head and the world shook with her. Her tongue burned with peppers. Her heart pumped angrily, blooming in her eardrums, and she felt as if an invisible hand was crammed invasively inside her chest with fingers wrapped around her right lung and slowly, oh-so-slowly, squeezing. With every breath she heard a crinkle of plastic under her arm

and sensed a whisper of moving air. James had engineered
. . . *something* there that seemed to operate on Looney
Tunes physics. It didn't seem real. *Am I real? Is this real?*
She couldn't remember anything after sprinting back to the
safety of the Rav4 and finding her tank top suddenly slick
with blood. She felt displaced, as if she had time-traveled
through surgical anesthesia or a night of brutal drinking.

The Soviet clasped one hand to his belly where James
had stabbed him. She saw a greasy splotch on his duster, as
if his blood was part crude oil. His other hand, the one
that frightened her, hovered by his flank with his fingers
busily kneading air. Like a cowboy in an old movie, fixing
to draw. She could read his little mind. Right now the man
was considering precisely how fast, in fractions of seconds,
he could draw his chunky little weapon and hose them
with automatic fire.

Her index finger hadn't touched the trigger until now.
It was one of Eowen's cardinal rules: *Never touch the trigger
unless you're about to fire.*

Elle was about to fire.

"No!" James grabbed her wrist but she barely felt it.
"Elle, don't shoot him."

"His hand is on his gun," she said.

It was. The Soviet had already parted his duster and the
butt of his machine pistol glimmered in the shoulder
holster. His eyes were still locked on her but his
outstretched fingers were doing that feathery dance just a
few inches from the weapon—

"Stop!" she shouted. She didn't recognize her voice.
"Stop or I shoot."

He touched steel with one index finger.

"*Stop.* Don't move."

One by one, the Soviet extended his other fingers and
wrapped them comfortably around the weapon's grip. His
eyes never left her, and she forced herself not to look
away. How she hated eye contact . . .

139

"I said don't move." The revolver's hammer cocked hungrily in her hands, startling her. She hadn't realized she was unconsciously squeezing the trigger. It was tightening and creaking under her finger, like a bicycle changing gears. There couldn't be much more to it. An ounce left, maybe? Just another millimeter and the tensed metal would release. It wasn't something she wanted to do, but the Soviet was making it easier by the second—

"Please." James crawled his hand up her wrist. Toward the gun. "Please."

She shoved her husband away. What the hell was he thinking? The Soviet was a half second from killing them both. A single distraction was all it might take. The bastard had his entire hand wrapped around the machine pistol now.

"Let go of your gun," she commanded.

He didn't.

"Let go."

He didn't blink. He was the only one here who didn't seem to give a damn. He had been more emotionally invested in his art show than he was here at gunpoint.

"Let go, or I shoot you."

"Elle." James was close, his lips to her ear and his hand on the back of her neck. "Think."

Think?

She hated when he told her to think. It was one of his go-to maneuvers in an argument, guaranteed to push her buttons: *Elle, think. Think about how wrong you are, and therefore how right I am. I flipped the bird to this murderer at the gas station and apparently that was okay, but right now I'm lecturing you on thinking.*

The Soviet slid the machine pistol an inch out of its holster. He was testing the water, and apparently it felt just fine.

Think.

140

Her mind shuttered. Against her pride, she admitted to herself that something about this revolver did feel wrong. As she slid back into the world one scattered thought at a time, she wondered why James and Roy would choose to fight the man hand-to-hand when they had a loaded gun. She tried to remember but her memory was slippery; as detailed as an IMAX in places but utterly barren in others. She had been so pleasantly surprised to find Glen's pistol resting in the dirt beside her. Had it been knocked aside in the scuffle? Maybe. It had felt so cool in her hands, like it had been inside an air-conditioned room this entire time.

Could she do it? She honestly didn't know at this point. She suspected this new version of herself – talking coldly, holding a gun, squeezing the trigger without realizing it – wasn't really working and the Soviet wasn't buying any of it. Maybe Eowen could have filled these shoes better, and maybe she could have delivered the action-movie dialogue with more zest. Elle, the quieter sister with the less interesting name, didn't have any of that right now. She didn't want to kill this childlike man, even if he was a muscle-twitch from killing James, Roy, and her.

That was when the Soviet's machine pistol came up and out.

* * *

James exhaled and sagged with relief.

Elle hadn't fired. She'd come within maybe a millimeter, maybe less, but thank God she hadn't fired and given away the whole bluff.

The Soviet held his boxy weapon with two fingers and dropped it. The evil little Venezuelan-drug-lord automatic clacked on the road with its barrel pointed at James. Hands half-raised, the greasy man glowered up at Elle again, only Elle. As far as he seemed to be concerned, Elle was the only thing here worth listening to or possibly saving. Had

James or Roy aimed the revolver at him, he likely would have just grunted and shot back.

"Okay," James said. "Do you have any other guns?"

The Soviet shook his head.

Of course, he could be lying. Why would he tell the truth?

"Kick the gun to us." James widened his stance. Once that weapon was in his hands, he knew he would need to execute the Soviet with it. Any other course of action would be irresponsible; the man was too dangerous to remain alive and in play on this long-distance chessboard. James dreaded that part and hoped Roy was still up for shooting the bastard in the face, to use his exact words. He wasn't judging him for that. Hell, if he'd been asked five minutes ago he would have given the same answer.

The man hesitated, like a cautious child in the company of a parent.

"Kick it," James said again. "Kick it toward—"

"Throw it," said a disembodied voice floating in shallow static.

Silence.

The Soviet glanced to his radio unit, resting in the dirt by James' left knee. So did James.

"Throw it, Svatomir. Right now." The weedy voice clipped under electronic garble and James recognized it from earlier today. The signal bleed on 92.7 FM! Of course. He tried to recall what the two mystery phrases had been, but then the ghost of Abraham Lincoln spoke again: "Field-strip the Mac-11 and throw every piece out into the desert."

Roy gasped. "No, no, no."

Elle squeezed the revolver, but what could she do?

The Soviet, caught between two guns, obediently scooped up his machine pistol. In a flash, the weapon was in two parts, then three, and then he extracted a long, oily spring and made four. Wincing with pain, he wound up and hurled each piece deep into the sky, and they touched down soundlessly somewhere in the distant scrub grass to the east.

James saw only one of them land, and even then he didn't see the actual piece landing – just a quiver of disturbed brush. He relaxed, but only a little. At least now all of the guns had been removed from the equation (excluding one very important one a mile away). He reached for the radio, a gnarled Motorola two-way unit wrapped in electrical tape. It was hot and damp with a malty odor that reminded him of wet paint. He turned it over and found a rectangular button on the top-right, built into the contour, stenciled PUSH TO TALK. He thumbed it and heard feedback static.

Elle and Roy looked at him. So did the Soviet, grudgingly, as he rubbed his irritated eyes at gunpoint.

"Who . . ." James fumbled words, but only for a second. He pulled the radio closer to his teeth and found his voice:

"Who am I speaking to?"

* * *

Tapp hesitated.

The husband's voice, timid but gathering conviction, reached across the gulf and touched him like an ice cube between the shoulder blades. He felt a shade of panic, as if he was suddenly under close assault, and flattened his body to feel strands of dead grass and jute threads pool at his sides. He wanted to liquefy and sink into the earth like something molten, to quietly morph into it and not exist at all.

Say something.

Even in the real world Tapp hated conversation. When you got down to it, it was fundamentally false. When someone asked you how your day had been, they weren't really asking if you'd passed a kidney stone that morning (quick hint – don't talk about the kidney stone). And every barber, clerk, and waitress just *had* to share all the tedious details and small dramas of their lives, as if someone's boyfriend's father's new Buick with a bad muffler was supposed to leave William Tapp starry-eyed. Sometimes he felt like a man with a fork trapped in a world of soup.

Say anything.

In his scope he could only see Svatomir's upper half, a few paces from the Toyota, standing dumbly at gunpoint. Hopefully this would be a learning experience for him. He had been warned about the (possible) revolver, but he hadn't been able to resist showing off his personal art gallery.

Svatomir was like that. He had always been a sensitive fortysomething prone to inexplicable, white-hot tantrums – breaking car windows with rocks, shooting armadillos on the road, spitting on the Fuel-N-Food hot dogs after the old man asked him to leave for bringing porn into their bathroom – and one day he'd taken an odd stumble off a dirt berm, concussed himself, and somehow got even weirder. His drawings got worse. He spoke less. He stopped picking up new English words. He got a little tougher to handle every year, too, like a baby gorilla transforming into dangerous adulthood.

Maybe they'll kill him for me, Tapp thought. That'd be nice.

He freed his right hand from the rifle's grip and it made a Velcro hiss. Sweat and pressure had formed a fierce suction between his fingers, transforming the cozy polymer into a sticky bed on a summer night. He cracked his knuckles one-handed, a five-shot salvo of wet blasts, then resumed his firing stance.

Really, nothing much had changed. He knew that even with this unexpected wrinkle, all possible outcomes remained the same. *They kill Svatomir – they're still trapped. They run for Svatomir's jeep – I kill them. They remain behind the*

Toyota — I relocate and kill them. The only question was how many extra minutes these three would buy themselves. This engagement was deliciously thrilling but in a manageable, safety-netted way because he still knew how it would end. It was like munching candy and enjoying a rousing summer blockbuster while knowing that no matter how hairy it gets, the dinosaurs won't eat the kids.

The husband tried again. "Hello?"

Tapp considered pretending to not be there. He didn't want to respond and make it personal, because there was absolutely nothing personal about any of this. They had nothing to discuss.

I kill people. So do car accidents. I am a neutral force. Just like car accidents. What would a car accident say if it could speak?

Clouds gathered and reached over the sky like gray tentacles. The storm was pushing in from the west a little sooner than the forecast had suggested. The air loosened and shifted over his crater and he imagined he could feel tectonic plates groaning and creaking in anticipation. This moment felt huge, somehow, even though it shouldn't have.

What would a brain tumor say if you asked it who it was? Or why it killed its host?

* * *

"William Tapp."

James couldn't imagine such evil owning a mundane name like William, or Will, or Willie, or Bill. It didn't seem possible that the eyes behind the scope could turn their attention from severing a nineteen-year-old girl's leg to mortal business like eating a burger, filling out a change of address form, or taking a leak. This William Tapp had to have a social security number, a driver's license, and a day job. Friends, family, holiday plans. He paid taxes, probably.

145

The invisible killer was just a man, James reminded himself. A man could make errors. A man could be reasoned with. And if need be, a man could be killed.

"James Eversman," he said meekly into the radio receiver. This fumbling connection between worlds felt so fragile and tenuous that anything louder than a whisper would crush it. He hadn't been asked for his name but his polite sales instincts told him to offer it.

The sniper said nothing.

Elle adjusted her grip on the revolver and it wobbled in her hands. The Soviet studied it intently. The skin above and below his eyes had swollen beet red, either from fierce rubbing or contact irritation.

"Here . . . here's the deal, William." James scooted against the Rav4's driver door and almost poked his eye on the rubbery Motorola antenna. No one saw except the Soviet, who smirked. "We have a gun on your smelly Lone Ranger friend here. If he moves, he dies."

He gave the sniper a moment to answer.

Still nothing.

"So . . . here's what's going to happen in the next two minutes." He unpeeled Elle's hands from the revolver and took it himself. She didn't protest. He trained it on the greasy man with his index finger pointed forward, off the trigger, in an attempt to treat the pistol as though it were actually loaded. Aiming a gun felt awkward and made him vaguely self-conscious, like he was posing tough with a prop. James Eversman: full-time account executive, part-time badass.

The Soviet's clammy eyes had followed the weapon while it changed hands.

"I'm . . ." He felt his voice waver and steadied. "I'm going to stay right here behind my car with your friend. My wife and Roy will walk to his jeep and drive away. If I even suspect you're about to take a shot at either of them,

I will blow this son of a bitch's face all over your stupidly-named Sesame Street road."

"James, no." Elle took a scraping breath. "We can think of something else—"

Roy glared at the Soviet. "Keys. Now."

The big man's jaw curled into another smirk and he plucked a jingling ring lined with many keys, many brands – Honda, Lexus, Ford, Chevrolet, dozens of bronze and silver home and apartment keys – and underhanded them to the ground at Roy's feet.

"There has to be another way," Elle hissed. "We can stall, buy time—"

"Every second we wait, we're giving him time to move. Then he shoots whoever is holding the gun and it's all over." He made sure the PUSH TO TALK button wasn't still depressed. "We'll do this now, and someone has to stay behind. I'm volunteering."

Roy pretended not to hear.

She pouted. "It's a stupid plan, James."

"I'm all out of smart ones." He looked her in the eye. "Also, you have a hole in your chest."

"Yeah, but a small one."

He laughed, a bitter tired thing. She pressed her forehead to his. He smelled green apple shampoo from the motel that morning, the floral tang of her antiperspirant, and her salty sweat. Somehow this, the smell of her hair and body, made it sink in – the gravity of what he was doing. It wasn't even a choice; it was a reflex. It might get him killed just the same.

"I want to stay with you," she said quietly. Stupidly.

He remembered something and handed the revolver to Roy, who took guard.

"What are you doing?" she asked.

He lifted her arm by the elbow and grabbed the duct tape from beside the tool bag. The one-way valve – three sides of the plastic taped and one flapping freely – seemed to be holding up. It just needed one final adjustment. He tore off a snarling piece and securely taped off the fourth side.

"James?"

"I'm sealing it."

"I don't—"

"The bag pumped the extra air out of your chest. Now I'm sealing it so it can't leak back inside." He stuck a long diagonal stretch of tape across the bag, and then another, pressing all corners flat against her warm skin. He pressed hard and she wobbled under his hands, exhaling.

"I'm not leaving you," she said.

"Yes, you are. Don't lose this, whatever you do, or you'll suffocate in minutes. You still have a little chunk of a bullet lodged inside you somewhere. I have no idea how bad it is, or how bad it could be getting. Consider it a ticking clock. You need to be in a hospital *five minutes ago*." He slapped on a final piece and she lowered her arm.

Her eyes brimmed with tears. "You can do that but you can't fix the bathroom sink?"

"Jaaaaaames." The sniper's voice crackled. "You're bluffing."

The Soviet smirked his biggest one yet, revealing yellow horse teeth.

James snatched the pistol from Roy, scooped up the radio receiver and gathered his confidence. "Yeah? Try and prove—"

"Shut your *fuckin' mouth*." Tapp's words came unevenly, like coiled rope unwinding in lumps. "So your friend over there. Mr. Glen Floyd, Clements County, MPR. Strolling down the road, probably . . . feeling a little more wind in his hair than usual. Making good . . . *headway*, you could say. Did he tell you anything?"

James tasted stomach acid.

Roy twirled the keys nervously.

"Because he told me lots." The sniper's voice was wavering, oddly unstable. "But let me back up. So it's noon. I'm driving up here on the Plainsway – that's what locals call the highway that skims through town, the Plainsway – and then I see this truck pulled off on the shoulder. And . . . then here comes Mr. Clements County, all wheezy and red, with a compact wheel gun in his hand. The one you're holding right now, James."

James knew where this was headed.

Elle held her breath.

Roy closed a tight fist around the keys.

"He tells me . . . this is amazing. You can't make up these coincidences. He tells me he saw a coyote." The killer smacked his lips and his voice settled into a pattern of tonal whiplash, rubber-banding from high to low, tense to relaxed, cordial to vicious. "And this coyote . . . had an arm in its mouth. A little mummified hand severed at the wrist, all black and ropy and burnt up. He tells me he slammed on his brakes, got out, and chased it a little ways, but you know how coyotes are, especially in daylight. So I tell him . . . I've got a four-wheel drive here. Let's track this little bastard to his rout, or at least see if he drops the arm somewhere. He can't chew on it forever. And Mr. Clements County is a pretty nice guy, and we hit it off while we're cruising up and over the hardpan, and we share a little male pattern baldness bonding. Young guy like you wouldn't understand, James. And we spot a little . . . blood trail in the sand, which is good, because he was certain this was a crime scene in progress, and shot his .38 special at the pup but thought he'd missed—"

"You talk too much," James said.

"You radioed me."

"I liked you better when you were shooting at us."

"He fired five shots," Tapp said with an exaggerated country twang. "You, James, have no leverage, because

149

you are holding my spotter hostage with an empty five-shooter."

James didn't have a smartass remark for that. The silence stung.

Elle and Roy exhaled in unison.

Look at us, he thought. *We're already dead.*

He clicked PRESS TO TALK again and tried to answer. He worked his jaw, pushed warm air through his teeth, and desperately willed for words to form in his breath, any words, but it was pointless. The sniper had already won. He knew it and now they knew it. He had been destined to win the microsecond James turned off the Plainsway and onto Shady Slope Road. Nothing else mattered.

James thought of the most pitiful of the live feeder mice at Elle's reptile store – the naked little newborn 'pinkies' less than a week old, unable to walk, making mewing sounds with their eyes clammed shut, dropped into a Rubbermaid bin with a fat python coiled and waiting. God, he had always hated snakes. Even Gray and Iris. Sure, the prey can dodge the strike, circle the outskirts, and paw uselessly at the curved walls (*Just like what we've been doing here with the distractions, the pepper spray, and now this failed bluff*) but ultimately those tactics only bought time. The mouse was trapped in a forced scenario where only the snake could win. Maybe there was a certain dignity in accepting that?

Relaxing, the Soviet stepped forward—

"Six." Roy grabbed the radio from James and groped for the button. "This revolver holds six bullets, asshole."

The Soviet froze mid-step.

Tapp paused, too. Then he made a dry crackling sound, as if he was sucking on his lower lip thoughtfully, or eating crunchy potato chips. A steady stream of background static hiss (*room tone,* the techies called it at his old radio building) meaning the sniper was holding the input button.

Maybe he was flustered and second-guessing himself. It made sense, too – even at close range, he couldn't have gotten a good look at the revolver before Glen had holstered it. You couldn't really see the ringed chambers until the cylinder was open. It could just as easily hold six, like the movies. Right?

Brilliant, Roy.

James grabbed the radio back and forced a cocky grin. "Yeah."

Tapp sounded deliciously uncertain. "Do you . . . ?"

"Yeah."

"Prove it." The sniper coughed. "Prove it and shoot my spotter in the face. Right now."

Roy looked at James.

"If I . . ." He felt cold fingers on his spine. "If I do that, I can't use him as a hostage."

"You already can't." Tapp suppressed a wet belch and sighed irritably, like he was explaining something to a child. "This is the second reason you have no leverage, James. You're operating under the assumption that I care about the man you're pointing a gun at. You see, I just . . . don't. Not even a little. So again, I courteously invite you to *shoot him*. Do it. Don't overthink it. This one's on the house."

James drew a bead between the Soviet's eyes and tried to read the man's face for fear, but like a stone, he gave nothing. Truly, he feared death less than he feared Elle's disapproval of his charcoal drawings. "Your friend . . . or spotter. Does he know that?"

"He understands."

"Understands what?"

"That there are millions of ways the world could end before you . . . well, before I eat supper tonight. A rogue black hole could pass through our solar system. A radiation burst could microwave our atmosphere. A star could go nova. We could take a meteor. A dormant supervolcano could create a nuclear winter. Or we could even get something called a Verneshot, which is basically when . . . your supervolcano explodes so violently that it blows a chunk of the earth's crust into space, and then it comes back down like a meteor. Sort of a buy one, get one free—"

James shrugged. "I'll be dead. Won't be my problem."

"Exactly," Tapp said. "Welcome aboard."

A dry popping came in over the radio. At first it sounded like signal interference, and then he realized it was the sniper slow-clapping with approval.

Welcome aboard.

James fell back into sales mode. What was life, if not a series of dilemmas to be unfucked? So the client blacklisted a time period. The show under-delivered ratings points. The promo didn't run because the eggheads in the control room forgot to carry the remainder. Whatever. James could fix it. Let James fix it for you. He always had a second chair in his office to rest his feet on, and he badly missed it now.

"We can negotiate," he said hollowly, as if William Tapp was a media buyer in an office somewhere hunched over an Excel sheet.

The sniper said nothing.

"What do you want?"

Silence.

"Everyone . . . wants something. So what can I offer you, Tapp?"

Nothing.

"You don't have to do this." James shut his eyes and felt himself rolling over in submission to a force he didn't understand. It was deeply embarrassing. He wished Elle wasn't there to see him like this. "I've . . . I've never done anything to you. We don't know who you are and we don't wish you any harm. We're not even from around here. We're moving from California to Tulsa and the only reason we even crossed the Plainsway is because of an impulsive trip to a crappy Wax Gore Museum. Listen to me, Tapp, there is nothing *fair* about this."

No answer came.

He couldn't believe he was pleading for fairness from a man who shot unarmed strangers from a mile away. In the face of this towering evil he felt small. Worse than small, he felt like he was already dead and his body sinking into the earth, decomposing, becoming dirt.

Drunk one night beside the embers of a beach bonfire, Elle had asked James if he remembered his father's suicide. He had lied, of course, and claimed he had been deeply asleep. He'd seen a tinge of quiet pain in her eyes, like she sensed there was more to it (much more) and couldn't help him without him first admitting that.

The gunshot had filled the inlet kitchen, rattled pans, rung off jungle-green tile, cracked windows in their frames, and the echo still lingered somewhere in the back of the house like trapped thunder. The air stank with wet fireworks. A splat of blood powdered the ceiling by the light and the rest was wafting back down like coal dust. Nine-year-old James had watched from the doorway, drawn by the noise and now shivering with his socks half on ceramic tile, half on spotted carpet. He hadn't known if he should approach or stay put.

His father had stood motionless in the kitchen for a long moment. His posture was so stilted and strange, he didn't seem to be attached to the floor. Like he was hanging from a hook between the shoulders. Then he sat down with his legs folded and his back against the dishwasher, and he looked up at James with only his right eye. His left was a black tunnel with a single upper eyelid, hanging white and bloodless like a window shutter. No explanation. No words. No emotion at all, just a cool indifference. This little moment of eye contact lasted a minute or two, and then the right eye turned milky and looked up at the blood on the ceiling.

James stood and watched until he was certain his father was dead. It kept looking like it would happen, and then another lax breath would croak out or another little twitch would squeal his boot against tile. Finally his chest stilled, and James quietly counted to one hundred. When his father still hadn't moved, he walked to the cigarette-burned sofa in the living room and curled up in a little fetal ball. Had he cried? He couldn't remember. What he had felt was something worse than grief. Something hollow. Wastefulness.

James hadn't known what the Tip-over was or why it was so important, but he would have pretended to in a heartbeat. He would have loved to be in the living room with the Anti-Weathermen, slurping a beer, bullshitting about the coming revolution with his father and the Tall Man. In the end, he just wanted a dad. Any dad. Even an awful one.

"Why are you doing this?" James asked the sniper.

"Because I can."

"How long have you done it?"

"Years."

"How many . . ." Flecks of sand stuck in his throat. "How many have you killed?"

"Fifty-seven," Tapp said. "Counting you."

Elle sighed hopelessly.

"That's impossible," Roy whispered.

James nodded in tacit agreement. No way. You couldn't possibly conceal fifty-seven missing people, all last seen traveling down the same rural highway. Not in this age of smartphones and geosynchronous satellites. Local law enforcement would be all over the disappearances in their jurisdiction – no, it would be a federal thing. These were serial killings. Helicopters would come, special agents and criminal profilers. It would be plastered over the news and net. A nation full of 'gore hounds,' Elle's people, would gobble it up, waiting hungrily for the made-for-television docudrama to churn out like cynical clockwork. The media would even brand Tapp with an insipid name, like the Shady Slope Sniper or some crap.

"Oh, no," his wife whispered.

"What?"

The Soviet had been staring intently down the bore of the revolver and now stiffened as if jolted by an electric current. Something flickered behind his eyes and a leering smile crept up his face, rippling the ash streaks in his beard. It was the grin of a child winning an argument with an adult. He looked south to the distant crater wall, to Tapp, and raised his left hand skyward with all fingers out.

James understood and his heart plunged. Five fingers, for five shots.

"Yep, I knew it," Tapp said. "The cylinder of a five-shooter is visibly different from that of a six-shooter. You . . . yeah, you really should have covered it up with your hand, James. Big fat mistake."

The Soviet leaned forward and spat a yellow mouthful in James' eye. Then he snatched his key ring back from Roy and pivoted hard, kicking a spray of dust to draw ocher shafts of sunlight, and marched off the road. The land took a dip and coarsened so he took high steps. Dead grass crackled under his feet like firewood.

"Good try." The sniper exhaled. "It was like . . . woo-hoo! Fuckin' *plot twist*."

Elle watched the Soviet leave. "Where's he going?"

"To rebuild his gun," James said, wiping warm saliva from his eye.

"Well." Roy shrugged. "That's that."

James nodded brokenly.

"You . . . you three almost survived to nightfall. Just amazing." Tapp took a hissing breath. His voice fluctuated and rearranged itself again, doubling back into something whimsical and curious. Almost friendly. "James, let me ask you something. How do . . . how do you see today ending?"

"I don't know." He raised the revolver again and drew a shaky bead on the Soviet's back while he clambered through knee-deep brush. He tugged the trigger and a pathetic part of himself hoped that maybe, just maybe, they had all been wrong and there was somehow a single miraculous round of live ammunition left in there.

The hammer dropped. CLICK.

Elle buried her face in her hands.

"Alright." Tapp audibly smiled. "How do you want it end?"

"With me. Driving to Oklahoma with my wife." He let the worthless gun drop from his fingers and clatter on the road. "We left good jobs behind. Some friends. Some roots. We left because we didn't like our lives and, truthfully, maybe we didn't even like each other anymore. So we rebooted. New place. New home. New everything." His eyes watered and he took a gulp of salty air. "And we were going to start a family. We had to keep trying. Maybe somewhere else, our luck would be . . . I don't know."

Elle squeezed his shoulder. He didn't want her to see him cry so he turned away into the amber fire of the lowering sun.

"Kids?" the sniper asked softly.

"Yeah."

"Why couldn't you?"

"Medical stuff."

Tapp sighed. "I'm . . . sorry to hear that."

"No, you're not," James said.

"You're right. I'm not." The marksman spat under his breath and again his voice morphed. This time it curdled the way room temperature stews milk in the carton, fermenting into something else entirely, cloudy and sour:

"It's a blessing, though. Really. Be glad . . . be glad you two never made any kiddies. Because if you had, I would have shot them last, so that they could first watch Mommy and Daddy die."

James pressed the receiver to his teeth and felt his own hot breath curling back at him. He surprised himself by saying it, and by meaning it:

"Before today is over, William Tapp, I will kill you."

14

A mile away, the sniper bristled. White-hot emotions and half-thoughts fluttered through his mind like trapped birds but he wasn't articulate enough to make them real, so he tried them out inside the safe echo chamber of his own mind.

Alright, James. Okay. Fine. Let's examine your options here.

You run . . . You die.

You stay behind the car . . . You die.

Even if you somehow achieve the impossible, something no else has ever done, and walk across hundreds of meters of descending open prairie, cross the arroyo, climb another four hundred meters up my perch of shorn rock, and somehow reach up toward me with bloody, desperate hands grasping to touch the face of God . . . God is dug in, ghillied up, and armed.

You still die.

With feline reflexes he clicked open the bolt and caught the ejected cartridge mid-spin. He thumbed three handloads into the dark breech, topping off his ten-count magazine, and inserted an eleventh directly into the chamber. He stared at that final bullet for a long moment

— a gleaming gold missile, curved to a perfect aerodynamic point — before sliding it into battery and closing the bolt behind it, and reminded himself that this James Eversman, for all his frightening unpredictability, was still 1,545 meters away.

* * *

"We're kicking the car into neutral," James told them. "And we're rolling it at him."

Elle gasped. "You're serious?"

"Roy. You said you worked on cars?"

He nodded.

"Good. Okay. I can't change gears because we don't have the keys." James drummed the door with his knuckles. This plan was pure, hot-blooded inspiration, coming to him while he spoke it. "Can you change gears without the engine, and without using the shifter?"

"Yeah," Roy said. "If I get under it."

"Fast?"

He unzipped the tool bag. "No promises."

"We have a minute. Maybe two." James squinted and saw the Soviet clambering thirty yards out in the ocher brush, scanning in methodical sweeps. One hand packed tightly to his bleeding gut, the other holding a recovered piece of his subgun — the stout barrel. "Until he finds all the pieces of his gun. And he comes back and he . . . you know, kills us."

"Anywhere but here," Elle whispered, giving him a jolt of déjà vu.

"Amen. Anywhere but here."

Roy twirled a screwdriver. "There's more to this idea, right?"

"Yeah." James blinked grit from his eyes and pointed around the headlights, downhill. "We push the car until it rolls and jump inside. We ride it downhill, to the gully down there. See it? At the bottom of this big valley. That dark area."

Elle squinted. "Right at the sniper's front door? *That* dark area?"

"That's the point." He fought a grin. "Since he's up there on that big rise, he might not have an angle to see down into the little channel. He might not be able to see us in there, and if so, he'll—"

"Might not?"

"Fifty-fifty."

She smiled weakly. "Those are the best odds we've had all day."

"Great," Roy said. "Another plan."

"The last one worked," James said.

"Your wife got shot."

"Other than that, it worked."

"Sniper-guy. Tapp. He'll shoot us." Roy rolled on his back and scooted under the Rav4, mumbling with a screwdriver in his mouth. "While we're in the rolling car. Through the windows."

"He'll try. But we'll duck low to the floor, heads down, bodies flattened under the seats. The engine block will shield us from the front. And all this crap will help." He pointed at the detritus of their old life – the television stand, the bookshelf, the sandwiched boxes in the back seats. He couldn't fight it anymore and let it wash over his face, a shit-eating grin of stupid excitement. Reckless hope. He knew it was crazy but that somehow made it even better. Every second was a celebration because it was a second Tapp had failed to take from them.

"The angle will change." Roy's voice was a flat echo under the car. "It'll steepen. He'll see up, over the engine. And he's thirty degrees off the road. That angle will widen as we get closer, and he could put a bullet through a door—"

"You can stay here if you'd like."

160

"I'm just saying, man, there's problems."

James was well aware of that. He turned to Elle, breathless. "You and I will be in the front seats. We just . . . we have to clear room in the back for Roy."

"What's the plan when we get to the gully?" she asked.

He swung open the other door. "We'll make it up as we go."

"Not funny."

"That literally is the plan."

"Still not funny."

James looked over his shoulder and squinted. The Soviet was fifty yards out now, a hunched silhouette half-obscured by wiregrass. He took a lurching step and his arm came into view with at least two pieces of his gun clasped underhand. Two to go.

"And him," Elle said. "He'll be behind us. Chasing us."

"Yep."

"And shooting at us."

"Probably." He grabbed a swollen cardboard box with both hands – their desktop Mac, purchased on credit after graduation. The hard drive contained Elle's demo reel, her thesis, and thousands of hours of raw work. "Roy! How's it going down there?"

"Got the cable." His foot jerked. "Give me thirty seconds."

"Tell us when you put it in neutral. So we can hold the car if it rolls." James braced a foot to the door, wrenched the computer box free, and let it crash to the road. Something broke inside with a pressurized pop and the monitor rolled out like a hubcap.

Elle winced.

"It's just stuff, Elle. It's not us."

"I know."

He tore out the bookcase next, dumping crispy hardcovers and yellowed paperbacks, and then their maroon bedding. Electric candles. A juicer. A cardboard box of Snow Village models – painted glass houses and sledding children – slid out and crunched. Did they belong to Elle's mother or aunt? He couldn't remember. He wiped sweat from his eyes and realized that if they died today, these relics would be the only physical evidence they'd existed at all. He felt like he was willfully vanishing, shoveling dirt over his own grave.

It's just stuff, he had to remind himself.

He had cleared almost enough room for Roy in the back seats, if he lay on his belly in the floor space. All that needed go now was Elle's grandmother's crib, that hulking eyesore that had survived the Nazi occupation of Poland and a house fire. It was a slab of dark chocolate oak as dense as cement. *Your grandmother could have left it in Lublin*, he'd told her once. *The Nazis would have mistaken it for the Ark of the Covenant.*

She watched him pull the creaking beast free and dump it on the side of the road to join the rest of their junked things, heaped indifferently like trash. "Tell me we're going to make it out of this," she said faintly. "And we're going to have kids."

"We're going to have kids."

She swallowed. "Okay."

"I promise—"

"Say it again."

"We're *going to have kids*, Elle." He grabbed her by the shoulders and kissed her, feeling the tremor in her breaths, while a bullet sliced through the air somewhere above them, flushing a warm breeze and quivering her hair.

* * *

Tapp threw the bolt and let out a hot breath. He was better than this. He shouldn't be firing at half-discerned shapes like some runny-nosed Walmart shopper with a deer rifle. In the jittery glass of his spotting scope he saw – or thought he saw – two blurred scalps skimming over the

Toyota's hood, so he rolled over to his rifle, guestimated, and fired off a dumb luck Hail Mary of a shot. Why did he do that?

He made those shots sometimes, often late in the afternoon when he was growing fanciful and bored. They were almost always misses, embarrassing misses, and he loathed himself for the wasted handload and worse, the sloppiness.

He was fatiguing and he knew it. His eyes were drying, spider-webbing with blood vessels, and his eyelids made a *squish* with every blink, like a grapefruit crushed under a boot. The muscles in his right wrist, his index finger, and his inner forearms were throbbing. Worst of all, he was out of Cheetos – a grand total of one hundred and twenty-seven in that bag.

He knew what was happening – he had reached that unpleasant point where his heart simply wasn't in it. He was shooting for a result, not enjoyment. He had to knuckle down on his wandering mind and force himself to remember that this was still happening, that the heat and sweat and burnt gunpowder was real, and hadn't gotten any less real in last three hours. Staying in the zone was exhausting.

Snipers – true military snipers – were machines. Tapp had been in their presence before at gun shows. Ironically (given their particular skill set) he could spot them from across a crowded fairground building every damn time. Even in flannel and jeans with their all-American blonde wives hooked on their arms, these men never took a false step. He could see it behind their eyes – this subconscious situational alertness – as they processed the license plates of every parked vehicle outside and quietly tallied the number of bodies in the room and exits available. In the field, these men would lie motionless for days with every cell in their bodies perfectly trained and waiting for a single window, suspended uneasily on a single chancy moment, to then take a single shot. Or most impressive of all, to recognize that this correct moment never materialized – the wind flared, the morning mist never burned off, the Sudanese general walked his Labrador behind the barracks instead of beside them, whatever – and then quietly cancel the mission and extract without a shot fired.

Tapp knew he never could have been a Marine Scout Sniper or an Army sniper, and he was too old and too fat to even be a designated marksman. He didn't possess the discipline or mental hardness for the role, even if his raw talent placed him among the best shooters currently alive. His mind wandered. He was prone to fantasy, distraction, and curious little impulses. And most damning of all, he was deeply impatient. He knew this. He had long known all of these things, so it didn't sting now as it had when he was twenty-two. But it still ached somewhere dark inside him, where he forever knew that 'sniper' was a term that would only apply to him in uninformed civilian shorthand. The way they call magazines 'clips.'

You're a demon, said Sergei Koal.

You just don't know it yet.

He dialed his spotting scope down to 80x to brighten the image and nudged it a few jittery millimeters right to find Svatomir wading in scrub brush. He had the Mac-11's upper, lower, and recoil spring in his oven mitt hands. All he needed now was the skinny little bolt, about the size of a cigar, hidden somewhere in the low grass. He would find it eventually. Might take seconds, might take minutes, might take until after sundown. Tapp wanted, and wanted badly, to simply radio him and tell him to forget about his stupid little subgun and just tow the damn Toyota. But that resourceful bastard James had Svatomir's radio now.

Which gave Tapp another idea.

"Roy Burke," he said into his headset. "Kill James. Or your family dies."

* * *

Everyone froze.

James sighed tiredly. "Of course."

"What?" Roy slid out from under the car. "What did he say?"

"How did he know your last name?" Elle asked.

No static. Silence.

The Soviet's radio lay in the packed soil at the edge of the Toyota's shadow. James reached for it but Roy snatched it with both hands and clasped it, squirrel-like. He turned it over and over, searching busily for the PUSH TO TALK button. "I'm serious," he snarled. "What the hell did he say about me?"

Elle chewed her lip.

"Roy Burk," James said placidly, testing it on his tongue. He looked up at Roy, who had suddenly become a stranger again. "He knows you."

He swallowed. "I don't know how."

"Are you lying?"

"Why would I lie?"

"He's lying," Elle hissed.

"Fuck you." Roy spat a little. "I'm not—"

"Roy, this offer will only stand once." Tapp's voice came dribbling through the radio and Roy's fingers parted as if it was corrosive. "And you can't save yourself. So we're clear, I will kill you today and nothing will change that."

Roy tried to speak but had no words.

"I hate him," Elle whispered. "I hate him so much."

James listened thoughtfully.

"Roy Burke, here's my offer." Tapp paused for half a breath and let it sink in. "If you kill James, I'll . . . kill you and our business is done. If you don't kill James, I still kill you. But then our business isn't done. I go after your family."

"Don't listen to him," Elle said. "He's playing you."

Roy winced. "Shut up."

165

"He's trying to turn us on each other. He's afraid of James—"

"Your house, Roy-boy, is on 126 Tyler Road in the town of Prim. Sixty miles down the Plainsway, give or take." Tapp's voice came in startlingly clear, like he was crouched among them. "I don't know what you were doing with those two girls, but it's not my business. Your wife Liza is . . . ah, twenty-three. Your daughter is almost two. I'll come in tonight, after dark, when things have settled and Emma is in her crib. I'll kick in the back door and I'll come in with a suppressed pistol. I'll go room by room, inch by inch, and I will kill everyone I find with two shots to the sternum and one to the forehead. Young. Old. Awake. Sleeping. Nothing in that house will survive. Do you have a dog or cat? I'll kill them, too. I'll . . . I'll pour bleach in the fucking *fish tank*. Do you hear me, Roy Burke? Is this getting to you?"

Roy shuddered.

Elle pressed her hands to her mouth. "How does he *know this*?"

"Kill James Eversman." Tapp sniffed and spat. "Kill him now."

Silence.

Roy quietly set the radio down.

"I . . ." James hesitated. What can you possibly say to that?

Roy stared at the radio on the ground for a long moment, broad shoulders sloped, eyelids fluttering, and then he slowly crawled his eyes up to find James. His palms were flat on his knees but his knuckles had subtly tightened. Gears were turning behind his eyes.

"Trust me," James said unconvincingly. "Just . . . trust me."

He tried to put himself in Roy's shoes but couldn't. A small part of him wondered if maybe this was the preferable outcome. By getting killed here by Roy he could

166

potentially save two lives. Viewed from another angle, wasn't that the morally correct choice? Sacrifice of self for strangers? Maybe the old James would have bought that. This new James sure didn't. In fact, new James was just getting pissed off.

"Trust me," he said again with more force. "I'll get us out."

"No," Roy said airily. "I don't think you will."

James realized the screwdriver – the flathead screwdriver from his tool bag – was in Roy's left hand, tucked in such a way that his wrist almost concealed it. Without question, that was deliberate. The bladed edge caught a gleam of sunlight, looking quite sharp. In twenty-twenty hindsight, it would have been a much more effective weapon against the Soviet than that stupid Korean multitool. And now here it was, in the hands of a man much bigger and stronger than James.

"Kill him," the radio crackled between them. "Roy, what are you waiting for?"

"Roy, I'm asking you a question." James looked at him bluntly, feeling Elle's fingertips digging protectively into his shoulders. "Do you want to kill me? Or him? Because we're not escaping the sniper anymore. We're *charging* him. We're going to trick him, and lure him, and you and I – we're going to kill the bastard. And I need you on my side to pull it off."

"You're a dangerous optimist," Roy said grimly.

"You're goddamn right I'm dangerous."

"Stop it."

"Are you with me or not?"

But big, tough, tattooed Roy had no fight in his eyes. They were just melancholy pools. "We're dead. I'm sorry, but we don't stand a—"

"He's *coming back*!" Elle pointed hard. "He has his gun and he's coming back."

"Help me push the car." James shoved past Roy, scraping his heels, and braced both palms flat to the hot tailgate, half-expecting to feel a screwdriver plunge into his back. "You'll just have to kill me later."

* * *

"Go. Go. Go."

In the disconnected silence of the scope, Tapp watched Svatomir race back to Shady Slope Road, kicking his knees high in the grass. The Mac-11 was reassembled, back in play on today's chessboard, and carried now over his head, barrel up, his sausage finger curled stupidly around the trigger like the amateur he was. His free hand clamped to his gut like a runner fending off a hellish side cramp. He was certainly wounded from that earlier scuffle with James, but how badly?

The Toyota bumped a few inches forward.

Tapp blinked – *squish.*

He rolled into his rifle scope and glided his black razor lines over the vehicle, its suspension now rocking back to stillness. He waited for it to happen again and didn't have to wait long. The yellow car budged again, harder, like an invisible fault line had shifted the ground beneath it. The rear end lifted, the front tires sank and dug into earth, and a wave of accumulated dust slid down the windshield.

Squish-squish. He didn't know what to make of this.

Svatomir saw it too and hesitated. He was still fifty meters east with the falling sun in his eyes. Even if he took a knee and a firm two-hand hold, taking them out with his squirmy little .380 was unlikely. More so, given his refusal to pick up even the most basic principles of marksmanship. He was a hip-shooter through and through, preferring to spit lead and fire with his back arched and his teeth bared. He used automatic pistols and automatic shotguns, close-quarters, spray-and-pray, quantity over quality, all of it. He had no respect for the nuance of the rifle, and right now, Tapp was wishing he did.

"Svatomir, hurry."

The Toyota lurched again and again in rhythmic shocks. Drawn tight across the badlands, three shadows huddled into one. The front tires fought their ruts and pushed, exhumed waves of stubborn earth, and tore fresh gashes in the road. Under a growing cloud of dust he saw flashes of motion, arms and legs and fingers a few inches behind the tailgate, but nothing to fire at. Just images, half-drawn shapes, uncertainties, and teases. Each motion wrested the rubber a few inches from the quicksand soil, and a few more, and suddenly the vehicle was moving. Rolling.

They were pushing the car.

Toward him.

His heart solidified into lead, his nerves tightened, and his rifle discharged without permission.

* * *

"Get inside, Elle."

"Now?"

"Get inside. We'll keep pushing."

She broke away from James and Roy and sprinted along the Rav4's safe side. She went for the driver door, which was hanging open clumsily, framing the far wall of the valley with jagged glass teeth. It was oddly beautiful – distant cliffs shadowed in firelight against a graying sky – and for a sad second her mind darted to her destroyed cameras, her ruined portfolio on the side of the road, her failures.

Molten pain stabbed in her chest. She couldn't breathe quite right, nor run quite as fast as she knew she could. Her body felt wrong. Her legs were spaghetti and for a sickening moment, she nearly lost balance and fell under the back tire. Wouldn't that be great? *Here lies Elle Eversman: Ran herself over, somehow.*

She reached for the driver door but it was just beyond her fingertips.

The vehicle was rolling fast beside her now, grinding along the beveled edge of the road. It was eerily quiet. No driver, no loping engine, only the rush of wind in her ears and the gentle crumble of packed earth beneath tires. Every sound scattered into the desert without an echo.

"Almost fast enough!" James shouted behind her.

Roy said something else. She didn't hear what it was.

She was reaching for the driver door a second time when it whipped shut and a hail of glass fragments exploded in her face. She flinched, blocking crunchy shards with her elbow. Something exploded into the ground behind her and pelted her back with rock chips. She lowered her arm and told herself to keep running for that door.

Tapp missed.

I'm okay. Keep running. She lunged for the door handle (third attempt) but missed again, stumbled, and lost a few paces. Her chest throbbed with every breath, filling her mind with red. God, it hurt. She couldn't keep up.

"Fast enough!" Roy yelled. "Everyone in."

"No." It was James again. "No, not yet."

"It's fine—"

"Not fast enough."

Elle dove for the door handle and caught it. The car seemed plenty fast to her. She swung the door open and hurled herself inside, bruising both shins on the frame and landing directly on the shifter. The metal knob jammed into her breast like a dagger. She gasped.

"It's off the road!" Roy panted somewhere behind her. "Elle, steer us."

She slipped her legs inside, tucked her knees to the pedals and grabbed the wheel. No power steering. The familiar contours barely budged. James screamed something behind her, lost in the noise. She knuckled both hands on the steering wheel, braced herself to the floor, and threw her stomach and spine into it until . . . yes, yes, she forced it to give and heard the crunching gravel change pitch. The tires rediscovered Shady Slope Road – first the right, then the left.

"Great!" Roy opened the side door and she felt the Toyota rock as he crashed into the back seats. "Great job, Elle."

"James!" She lost track of him. "Where is he?"

"I . . ." Roy gasped. "Oh, shit."

"Did we leave him?"

"Shit."

Panic rose inside her. "Did *you* leave him?"

"I don't—"

She pivoted on her knees and raised her head, craned her neck to see over and around the driver headrest, blinking in the amber warmth of the setting sun. Then a hand grabbed a fistful of her hair and slammed her facedown into the seat, her teeth clicking against shards of glass and plastic, and she recognized her husband's voice, calm but urgent, in her left ear:

"Get down. This is gonna be bad."

15

James had run along the unprotected side of the Toyota and hurled himself over the passenger seat, his legs dangling out the door. A Fritos bag crackled under his knee. One foot skimmed the road and kicked pinging rocks against the doors. He pressed Elle down into the driver seat, his palm to the back of her neck, crushing her low beneath the dash, low, low, low, as low as they could possibly squeeze.

"James—"

Even injured, the Soviet had closed the distance quickly. He reached Shady Slope Road's left shoulder and took a firing stance, machine pistol wrapped in beefy hands, his lips curled, trail duster flaring out like a cape. That was the last thing James had seen through the broken windows – a man shaded Rottweiler black and brown, flash-burnt into his mind – before he slammed his head down to the seat beside Elle's. There was an uneasy silence where he was expecting a gunshot and nothing happened. Then it did.

The subgun screamed a shrill rattle, like a soda can filled with pocket change and violently shaken. Swarms of little impacts peppered the Rav4 above and around them, ripping frothy tunnels in the seats and headrests, punching holes in cardboard and finished wood, and pulverizing the windshield in a crystal shower. The air thickened with splinters and tufts of bright yellow seat foam. It went on and on – like furniture tumbling down endless stairs – as more and more bullets, more than James ever imagined could fit inside a handheld weapon, growled and hissed through the air. Another window imploded. The back passenger door warped and snapped open. The rearview mirror dropped to the seat beside his cheek, fissured with cracks. In all the noise and violence, he held his head close to Elle's, his scalp against hers, because she was the only thing in this disintegrating world that mattered.

Finally, silence. He smelled burnt plastic, burnt fabric, burnt hair.

"Everyone still alive?"

Elle picked gummy glass shards from her hair. "Alive."

"I'm okay," Roy called from the back seat.

James bounced upright and clicked the passenger door shut. It had two blistered holes punched through the handhold. With his nose to the dashboard, careful to keep his scalp below Tapp's sight, he spotted the Soviet in the side view mirror. He had turned and was running back to his jeep. He flicked his subgun sharply to the right, throwing a spent magazine, and plucked a new one from his left.

The Rav4 hit a dirt bank and jolted. The mirror flashed sunlight.

"We almost lost the road."

"I got it." Elle twisted her body and raised one eye over the dashboard, correcting the wheel with gritted teeth.

He pressed the rearview mirror into her hand. "Use this to see."

"I am *so* tired of being shot at today."

"Don't touch the brakes. Don't slow down. We can't lose our momentum," James said. The chassis banged against another pothole and something tore loose and dragged underneath with a vibrating metal scream. The rest of the glass fell out of the rear passenger window. The car was rattling apart, one piece at a time.

And worse, it was definitely slowing. Then what?

"Not fast enough," Elle said. "We're stopping."

Roy contributed his obligatory bitch: "I could get out and run faster."

"Feel free." James brushed a pool of glass off the speedometer but the needle hung at zero. He estimated they were rolling five, six miles an hour at the very most. And bleeding more precious momentum every second on the mucky road, which might as well have been made of sand.

"The road steepens." Elle braced the rearview mirror against the curve of the dashboard like a periscope. "I can see it gets steeper, going down into the valley. We'll pick up more speed, if we can just get to it."

James nodded hopefully.

"Then what?" she asked. "We crash into the gully?"

"Crash isn't the best word."

"It hasn't been the best day."

He leaned forward and kissed her, because now seemed like an appropriate time to do so – in a powerless car guided only by a mirror, with one murderer somewhere behind them and another concealed a mile ahead. He had no plan. He wouldn't dare think more than thirty seconds ahead. Every idea and every move was an improvised reaction to a world under Tapp's command and closing on all sides. James whispered a little prayer somewhere in the back of his mind. He wasn't even sure he believed in a higher power but here it was, a simple, modest plea: *God, please keep me thirty seconds ahead of the curve.*

The Toyota spent its last gasp of momentum and scraped to a halt. Everyone gasped. The trailing dust cloud caught up, swept past, and settled.

James punched the glove box. "Shit."

Elle sighed. "So . . . we relocated ourselves a hundred feet *closer* to the sniper."

"Basically, yeah."

"Goddamnit."

"We have to . . ." James felt words gunk up in his throat, thick as peanut butter. "We need to get out and push the car again."

Roy moaned. "Aw, hell."

James almost asked what it was, and then he recognized the familiar throaty roar of the Soviet's jeep, pounding pistons and spurting hot oil, rumbling up on them from behind. He wasn't far back up the road, and rapidly gaining.

"Push us," Elle whispered. "Push us now."

Something pinged off the hood, like a small rock thrown impossibly fast.

* * *

Tapp threw the bolt and ejected a twirling .338 casing. That was his final shot in this magazine, harmlessly stopped somewhere in the Toyota's engine block. He didn't have an angle on them. Even though they were rolling directly toward him, surging on a breathless wave of nuthouse adrenaline, he had no shot on them. James had turned the vehicle into a moving shield because of the *goddamn fucking engine block*—

No matter.

Breathe.

The Toyota had groaned to a halt again, ragged and peppered with dark holes. He guessed that James and the other two were still alive in there, since most of Svatomir's piss-poor shooting had gravitated over the vehicle's roof

175

under the Mac-11's notoriously wild recoil. His jeep was racing up behind the Toyota right now to finish them off, smoothly gliding through glass and prairie like a black shark fin.

See?

It's fine.

Breathe.

Tapp forced a good ol' boy chuckle as he peeked through his rangefinder and squirted off an invisible laser at the Toyota's grill. It bounced back at the speed of light and the digital readout pulsed: 1,402 meters. They had rolled over a hundred meters closer, enough to wreck his presets for elevation and bullet drop. He click-click-clicked his scope and adjusted for eighteen meters of vertical rise. The incline made it trickier because his rangefinder only tracked distance as a straight line, not in relation to the parabolic tug of gravity—

Breathe.

This is what you do.

Let's not be . . . gun-shy.

He changed magazines without looking; a reptilian muscle memory that lived somewhere low in his brain stem. He knew that with Svatomir bearing down on them, James and the others would need to step outside and push their car again, and this time they would need to push from the sides, not the tailgate. Further, their angle of approach had straightened to follow the road into something damn near perpendicular, giving him a clean shot at both the driver and passenger sides. He didn't have to wait long. To his delight, the shadows unfurled like twin jack-in-the-boxes, two doors swung open, and in the delicious hot panic that followed, Tapp fired at the first human shape he saw.

* * *

"Fast enough. Get back in!" James shouted with grit in his throat. They had given the passenger doorframe two heaving pushes on the inclined road and (thank God) that was all it needed. They were rolling again. Roy fell back into his seat screaming. Something guttural, howling, deep in his throat. The car bounced off another pothole. Elle cracked her cheekbone on the steering wheel and cursed.

"Roy!" James tucked the door shut behind him. The sun visor dropped on him and he swatted it away. "Roy, did he get you?"

The back seat was silent.

"Roy!"

Nothing.

"Roy, talk to me—"

"James." Elle's voice was low, all business. "Where's the jeep? How close?"

He checked the side view mirror and saw the evil black thing bank hard and hungrily accelerate behind them, rapidly closing the distance to ten yards. Then closer, and closer still, the bruised silver slats of its grill becoming teeth in the sunlight. "He's . . . he's right on us. Coming up."

"We're not going to outrun him," she said with icy calmness. "We can't."

"I know."

She swerved to dodge another hole but hit it anyway. The Rav4 nosed skyward, glass shards snow-globed everywhere, and furniture groaned and shifted. Roy gasped something muffled back there, meaning he was fortunately still alive, or at least not quite dead yet. James watched the Soviet's jeep draw closer and hit the same dip, smoothly rising and falling on titanic shocks like a speedboat on choppy water. The unpainted bumper touched down with a fireworks splash of sparks. The tinted windshield stuttered flashes of mottled sunlight – just like at the Fuel-N-Food, it afforded only a silhouette of the man inside.

"Roy." Elle looked back but couldn't see past the blossomed driver seat. "Are you okay?"

Through the gap over the center console, James could see Roy's scalp buried under debris and shifting shadows. He was shaking his head, eyes clenched to slits. "My hand," he said hoarsely. "It's messed up."

"How bad?"

"*Bad.*"

James checked the side mirror for the jeep but the Soviet was too close. The hulking vehicle pulled up alongside them, matching their speed, as if preparing for a drive-by shooting. He chewed his lip thoughtfully. "We're . . ."

Elle looked at him. "What?"

He had an idea. "We're going to pit him."

"Pit him?"

"Yeah. The P.I.T. maneuver." James leaned back against the bullet-riddled dashboard, head hunched, watching the roof of the Soviet's jeep over a window frame lined with glass daggers. "I . . . I saw it on an episode of Cops once."

"What do the letters stand for?"

"I don't know."

"That's not reassuring."

Beside him, just a few feet away, passenger door to driver door, the Soviet was pulling closer to make his kill. The motor gave another cycling roar and James felt it vibrating the fillings in his molars. "Basically," he shouted over the noise, "we'll bash his car at just the right point on the back end, so he loses traction with his back two wheels and spins. He'll fishtail."

"Okay."

"I'll tell you when." He squeezed her shoulder. "Okay?"

She nodded fast.

The cars were perfectly side-to-side now. If she missed, or hit the jeep at the wrong spot, they would stall and lose their momentum. Or worse, pivot and spin like a stunt car, leaving them disoriented and defenseless from Tapp's scope. This would need to be precise. Impossibly precise. Like performing brain surgery while riding a jet ski.

"Alright." He steadied himself. "Lose some speed, Elle."

She pressed the brake with her knee.

Nothing happened.

"Huh." She pumped the pedal with her hand. "So, there's that."

James cursed under his breath.

"This'll work, too." She swerved onto the left shoulder. The driver side tires dug into coarse dirt and fought the passenger side, throwing the SUV into an indecisive skid. More boxes crashed around Roy and he moaned again. The television stand dumped a shelf into the console, where it sliced down an inch from James' knuckles like a guillotine blade. Elle cranked the wheel hard to the other side, overcompensated, and the rear passenger door swung open and slammed shut like a gunshot. Had Roy not been holding on back there, he could have been thrown out the side like a ragdoll.

"You got it?" James asked, breathless.

"Yeah."

It worked. The jeep crept a few feet ahead. Through thick glass, James saw the Soviet's unmistakable profile, head down, fumbling busily with something in his lap. What else? That wicked little subgun.

"Ram him?" Elle asked.

James shook his head. It didn't feel right yet.

Over the passenger window frame he watched the jeep inch further ahead. The Soviet reached for the window crank (of course he would have those dinosaur hand-powered windows) and scraped the glass down. It cried as it lowered, a brittle squeal, and the man's bloodshot eyes came into view. The rest of him was still shrouded in shadow except for those wet eyes. It was absurd, but James would have sworn that the Soviet was still somehow looking at Elle, only Elle, forever Elle, like she was a campfire in a dark forest and all the creeping things were drawn to her.

She tensed. "Ram him?"

"Do it!" Roy shouted. "He's going to shoot us—"

"Don't." James dug his fingernails into the door. "Wait a second more."

The Soviet shoved his hand out the window, holding that vicious scratched machine pistol. His entire arm was slimy with rusty blood now, like his skin was sloughing off inside his sleeve. He leaned out, cocked his head to face them with the wind tugging his beard, and pulled the sights up to align with his red eyes. Finger on the trigger, curling—

"Shit," Roy screamed. "*Now! Now! Now!*"

"Now?" Elle looked at James, her eyes wide. Her calm sarcasm was gone. She was terrified, her jaw quivering, her stomach rising in her throat, waiting for her husband to say it, to *please just say it.*

He waited a half second, and then a half second more, as the jeep nudged a few more inches ahead, and the Soviet had to cross his arm to track them, and lean up and out his window to follow them down the stubby iron sights, and (yes!) their right tire was just about even with his back tire—

"Now!" James screamed in her ear.

She wrenched the wheel hard right.

16

To Tapp, they looked like toy cars colliding down a long hallway. Svatomir's jeep swung a silent jackknife in front of the SUV and its tires lifted free of the road while its right dug into it, spewing dust in a graceful arc, like a handful of sand thrown into the wind. The cloud obscured both vehicles and billowed lazily. Then the Toyota, James Eversman's goddamn powerless Toyota, punched through the curtain. Still coming, still rolling, still growing inside his scope, leaving Svatomir sideways, stalled, and far behind.

How the . . .?

James' vehicle tore past the nine hundred meter flag, fearless and unstoppable. For a terrible half second, Tapp entered free-fall. A sour tequila shot of panic. He was terrified. This was so wrong. Everything had gone wrong today. He found himself nurturing such an awful thought, he could only whisper it in the back of his mind and approach it from oblique angles, just a meek little voice . . . *The situation is slipping out of my control.*

And even worse . . . *I might not win this.*

"William Tapp!" James shouted triumphantly into his ear, his voice tinny and crackling. "Are you afraid yet?"

* * *

The impact had scooted the Motorola across the floor and James found it by his ankle. He held it to his teeth as he spoke, shivering with a wild adrenaline high. Elle punched the steering wheel and whooped – the sound college girls made when they took shots together – and he saw she was smiling, laughing, and crying all at once. "How's my driving, *asshole*?"

"He almost flipped back there," Roy said. "He's off the road, in a ditch. He's gonna be stuck awhile."

Elle looked to James. "Was that the easy part or the hard part?"

"Not sure yet." He reached through the broken window and grabbed the side view mirror – crushed by the collision, dangling by bent fiberglass – and scanned the cracked reflection for the Soviet. No luck. All he saw was a wall of dust, boiling and churning like a Mount St. Helens-esque pyroclastic cloud, sliced by shafts of orange sunlight. He would have to take Roy's word for it.

"Four hours left," Elle whispered cryptically.

"What?"

"Four hours left," she said again, as if it should be obvious. "Remember?"

"Yeah. Tapp said it on our car radio."

"He said it over three hours ago." She grinned. "And now I know what he was talking about. *Daylight.* I should have figured – a scope is like any other lens. Camera, binocular, telescope – it needs light to work. He only has so much daylight left to kill us. He has less than an hour, in fact, until the sun is down."

James let out a shocked sigh. The sniper's words whiplashed back at him: *You almost made it to nightfall.* Of course! How had he missed that? The sun was the timer, the big-ass ticking clock in the sky, dimming behind pink clouds with every passing second. Through the hollowed windows he could see the eastern sky was already fading to a deep purple against jagged crater walls. A shadowed twilight was descending over Tapp's land as they raced toward the killer. If only it would descend a little faster.

"That would . . ." Elle's voice was muffled by something scraping off the chassis and tumbling. "That would explain why he wanted Roy to kill you. He's getting desperate but he can't show it, like a poker player with too much on the table and a shit hand. He's running out of time, out of usable daylight, and he knows it."

Tapp, getting desperate. James couldn't imagine a happier thought.

"Sundown in a half hour," Roy said. "Maybe less."

"Survive thirty minutes." Elle waved her hand. "Easy."

The world came alive with possibility again. After night fell, would Tapp really be blinded? That would be an incredible reversal. If so, they would only have to outrun the Soviet. In the dark they would have an edge over the injured man, and if he were stupid enough to fire up a flashlight, they'd literally see him coming for miles. They could follow the arroyo east, as far as it went, and cross the valley under cover of darkness to reach the rough hills by the highway. Once they reached the highway they'd be as good as free. Could it really be that easy? Just survive four hours, until the killer ran out of light?

Now it turned to acid in his stomach. When was anything ever that easy? And of course, he remembered, that hadn't been all. Tapp had said one more thing on that scratchy signal bleed three hours ago.

"Black eye," James said. "What's that?"

The Rav4 hit a violent rut and knocked his head against the glove box. That was when he noticed the dry rushing sound — like the wind at Gray beach, or the army of cooling fans in his radio station control room — and realized it was the desert air blowing through the windshield. It tugged hair and flapped bloodstained clothes. The Toyota had picked up speed as the incline steepened.

"Too fast. No brakes." Roy winced, choked with pain. "We land in the riverbed like this and we're crash test dummies."

Curiously tomato-like. James remembered nearly rear-ending that dumbass deputy four hours ago and thanking God he hadn't, because back then, that had been the worst nightmare he could envision. Wasn't that funny? He and Elle had narrowly avoided a fatal car accident, only to fall into the trap of a psychotic killer, and while trying to escape said killer, were now fixed to die in another fatal car accident.

He supposed the parking brake was an option, but on this terrain, it could just as easily flip them over. And it wouldn't get them inside the gully – *that* was the goal. Getting inside the gully, sheltered from Tapp's scope, forcing the sniper to move in close. Everything else was secondary.

"Seatbelts," he said, groping for the first buckle in the seat behind him. It felt comically futile, like those old photos of Cold War children ducking under their desks to survive a nuclear attack.

"I lost the mirror," Elle said. "How close is it?"

He peeked over the dashboard, into Tapp's no-man's-land, and squinted hard into the low sunlight. They were well off the road now, jangling and crashing. The arroyo itself, a winding talus floor following the crease of the valley, loomed three hundred yards downhill and raced closer every second. Flash floods wouldn't come more than once every few years out here, but he could read the erosive imprint on the land; where the waters had swept away sand and silt but left jutting monoliths of exposed granite and car-sized basalt pillows, oxidizing bright red and choked with huddled plants. He couldn't tell how deep it was. It might be a shallow creek trail or it might be a cousin of the Grand Canyon. There was no way to tell.

"Guess we'll find out if seatbelts really save lives," Roy said flatly. It might have been a joke or it might have been hopeless resignation. Again, no way to tell.

James looked at Elle. "Remember how we met?"

"I like that story." She smiled and gritted her teeth. "Tell it."

A yucca sapling crunched against the Rav4's grill and branches stabbed through the windshield. Elle gave a muffled cry. Bony fingers grasped over them, slashing exposed skin. A big frond stuck in the passenger headrest and flapped furiously, like a tarpaulin in the wind.

"Okay. Riverside Apartments." He collected his thoughts, closed his eyes, and felt the seat vibrating under his chin. "I'm walking to my door. And I see this plate of brownies sitting on the floor with a little red bow, maybe two feet from my front door."

"No," she said. "It was *his* door."

"It was like, fifty-fifty. Between my door . . . my door and the neighbor's door." The Toyota took another crashing rise and fall. Rocks pinged like bullets.

"You should've assumed they weren't for you," she said.

"I gave the brownies the benefit of the doubt."

"You deserved it—"

The rear bay door rattled open, caught a rush of air, and slammed shut.

"I had . . ." He flinched. "I saw you when you visited him. Next door. Always on Thursdays. I thought your were so beautiful. I didn't dare look you in the eye, even when we passed at the mailbox—"

"I remember that." She was crinkling her nose, trying not to cry.

He checked over the dash again. The arroyo was a hundred meters away now, coming fast.

"He was an idiot for what he did to you, Elle. And thinking you wouldn't find out." He reached over, grabbed the driver seatbelt, and wrapped it around her shoulder. "So *of course* you'd make him a plate of laxative brownies."

She smiled guiltily as he raised her arm and looped the belt under her. The buckles met with a piercing click.

"Roy," he gasped. "Hang on back there." He grabbed the passenger seatbelt and twisted it around his own shoulder, then arched his back, lifted a thigh, and brought the buckles together. Another cold click.

"I used the whole box of laxatives, too." Elle sniffed. "Like, twenty-four doses. I only expected him to eat one or two—"

"I love brownies, Elle."

"He didn't like chocolate."

"I ate *eleven*."

She laughed and he felt her breath on his face.

He squeezed her fingers. "Worst forty-eight hours of my life."

Somehow all the noise and glass and metal and wind drained away, and it was just them, their small voices, and the scent of her green apple shampoo.

"It was worth it." He closed his eyes and braced. "Because it gave me something to talk about when—"

* * *

Tapp couldn't see the vehicle crash down into the arroyo (his view was obscured by the rising land) but the hollow crack reached him in just over a second. It sounded like a femur breaking. The flashflood crevasse was only four hundred meters downhill from his roost. Just over four football fields. By a sniper's measure, that was pissing distance.

186

He worked a jittery chill out of his spine and darted his scope to Svatomir, five hundred meters back up the hill, right where James' tire tracks left the road. The big man now stood at the lip of a ditch where his jeep rested brokenly, one tire canted hard. He was bending low and circling a crusty basalt boulder – in his hands was that loop of ever-useful winching cable – and he tucked the hook, planted his boot to the lava rock, and drew the cable tight. He would be out of that rut in a minute. Two, tops. Then he would descend the slope and corner James Eversman and his gang of moving targets inside the riverbed and hose them down with his Mac-11.

Unless, of course, James somehow managed again to—

Stop.

He could maybe—

Nope. He can't. He won't.

Tapp needed another energy drink. Without caffeine his mind unraveled like mummy bandages. Questions fluttered. *How badly is Svatomir injured? Is there enough sunlight for my objective lens? Do I have to pee again?* And lesser thoughts, half-formed, coming faster than he could handle them – that coyote with a black skeleton arm in its jaws, credit card interest, drool crusted on his pillow, variable winds. Too many things to catch at once, all emergencies. His body was curling into a defensive fetal pose, his thighs creeping to his elbows. He felt his heartbeat revving up like railroad ties under a locomotive. He hated himself. He never could have been a real sniper, and *this* was why.

He grabbed his third energy drink, popped the tab, and swigged half the thing. His hyperactive mind – what an unbecoming trait for a marksman, to be cursed with a brain like a bag of cats – leapt now to his homemade camouflage suit. His familiar coat of threads and crispy grass, rank with sweat and gun smoke. His costume, his masterpiece, his *ghillie suit.*

He tipped his beverage. Empty. He hurled it and grabbed another.

Ghillie suit. Noun. Derived from 'gille.' Scottish Gaelic word for 'lad' or 'servant.' In feudal times, gille gamekeepers under the employ of their lords would don this shaggy mesh of netting, scrub their skin with dirt and moss, and melt into the trees. There these men would lay concealed in plain view, waiting weaponless for their prey to—

Shit! He slashed his thumb on the drink tab. Hot blood all over the sipping edge. He didn't care. He drank anyway.

After hours or days, the buck would draw near. It'd be a wraith in the trees; a magnificent huffing beast made of rippling muscles and tightened nerves. And the invisible, scentless gille crawls and creeps – sometimes taking an hour to move a single meter – to within whisper-distance and ambushes the animal with his bare hands. Pins it, binds its legs. Then he drags his quarry back into town, into his lord's fenced arena, which is adorned with planted ferns and ringside audience seating, and cuts the buck loose. So some faggot Scottish prince can stroll in, dust off a bow, nock an arrow between clean fingernails, and kill the animal in a staged hunt. Cue polite applause – but everyone knows who the real badass is.

Which one am I?

He crunched another empty can on his forehead (four) and dropped it. He needed to focus. The stakes here and now were incredible. If James, or any of them, escaped his valley and reached the local authorities, it'd be over. Done. Fin. Do not pass Go. Do not collect two hundred dollars. He'd be strung up like the Unabomber, crucified and mainlining barbiturate.

A fresh shot of white-hot panic tore through him and he reached for energy drink number five, biting the tab open to protect his bloodied thumb. Nightmares came to him in flashes as he slurped his beverage down like warm medicine – some Google Maps asshole stumbling across Shady Slope Road, or one of his radio exchanges with Svatomir bleeding into a passing trucker's closed-band frequency, or his cell signal jammer somehow alerting some underpaid Verizon engineer climbing the cell tower ten-odd miles north. All possible. It was, after all, the details that killed you, and details were sneaky little bastards.

Tapp knew this wasn't a shoot anymore. This was a psychological battle with James. This was kill or die. What was Tapp willing to do to survive?

Anything.

He shot a little girl once to survive.

Yes. Yes, I did.

That had been hard.

This won't be.

The sore panic was finally receding. He started his final energy drink (six) and wished he had packed more Cheetos, or Swedish Fish, or at least some crackers. Already he could imagine the caffeine kicking in, filling his veins with hot life, unlocking new neural tunnels and wiring shortcuts inside his brain. His fingers were suddenly nimble, his reflexes instant. The energy crash would be brutal after this binge, but by then James would be dead. Long dead. If in five hours, Tapp's biggest problem was an icepick headache and sludgy memory, well then, he'd be doing just fine.

I'm still doing fine?

He was doing great.

Okay.

Around him the earth was falling into shadow, turning back to an ancient dark that existed before man and would exist long after. Sound carried differently in this air – sharper, cleaner, harder. Echoes vanished. His own gunshots would lose their bass and become whip cracks. The winds were coming now in timid spurts, touching his cheeks and aggravating his yellow flags. The distant storm wasn't distant anymore, towering over the horizon and shrouding the reddening sun. Everything was changing, morphing, rotating into a darker form.

* * *

James was staring into the sun for some reason.

It was setting, which pleased him, although he couldn't recall why, so he just grinned dumbly while he watched it dull like a lantern behind fog. He felt the heat touch his face and numbly remembered – eight minutes. It took eight minutes to travel from that distant nuclear fire, through the gulf of space, to this little rock.

"James."

He recognized her voice and the day exploded back at him – Glen Floyd's comb-over-in-a-car story, the soda can shriek of automatic gunfire, the way blood hardened into globs in the sand like donut glaze. And the crash. What about the crash? He tried to search his surroundings and decipher what the hell had happened but he couldn't pull his eyes from the sun. It held him transfixed.

"James, I . . . this is really bad."

Elle's tone was grave. No sarcasm, no understatement. An updraft washed through the Rav4, surprisingly cool, and he heard it jingling loose glass and blowing soft tufts of seat foam. He clamped his eyelids and blinked but saw only that damn sun, seared into his retinas in splashes of orange-violet-yellow-green. He felt like he was awakening after a night of dollar beers, and now establishing the basics – *Where am I? Did Elle and I have a fight? Where's my wallet? Can I taste vomit in the back of my mouth?* Somewhere in the car he sensed Elle moving and something wooden creaked in the back seats. The vehicle rocked a few inches like a teeter-totter, suggesting that they were high-centered. His chin rested against what he figured was the dashboard. He raised his head, turned his shoulders—

His arms didn't move.

"Yeah." He heard her shrug. "I was getting to that."

At least her sense of humor was back.

He blinked away sunspot colors and saw it. Both of his wrists were bound with sloppy loops of duct tape, swooping up, down, over, under, from his knuckles to his forearms, thoroughly sealing him to the Rav4's shifter. Much of it was stained with dollops of blood, running down folds and seams in hardening rivers, all of it belonging to someone else. He leaned back and tugged, and the shifter wobbled sympathetically in its socket, but he knew the next thing to give would be his shoulder blades. He was stuck.

He exhaled. "Roy?"

"Yep," Elle said.

"It's . . . more tape than I would have used."

"He hit me."

"What?" James looked at her, certain he'd misheard.

"He was crawling over me, tying you up. I tried to stop him, jabbed his eyes, grabbed his hurt hand, and one of his fingers tore off. And he pushed my face against the door and I think he . . . kicked the back of my head." She worked her jaw and he saw it, a blue shadow coalescing over her cheekbone. "I must have blacked out, and then he left. I'm sorry."

"It's okay."

Her eyes glimmered. "I'm *so sorry.*"

"It's fine." He was still hazy, like his head was sloshing full of cheap beer. "Find something to cut me out. The . . . multitool—"

"It's gone."

He knew that. "The tool bag—"

"A half mile up the road," she said hollowly. She moved and the sunlight drew her bruise like a Nike swoosh under her eye. Her skin was already puffing up.

Roy. James felt his cheeks burn and the delayed agony of his concussion headache hit like a wheelbarrow packed with cinder blocks. Goddamn Roy, and the family he neglected, and his stupid I PISS EXCELLENCE shirt. Goddamn him. No, *fuck* him. Fuck him for hitting beautiful, sweet Elle in the back of the head.

Anger is weird, he realized. More than a feeling. It has mass, somehow. It fills you up like hot food. James was ashamed of how good it felt. He wanted to kill Roy. It was wrong, everything in him said it was wrong, but he couldn't control it. None of his father's words came easily to him, but the one about having a plan to kill everyone you met was ringing cautiously true. After all, Roy sure did.

If I see you again, Roy . . .

"Wait." He hesitated. "Did you . . . did you say you pulled off his finger?"

She looked embarrassed.

"Wow, Elle."

"It was an accident."

"How do you accidentally pull off a finger?"

"His hand was shot. You're making it sound worse than it is."

"Is it . . . is it still in here?"

She pointed to the middle console, beside his elbow.

He looked and recoiled. "Oh, Jesus. What's it doing in the cup holder?"

"I had to put it somewhere."

"But the *cup holder?*"

Elle started giggling.

They both lost it. Exhausted, pitch-black belly laughs. For a few seconds, everything was okay and they were back in the Sacramento fire marshal's office and that mustached old man was offhandedly comparing the neighbor's meth lab explosion to Washington state's iconic 1980 volcanic eruption, and everything was just hilarious. He couldn't describe it.

"If Roy . . ." She gasped, an ugly dry scrape. "If he survives this, gloves are going to look *so stupid* on him."

A bellowing roar descended the hill and splashed down both ends of the creekbed. James threw his head back to see (what else?) the Soviet's jeep, three hundred yards back, framed by the toothed glass of the Rav4's back window. The rig skidded to face them and revved hungrily.

Elle looked up and sighed.

"Yeah." James chewed his lip. "We should probably start cutting this tape."

17

Safety glass turned out to be worthless for cutting duct tape. Who knew? Chunks crumbled in Elle's hands like ice, so she checked her purse for her car keys (*Oh, right*), then grabbed a triangular shard from the broken rearview mirror. Every layer of tape she sliced and peeled off exposed another underneath. Her fingers whitened and burned with sweaty friction. The sickly sweet odor of adhesive curdled the air. James' left wrist tugged free but his right hand was buried much deeper, his knuckles mummified unrecognizably around the shifter like a big lobster claw.

"Shit."

"I can't—"

Not fast enough. No time.

Every second, the Soviet's loping motor grew louder, turning the air into cotton. Glass chattered and debris shifted anxiously. James felt his molars vibrate. Who knew that cars could even sound like that? It deepened against rock walls until it sounded like a monster truck, approaching fast.

No words were needed. They both knew. She tore another crackling strip of tape free and looked up at him apologetically, jaw clenched, eyes wet, cheeks red.

He smiled at her.

A smile had always been the path of least resistance for him and it came naturally, even here. A strange calm was sliding over him and he was somehow certain everything would turn out okay. The sun was setting. Tapp's scope was dimming. She would make it. It wouldn't be easy, because the killers would hunt her with whatever gadgets and cruel tricks they had at their disposal, but she was tough and she could do it. She wasn't that hollow-eyed version of herself from the Fuel-N-Food anymore. She was the fighter he fell in love with, the girl who (probably) wasn't bluffing when she'd threatened to castrate Roy for punching her husband. She was the girl he'd seen on that USC running track, sophomore year. October, under a milky sky.

There had been a dreamy, soundless second when she'd clipped her shin on the zebra-striped hurdle. Then he watched her pile-drive into the ground and roll once, twice, three times. Not a murmur from the crowd. James had been in motion then, pushing people aside, bolting for the chest-high chain link fence cordoning off the oval track – but she was already back on her feet, standing dizzily, shaking off the blur. Both of her knees were slashed and thin rivers of blood raced down to her running shoes. She wavered once, looked at the crowd, and several hundred people waited in rapt confusion, like an airshow audience stunned by a fireball. Someone had said something about a medic – *Here he is, he's coming* – but it didn't matter because Elle DeSilva just dug her heels in and kept running. Three more jumps cleared on the final curve and she finished the hundred-meter hurdle with a gray face and a quart of blood staining the track behind her. *Badass*, James had thought. Badass – and he didn't even know about her snakes yet.

She was that woman again now, and she could do it. Collapsed lung or not.

"Elle, go." He pushed her away with his free hand, hanging tatters of tape.

She shook her head.

The Soviet's motor change pitch and cycled lower, rougher. He was slowing down at the rim of the gully, preparing to get out and descend on foot. His brakes whined. Rocks crunched under tires. A dry stick broke.

There were so many things James wanted to tell her but there was no time: *Run. He's lost a lot of blood because of me, so he'll be slow and easy to outrun. Keep moving, don't stop, follow the riverbed where Tapp can't see you. Keep putting boulders between yourself and the Soviet. When it gets dark enough – thirty more minutes, tops – you run out of here, up one of the valley walls, and race for Mosby. Tapp's gun will be useless, but he'll still search for you on foot. They'll need to get in close to find you, though, and they never will because you're fast. You'll make it.*

Or *I love you*. There was always that.

The Soviet cut his motor, not twenty yards up the hill behind them, filling the air with expectant silence. The last breath before the plunge, held with swollen lungs.

Elle was smiling now. She had an idea.

"What?"

She kissed him. Then she passed the shard of glass to his right hand like it was a prison shiv and whispered in his ear, shivering with adrenaline: "I'll buy you as much time as I can."

He felt her fingertips brush his one last time, and then she was out the swinging door and running, a desperate silhouette against a graying sky, going, going, gone.

* * *

Elle estimated the arroyo to be twenty yards wide and ten deep. A calcified creek bed wove between limestone faces and patches of prickly pear, all dulling blue in the twilight. She wanted to look back, to know where the jeep was relative to the wrecked Rav4, if the Soviet was out of it yet, if his subgun was in his hand or under his duster or in the process of being reloaded—

Just run. Don't stop.

Prickly pear everywhere. Dense clusters of the paddle-shaped cacti rising in bunny-ear patterns, most a yard deep but some approaching neck-height. The lowest reaches of the arroyo were filled with a rushing tide of green, cascading from one bank to the other and speckled with pink fruits like an alien garden. She couldn't see the thin barbs but she felt them piercing her jeans, slashing her ankles, sticking to her Converse in messy clumps.

She heard a door slam, up the hill.

The air chilled. She knew the Soviet had to see her by now, had to be drawing on her, seconds from pulling the trigger and stitching a bloody line down her back. She veered left and right over the floor of chipped shale, taking a running leap over a thorny patch and crashing down hard on her left ankle. Every breath was punctuated by a stabbing pain, like a molten dagger buried in her chest.

Chase me. Chase me, you son of a—

The subgun barked. A line of splashing dirt, right to left, crossed the desert floor at her feet. She stumbled through the flying grit, missed a step but caught herself. She stole a glimpse over her shoulder at the Soviet, descending the lip of the arroyo. He was skidding on both feet for traction, slowing, and she knew it was so he could hold the little weapon with two hands, brace the stubby thing to his shoulder, and squirt off an accurate burst. Next time, he wouldn't miss.

She stumbled, lungs burning. Ahead and to the right came a shadow of prickly pear. It was incredible, a towering pillar of outgrowths gashed with the whitened scars of a thousand frosts. Hundreds of paddles – some olive drab, some neon green, some standing rigidly, some sagging in tired pillows – all splintered with thorns. A cactus metropolis. If cacti had a nation, this would be its capital. Cactus legislation would be passed here, with cactus crowds lobbying outside for various cactus interests.

I'm not *jumping into that. Nope.*

But she was already running for it. She willed herself to enjoy this final half second of cool air on her cheeks. She didn't give herself time to think. There was no time anyway. She forced another breath into her broken lungs and dove. Again the subgun rattled behind her, and at this distance she could hear the individual shots pumping down the barrel in a rhythmic BRAP-BRAP-BRAP-BRAP. As her feet left the earth she was vaguely aware of barbs sticking and breaking off in her palms, her stomach, her ankles, the back of her neck. Then the rock floor came rushing up to meet her and she let her knees bend in a controlled runner's fall, tucked her shoulders, and rolled once, twice, to land on her back in a rippling sea of little bites. It didn't hurt yet – too much adrenaline – but it would. Oh yes, it would.

She remembered when she was five and her mother had taken her to Fred Meyer's, where she discovered potted cacti in the gardening department. Most were gnarly but some of them had no thorns at all, just little patches of yellow fur dotting the domed surfaces like pepperoni on a pizza. *Nice cactuses*, she called them, petting them like her aunt's cats. Only when they reached the car did she realize what those little monsters were – their thorns microscopic, leaving millions of hooked barbs in her fingertips. They hadn't stung until then, but they *really* stung. Her mother had laughed, which made her cry harder, because the tweezers were at home and it was a long drive. She remembered sitting in the backseat with hot tears on her cheeks, unable to wipe them away because her hands had been transformed into itchy red claws, pincushioned with tiny quills. *Nice cactuses*, her mother had chuckled as she drove, making petting motions against the steering wheel. *Nice cactuses, nice cactuses, nice—*

The Soviet fired again.

She rolled on her side, her cheek against the cool rocks, her hands over her face. Bullets slapped around and above her, quivering cactus paddles, punching out fleshy gouges, showering gooey chunks, thorns, and warm juices. A tower of prickly pear broke and fell, letting in a burst of daylight. Finally the world stopped shaking and the rattling echo of the subgun raced from one end of the valley to the other. That, too, faded until there was only the distant wind.

She couldn't see him. He hadn't used his whole magazine, either – he had at least five seconds of sustained fire in that thing and that had only been three. He might be advancing on her again. She rolled over and elbowed up, pushed a shredded paddle aside with her fingertips, and scanned the riverbed. Just rocks and brush. No Soviet.

She rose further. Her hair was matted with sticky cactus blood. It had drenched her. It was in her mouth, coating her teeth like wax, bitter enough to make your throat seal up tight like Eowen's disastrous attempt at an India Pale Ale—

There he was.

The Soviet was still at the edge of the riverbed – why hadn't he chased her further? He was standing oddly, like a statue, duster stirring in the wind, his left leg slick with glossy black. Blood. Even with a two-inch butter knife, James had managed to inflict some damage. The man hobbled a bit, lowered his subgun, and scraped out the stick-shaped magazine. He made a sour face and palmed it back in.

Bullets, she realized. Thank God. He was almost out of—

The Soviet turned around and walked a few paces back to the crashed Rav4. Where James was, duct-taped to the shifter. Helpless.

She screamed but the Soviet ignored her.

"No! Come back!"

He approached the Toyota where it had destroyed itself against lava boulders, headlights facing each other, windows blown out, tires bowed. The car didn't look totaled (which it certainly was) so much as corrupted, *twisted*, like something out of Wonderland. The Soviet grabbed the bruised passenger door handle, subgun up and at his hip in a practiced close-quarters entry maneuver. Instead of the sterile professionalism of a SWAT team, he had a relaxed confidence that was a thousand times more frightening.

"Hey. Your drawings *suck*!"

The Soviet wasn't listening. She wanted to stand, or throw something, or maybe futilely race up behind him to catch a machine gun spray in the chest, anything but nothing – and then it was too late. Life moves too fast, your window for the perfect comeback closes. The Soviet threw the door open, aimed inside, and she knew James didn't stand a chance – *This is my fault, I ran too fast and he lost interest—*

Nothing happened.

She watched in dumb silence. The Soviet leaned inside the mangled car, checked the back seats, and leaned out. He paused, placed his hands to his hips like a disapproving mother, and spat in the dirt. She could hear the glob land from fifty yards.

Her heart pounded. She saw rotten blasts of color in her vision. *James is alive. He's okay. He wasn't inside the Toyota, he ripped free of Roy's duct tape while the Hello Kitty Man chased me. My plan worked. I was a decoy. An excellent, five-star decoy. James is fine. He's somewhere else—*

Where?

The Soviet kicked the passenger door shut. He misjudged and stumbled instead, slapping a hand to the Toyota's yellow quarter panel and leaving a print of sticky red. He had to be hurting by now. He'd lost a lot of blood. That made Elle happy; happier than she ever thought she could be about blood loss.

She prairie-dogged further up and scanned both ends of the arroyo for James. She couldn't see him. Or Roy. There was a lot of winding terrain, though, and an exceptional amount of visual cover. You could play hide and seek down here. Which, to be fair, was the goal right now.

The Soviet tucked a hand under his duster and paced back up to his jeep, and then he threw open the black door and climbed inside, disturbing a handful of rolling rocks. He closed the door and sat there for a long moment, barely visible in the dimming red sunlight. Then he kicked the engine into gear and . . . skidded back up the rise.

He was leaving.

Like the evil birds in that old movie she had watched once with James – *They're flying south? Really?* – the villain was swiping a timecard and leaving because, well, that's the end. Why now, in real life?

He'd lost a lot of blood, she figured. He was probably seizing the opportunity to bandage his wound while Tapp's still-functioning scope kept them safely corralled in the arroyo. After all, when darkness fell, all bets would be off. Best to resupply now.

She felt her adrenaline high tapering off, but knew this wasn't the end. This was just a breather. The Soviet Cowboy would certainly be back before full dark. How long then? Twenty minutes? Fifteen? Until then, she was trapped in this crevasse in the center of Tapp's valley like a soldier pinned in a trench. She knew Roy was down there, too. If he wasn't, the sniper would have already blown his head off.

So where was James?

* * *

James was hanging underneath the Soviet's jeep.

He wished he wasn't. He was already regretting the idea. He braced both arms around some sort of lateral bar and tucked his feet up to what he guessed was the transmission case. This was the most familiar he'd ever gotten with the underside of a car. It sucked. He couldn't tell how much clearance he had with the rushing desert floor below and he honestly didn't want to know. He really, really wished he hadn't done this.

On the subject of wishes – he also wished the Soviet had left a gun in his unattended jeep. That had been James' first priority after he'd cut himself free and bolted to it, wincing while gunshots thumped from the gully. He had checked the Soviet's glove box, the console, under the slashed seats. Nothing. Just a sweaty jeep with three stiffening bodies in the back. No keys, either – the bastard carried them on that jingling ring. Before James had been able to think of anything else, he had heard Elle shouting and seen the Soviet doubling back to—

Jagged rocks scraped his back. A big one, then two smaller ones. Then a vicious one that felt like an ice pick in his collarbone, drawing warm blood. He gasped and his front teeth scraped against dirty steel, like biting a chalkboard. Everything hurt. His elbows quivered with Charlie Horse tightness, he badly needed to pee, and the muscles in his stomach threatened to burn through his skin. He adjusted and readjusted his feet but found no firm traction, only temporary holds and a slow slide. Gravity was a patient enemy that would never tire. James was already exhausted.

The Soviet stomped the gas and the engine snarled a few inches from his face. Smothering air stung his eyes. He tasted burnt oil. Dirt clods pelted the sides of his head, kicked up by monster truck tires. He felt like he was breathing into a hair dryer. All the while, the vehicle shuddered up and down over every imperfection in the terrain, threatening to slip free of his sweaty hands.

Yep, this was a bad idea.

But he couldn't drop to the ground and let the jeep pass overhead. Not an option anymore. The Soviet had chugged too far uphill. The vehicle was now certainly within Tapp's eyeshot – if James dropped or fell off the chassis now he would find himself exposed and very dead. It wasn't dark yet, either. Dusk, yes, but not dark.

At least Elle was still alive.

And so am I.

He shuddered with raw excitement, a guilty nervous glee he hadn't felt since he was twelve and grimacing at the acid taste of vodka in his friend's basement, as he imagined Tapp's thousand-dollar scope sweeping over the roof of the Soviet's jeep without knowing his prey clung underneath. Bad idea or not, this was a big step. For the first time all day, William Tapp didn't know exactly where James was.

He only *thought* he did.

Squeezing his eyes open, he saw the setting half sun rotate behind his left elbow and realized the jeep had changed direction from north to south. The bumpy ride had improved, too. The Soviet was back on the packed dirt of Shady Slope Road and was . . . yes, he was driving toward Tapp now, straight toward the sniper's side of the valley. Even better. Straight to the marksman's den as the night descended, where the coward was roosted and vulnerable up close. It was almost too good to be real.

James felt a tormented grin crawl over his face.

I'm coming for you, Tapp.

You may own every inch of this valley, but you can't own the night.

18

NIGHT VISION, read the military-style polymer case.

Tapp popped both latches under the wet thump of his own heartbeat. This gadget cost over three thousand dollars and he had operated it only once, last year. It was still an unfamiliar thing which he kept stashed in his nest the way one would keep a fire extinguisher, and he now wished he had thought to bundle the instruction manual with it. He was lousy with manuals anyway, often leafing through them once and discarding them to discover the subtleties with his own hands. Right now, those hands were shaking.

His BlackEye X3S wasn't military spec anymore, but it was damned close (close enough for some Brazilian SWAT teams, and at least one outfit of red beret hand-choppers in Nigeria). It was a bulbous optic swollen with curves and knobs. He thumbed in the silver disc battery and closed the trapdoor like a sewer lid. He couldn't peel the covers off and look through it yet – not quite dark enough. Fifteen more minutes, tops. The tech had come a long way from those primitive Starlight scopes in Vietnam, but light overload could still destroy a night optic. Although the BlackEye online ad boasted an automatic shutdown feature to save the image intensifier tube from such damage, did Tapp really trust it? Nope. No, sir. He was gravely protective of his nice things and this third generation night scope, capable of spotting a human at two miles in moonless darkness, was one of his nicest.

This particular model – the X3S – worked its magic by gathering whatever ambient or infrared light it could soak up and squeezing it through a photocathode tube, which turned photons into electrons. These electrons were multiplied thousands of times through a micro-channel plate and then reconverted back from electricity into visible light through a phosphor screen, creating that trademark green-tinted night vision that penetrated every shadow's secrets.

This is definitely a . . .

He tried to make another pun; something about the situation being a *sea change*, referencing the fact that the BlackEye allowed him to *see* in the dark, but it just wasn't happening. His heart wasn't in it. In fact, his heart was slamming against his ribs like a dryer with a brick in it. Slippery panic welled up inside him and every time he pushed it back down, it came up stronger. He just wanted to go home. Finish this shit show and hit the road and go to bed. Yes, sir.

Something growled downhill.

Clear to his naked eye, Svatomir's jeep was humming up the incline three hundred meters away. That Mac-11 had to be dry by now, so Svatomir was making a trip to the supply shed (the bungalow, Tapp affectionately called it) to retrieve his Saiga 12 – a chunky Russian 12-gauge mated with an AK-47 receiver. Picture an Osama bin Laden-style assault rifle that fired *shotgun shells*. Aiming optional. Two quick pulls would turn most creatures from solid to liquid. Birds become showers of red feathers and snakes become stringy clots of scales. Svatomir loved the Saiga 12 because it was the firearm equivalent of an 'easy button.' Tapp loved the Saiga 12 (right now) because it had an LED torchlight mounted under the barrel. With it, Svatomir could scrutinize every nook and cranny of the sheltered arroyo, while every other square centimeter of the valley would belong to Tapp and his BlackEye night vision. So yeah, the situation was under control.

Alright, James. What now?

You stay in the arroyo . . . Svatomir kills you.

You run for the hills under darkness . . . I kill you.

On autopilot, William Tapp's hands had already turned his rifle sideways, bolt-side up, to swap scopes. With a baby screwdriver he attacked the first eight screws on the cantilever, sealed with blue Loctite, and they dropped like black flies into his palm. He heard Svatomir's jeep grumble closer but ignored it.

* * *

Under that jeep, James hung on by fingernails and prayers.

Shady Slope Road crossed the arroyo on a black trestle and then halfway up Tapp's incline, the Soviet veered west off the road and followed a slithering horse trail over two ascending switchbacks. In the fading dusk he saw the destination over his elbow – a heap of scrap metal under Army-brown camouflage netting, and beside it, nestled snugly into the hillside like a Tibetan mountain temple, a small rectangular building. It was the building Elle had spotted in her Nikon screen. Two hours ago it had been a distant smudge in a lens, and now it was real.

His arms were clay. He couldn't hold on much longer. Twice he let his back dip to the racing ground. Twice it bit him and he recoiled up against the undercarriage, torn and gasping. Three times now – or was it four? – he'd sworn he was at his limit, and then he'd surprised himself each time and somehow kept holding on.

Don't. Let. Go. He pressed his cheekbone to the hot steel.

Barely glimpsed over the right tire, he saw the sun had sunk beneath the horizon and a crest of clouds had taken its place. The storm had overtaken half of the sky. Behind the left tire, he could see the very first stars pinpricking the eastern horizon. The world was falling into blues and blacks now and he hoped it would be enough to conceal Elle's escape. With any luck, the incoming storm would choke out the moonlight. Rain, if it happened, would be terrific and cut down visibility even further. It was at least six miles back to the highway and more to Mosby, but Elle could make it if she paced herself, took unpredictable routes, and moved intelligently. But what about her injuries?

She had a hole in her chest, sealed with hardened blood and a sandwich bag. There was a pernicious little shard of Tapp's bullet buried somewhere in her guts, drifting freely, slicing everything it touched like a razorblade. How long could she go without medical attention?

The Soviet tapped his brakes. James felt the discs squeal beside his head, slightly independent of each other. He rolled his head back to see the destination creeping closer, upside-down. Composed of maybe two or three rooms, the battered little structure seemed to be a plywood skeleton fleshed with mismatched plates of corrugated sheet metal. Some were corroded and pitted with rust and others gleamed fresh silver in the dying light. A gray door, heavy-looking and a few centimeters crooked, told him which side was the front. Dim yellow light poked through the seams. A lantern or a chemical light inside, James figured.

He pulled himself back up the moving chassis and decided this building was his objective. He supposed he could find some sort of bladed or blunt weapon in there at least, and at the very best, a gun. And if miracles did still occur on this godless stretch of Mojave, perhaps a CB radio or satellite phone. Maybe he'd be able to contact the police. If the next few minutes went truly, spectacularly well, he could distract the two killers long enough to secure Elle a head start. There was nothing better to hope for. He understood that he would likely die here, which was fine. All that mattered now was Elle. Saving Elle.

As the jeep slowed to a walking pace, James let his legs drop. They felt like noodles. His heels scraped the road, leaving tracks in the dirt. This was also fine. Acceptable.

Just keep holding on . . .

After the Soviet whined his brakes for a teasing eternity, the jeep cranked into park and the miserable ride ended. James let go and didn't register hitting the ground. He just sort of time-traveled a second into the future, sprawled flat. Spreading warmth on his scalp. Flashbulbs on the edges of his vision. He must have banged his head on a rock. Another concussion. Sure, why the hell not?

The Soviet killed his engine. Dry silence.

James rolled on his side and waited for the Soviet's boots to hit the ground a few inches from his face. Beyond, he saw the blackness of the scrap heap. But it wasn't a scrap heap at all.

Cars. A junkyard row of them, parked door to door with inches between them. There were eight or nine maybe, all different locales and stories. Two pickup trucks. A sleek black Jetta, like the one his old general manager had driven. Two station wagons, one with a racked canoe on top. And more, further down and out of view, parked with the same tedious efficiency. His mind darted to Auschwitz, of all places, to haystack heaps of shoes and scrounged dental fillings and pocket change catalogued in ledgers. Such dull evil. It made him feel cold.

The Soviet kicked the driver door open, and James held his breath. He got out, kicking dirt in James' face, and then took a gasping stumble, his duster slapping wetly against his thighs. One hand clasped to his stomach, darkened with blood. He walked straight to the building, leaving the driver door ajar but the keys jingling in his pocket, and threw the metal door open and ducked inside. He was in a hurry.

So was James.

He rolled out from under the jeep and sprung alongside the closest of the stashed cars, which happened to be Roy Burke's red Acura. Tapp hadn't seen him (or if he had, he hadn't fired yet). He flattened his back to the bumper with his palms on the ground. The rapidly cooling air stung his throat. His bladder felt the size of a basketball. His joints slushed. He peeked uphill and saw there was only another two hundred yards of terrain rising up to form a jagged horizon behind the building. He knew no sniper of such expertise would ever silhouette himself against the sky. This meant William Tapp was less than two hundred yards away.

He was so close.

Better yet, the shooter had no reason to be scrutinizing this little motor pool on his doorstep because as far as he knew, his three victims were safely herded inside the dry riverbed. James was in Tapp's blind spot.

I'm so close, and you don't know it yet.

He looked over the Acura's hood and estimated the strange shaggy-dog building to be twenty paces away. It was still his objective. He heard a mechanical humming from within, and the Soviet moving, pacing, huffing, opening a drawer, slamming it shut, opening another—

Something snarled beside him and he flinched. The radio! Still crammed in his back pocket through some minor miracle. He'd forgotten he had it.

Tapp's voice dribbled in. "James."

He said nothing.

"James? You . . . you still alive in there?"

In there. As in, *in the gully.*

209

So far, so good.

James wavered and then clicked the input button, keeping his eyes on that gray door as he waited for the Soviet to reemerge. The situation hung on a knife-edge and he didn't want to risk speaking aloud – but Christ, wasn't everything a risk now?

". . . James?"

"I'm here," he whispered through his teeth. "I'm still here."

"Good. Quick question, James."

"Shoot," he said.

Tapp made a gasping, croaking sound. At first James thought the sniper was choking on something, but no luck. It was laughter. Giddy laughter, rippling through his voice in waves: "That's a good one. That's a really, really . . . good one."

"Good what?"

"No one . . . ever appreciates puns." The sniper caught his breath and sniffed, audibly grinning. "It's like they're toxic or something. I don't . . . I don't get it. Folks say puns are the mark of an infantile mind. Wordplay for retards. The lowest form of humor. Thank you, James. It's been a long day. I needed that."

He nodded. "I, uh, figured it was worth . . . worth a *shot.*"

"Not bad, James. Not bad for being *under the gun.*"

"Well, I *aim* to please."

The killer belched. "I've always felt that a good pun is its own . . . re-word."

That one ambushed James. He laughed. It came out like a cough.

Tapp was pleased with himself. "Gotcha."

God help me, I just laughed at a pun. Elle would kill me.

He cleared his mind and focused on that gray door. Any second now, it would swing open and the Soviet would return to his jeep, and when he did, he would leave the building unguarded. Right under Tapp's nose. James would then bolt inside, search for a phone, gather information, recover weapons, do something. Anything.

I'm on the offensive now, he realized. *It's my move.*

Inside the shed, the Soviet slammed something. It sounded like a high-school locker, harsh and jangling.

"Know what scares me, James?" Tapp asked.

"Yeah?"

"I . . . I don't dream. Never have, ever." The sniper licked his lips and paused. "Why do you suppose that is? What's wrong with my brain?"

"Do you really want me to answer that?"

"When I was a little kid, I used to worry it was because I didn't have a soul. I couldn't conjure up dreams, because I had zero spiritual activity inside me. I thought maybe I was born without one. Or I signed a deal with the devil when I was very young, like three or four years old, and just didn't remember it. Who's to say you'd remember? Maybe the devil doesn't . . . let you. So for years, I'd go to bed desperate, eating a pound of Gummy Bears every night. Sugars kick-start dreams. I would pray, beg, hope, that that would be the night I'd dream about something. Even a nightmare. Because it would mean my soul was alright."

James said nothing.

"It's stupid, but it still gets to me. Because I know I'm not normal. Normal people can't do what I do." The killer exhaled and crackled static. "Isn't that just . . . rich, James? I fear that I'm missing something that I'm scientifically certain doesn't exist anyway."

The Soviet stomped past the door. Cracks of sulfurous light shifted.

James shrugged. "Are satanic contracts binding at age four?"

"Shut up."

"Just saying. Was there a notary present?"

"You're teasing me."

James was — kind of. But he couldn't stop. "Theoretically, then. If you did sign your soul away, what would you have asked for?"

"To be good at something," William Tapp answered immediately. "To be impossibly, superhumanly good at one thing. Whatever the cost."

A chill breathed over the dark prairie, and it seemed to echo the sniper's words.

Whatever the cost.

James pressed his forehead to the Acura logo on Roy's trunk, wishing the Soviet would hurry up in there. His little adrenaline high had abruptly gone sour. He felt insignificant. Like an insect, clinging desperately to the gears of Tapp's machinery. He was fighting back, sure, but how many victims had tried that before him? He was pushing back against a double-digit murder spree spanning decades. Resisting the momentum of history.

"What scares you, James?"

He felt obligated, too. Tapp had bared a wound, or a soft spot, and it felt oddly appropriate to return the gesture as a weird, old-timey 'respect thy enemy' thing while you loaded your flintlock pistol and awaited the dueling count. Because – being honest – that's what it was now: a duel. Between a man with a gun and a man who wished he had one. So, he decided, to hell with it.

"James? What scares you?"

"I . . ." He sighed, careful to keep his voice low. "Okay. I'm nine years old. And my parents are fighting in the other room, and I'm trying to watch the TV menu channel because I like to watch the little movie previews in the corner of the screen, but the volume doesn't go high enough to cover the yelling."

As he spoke, he heard the Soviet fidgeting with something inside the building – delicate, hollow clicks, muffled by the door.

"He's . . . God, my dad's so furious I can hear his teeth chattering. Through the wall. And for a while it just sounds like another fight. A loud fight. My mom is saying something about the cops. Something about the Anti-Weathermen. She knows something. The phone kept getting picked up, set down, picked up, set down. And then they both fall very quiet, scary quiet, for a long time. It's like they vanished. I'm confused, so I mute the TV. Then she screams."

Tapp fed static, but said nothing.

"It was an exercise weight." James closed his eyes and dug his teeth into his upper lip so his voice wouldn't shudder. "Like, one of those ten-pound dumbbells with the big knobbed edges. This one was bright pink, stupid-looking. He'd grabbed her wrist and held her right hand on the kitchen counter by the stove, like an executioner's block, and that silence must have been the disbelief. Like, *are you really doing that?* Maybe they'd had these moments before. I don't know."

"Did he?"

James said nothing.

"Did . . . did he smash her hand?"

The summer before that episode, eight-year-old James and his mother had gone to Gray Beach to stay with her sister and her kids. The house was even tinier than their farmhouse, with no electricity or running water, but it was a half mile from the ocean. A barefoot walk through the dunes, soaking up fleabites, and you were there on the edge of the world under an Atlantic sky. The sand was pockmarked with dead crab shells. They looked like bleached tombstones, dried out and rotted, and James had made it his personal mission to stomp and shatter every one he encountered on those six miles of coastline. That particular sound – the porcelain crack, the fleshy squish underneath, muffled by sand – was exactly what his mother's right hand sounded like when the exercise weight came down.

"James," Tapp prodded. "Did he—"

"*Yes.*"

From the building came the sound of a wet spring compressing and releasing. A buffalo grunt. Then footsteps on slick concrete. The steel door banged open and James snapped back into survival mode. He clicked off the radio – "James?" – and sank to his belly beside the Acura's rear tire.

Under Roy's muffler, he watched the Soviet stomp back to his jeep. Now he had a new gun over his shoulder – a muscular black thing with a swollen, drum-shaped ammunition device on the bottom. A blue LED light bobbed under the muzzle, burning a circle in the ground as he walked. His duster bulged with extra rounds, and underneath, white bandages were taped to his gut in sloppy loops. His nostrils hissed an odd railroad whistle. Even at ten yards, James could smell the disinfectant dripping off him, condensing in the air like a gallon of spilled tequila. The Soviet climbed into his jeep and vanished behind tinted windows, pitch black in the descending night.

Was Elle running now? James hoped so. It was dark enough.

The motor growled and the Soviet Cowboy backed out urgently, hurling bucketfuls of dirt, and flicked on his high beams. He was heading back down to the arroyo, banking into the first switchback and drawing harsh patterns with his lights. Bandaged, rearmed, ready to finish off Elle and Roy.

No more waiting.

It was time.

James pulled himself upright, shivering, and raced for the unguarded door with his heart thumping in his neck. His clothes tugged. His footsteps crunched. He thumbed the radio back on and heard William Tapp's voice, mid-sentence: "—I like you, James. I wish you'd be the one to kill me."

"I'll try," James said sincerely. He reached that mysterious metal door, pushed it open, and stepped into the yellow glow. His mind raced.

He's coming back for you, Elle.

Run.

* * *

She watched the Soviet cross the trestle and park his jeep at the lip of the arroyo, just above where the Rav4 had crashed. Then he reentered the gully on foot. Even at a hundred yards and through a filter of thorny shadows she could discern a new gun in his hands with a mounted flashlight, throwing methodical sweeps of light as he descended. It was now or never.

She was crouched at the arroyo's westernmost point. Any further and the land flattened to lose its defilade. She looked out into Tapp's open valley, up hundreds of hopeless yards to the bowled, black horizons. The desert now appeared strangely two-dimensional, like the sort of matte paintings they used to use for backgrounds in sci-fi films before today's age of soulless CGI. It felt vast, lonely, and utterly indifferent to her and her tiny problems – her racking breaths, the blood hardening between her fingers, the jagged shale under her knees, the itchy barbs burrowed into her clothes and skin like mites. A particularly nasty one had nail-gunned itself deep under her thumbnail. She squeezed that hand into a fist.

Run, she told herself. Tapp couldn't see her in the dark. Right?

Somehow she kept punching the snooze button. Just a little more time, she begged herself. Another minute of relative comfort, one final whiff of safety and stillness before dashing into the open ground. A few more seconds for James to burst from the darkness – *I'm fine, let's get the hell out of here* – and they could flee this nightmare together. Waiting here was easy. To run was to leave her husband behind, likely forever, and she couldn't commit to that. So she kept waiting, while the Hello Kitty man drew closer and brighter, like they were playing some life-and-death version of flashlight tag.

Twenty seconds passed.

Thirty.

A minute.

She tried to rationalize that every second she procrastinated was a shade more darkness, but the sun was already long gone. Night had fallen. This was it – take it or leave it. The Soviet was too low in the riverbed to be visible now, but she saw his blue-white light dart up granite walls and cut jagged shadows as he scrutinized every inch in hungry sweeps, like a mobile lighthouse. In a flash of panic she wondered – had she left footprints in the packed soil for him to follow? Possibly. It's tough to pay attention to that sort of thing when you're being shot at and jumping face-first into plants you have no business jumping face-first into. She could cut herself some slack there.

Come on, Elle. Run.

She distracted herself again by taking mental inventory. Her purse had been dead weight so she dumped it – her makeup, eye drops, ballpoint pens, a checkbook, a yellowed paperback she had lost her place in – and kept only her wallet and her crappy cell phone. Between this and her heaped belongings on the side of Shady Slope Road, she felt as if she was being purified, distilled into whatever was left of a person when you rendered them homeless and hopeless. She considered setting an alarm (one of the few extra features her prehistoric flip-phone could manage) for fifteen minutes from now and hurling it somewhere in the gully to create a time-bomb diversion, but decided it was more valuable in her pocket. This signal dead zone couldn't stretch forever and the instant she escaped it, she needed to dial 911 and summon the full force of the law down on Tapp's little valley. There had to be a few cops out there over drinking age, right?

Elle. Stop screwing around. Run.

Still her mind wandered and wondered; how did Tapp know so much about Roy? He knew addresses, names, the age of his daughter. He knew everything. He must know something about her and James. He might have been watching them since they left California, or even before then. There was no telling what resources were at his fingertips. She wondered, with a stiletto-jab of fear, what would happen if the sniper went after her family. James had virtually none – no siblings, a reclusive mother, a dead father – but Elle Eversman was a gold mine of potential victims. She wondered if the sniper knew about her dad in Redding, or her copywriter cousins, or Eowen in Tulsa. Eowen thought she was gun-savvy enough to take care of herself but those were only power fantasies. How could anyone be prepared for a killer who could blow your jaw off from another area code?

The Soviet was coming closer. Cactus paddles crunched juicily under his boots and the shine of his light intensified.

One mile through Tapp's line of sight. Easy, right?

She steadied herself and formed a feeble runner's crouch, her knees bent, her shoes arched on brittle rock. One mile out of Tapp's valley, and then another . . . what, five or six to the highway? In the dark. Dehydrated. With a collapsed lung and wrenching pain. It had subsided now, but as soon as she exerted herself again she knew the invisible dagger would return and her chest would fill with broken glass. For a few bleak seconds, she hoped the Soviet would hurry up, find her and shoot her between the eyes so she could be spared this dilemma. She didn't actually want to die – but man, would it be easy. Much easier than running seven miles on broken lungs, being hounded by killers, and discovering the next day that they'd murdered her husband. Much, much, *much* easier—

James is watching me, she told herself.

Somehow this changed everything. She repeated it until it was a chorus in her mind. *James is watching me . . . James is watching me . . .*

This little chant had once carried her through the final curve of a hundred meter hurdles race after she had spectacularly biffed a jump and torn both knees open. White plywood pin-wheeling behind her. Blood everywhere, bright as a stop sign, running hot on her skin. So much of it, too. She knew that the human body was seventy percent water, but *come on*! What was the other thirty percent? Ketchup?

She hated running. She hated jumping. She hated running and jumping. She hated track and field the way she hated Republicans, slobbering dogs, cilantro, and documentaries. She had joined only because she was blessed with the lithe build of a runner and her scholarship required an extracurricular activity. So the instant she tumbled upright on that broken momentum, feeling the shame of a hundred eyes now focused only on her, she knew this was a fabulous excuse to limp over to the medic and sit down. Enough stitches to knock her out for the whole season. To hell with it. Running and jumping over things? When did that become a sport?

James is watching . . . James is watching . . .

She finished for him.

Not for herself. Not for the team. Not for the crowd. Not for the stupid scholarship, which rejected her the next year anyway. For James. And for years afterward, he spoke of that moment as if she had climbed Mount Everest or crossed the Delaware under a ray of golden sunlight with an American flag stirring behind her. All she'd done was limp over a finish line. Funny how the stupid shit we do for those we love hardens into legend.

James is watching. He's alive. He's watching.
Don't let him down.

"*Run,*" she hissed to herself, too loud, and winced at the echo. Down the riverbed, the Soviet's torchlight halted. Then it flashed in her direction.

Finally, Elle ran.

19

James closed the door behind him and locked the steel deadbolt. He stepped forward into a ring of yellow overhead light.

To his right was a workbench crowded with grimy tools, capped bottles, and a gaping horizontal vise. Towering gadgets of painted metal and glass rose to the ceiling like organ pipes, packed with dark powder and braced with knobbed levers and Rube Goldberg ramps. The array was workmanlike yet oddly gothic, reminding him of the skyline of some bleak future city – Chicago in the year 2050, as envisioned by H.R. Giger. Further back he saw what looked like a welding station, and two bulbous tanks rested beside it, marked C2H2. Acetylene. Flammable. Or inflammable. Same thing, right?

Plastic crackled under his shoes. He was standing on candy wrappers – a kaleidoscopic sea of them – and he noticed more heaped on the workbench, stuffed into crevices and drawers. Even more swelled from a cardboard box, which at one point must have been a trash bin.

Green, red, blue, pink. He fished one out and read the joke on the back: WHAT'S RED AND BLUE?

He turned it over.

PURPLE! LOL!

To his left, a human face watched from the darkness.

His gut sank fifty floors and he whirled. His shoe squealed. Letting the overhead light fall on this thing, he let out an involuntary breath when he saw it wasn't a person, but a rough approximation of a face, hammered into steel to pool shadows in sunken eye sockets. He saw more behind it, too. Huddled shapes crowded like World War I soldiers blinded by mustard gas, crawling and groping – some of them smoothly humanoid, others geometric with harsh edges, stacked against the far wall like folding chairs and just approaching the ringed light in fallen domino rows. Only the one at the front was fully visible; a formless torso on a stake without arms or legs. They were metal targets pockmarked with clusters of concave bullet hits. Tapp must have accumulated dozens of these, and fired hundreds of thousands of rounds into them, before graduating to the real thing.

The humming he'd heard outside was louder, deeper in here, rolling off the walls. It reminded him of a lawnmower. It came from further inside, as if luring him.

Ahead a standalone wall cut the way into an L-shape, curving around the left to form a separate room lit by a faint, radioactive green glow. He passed under the shop light and plunged back into darkness, his hands outstretched, with the yellow glow shrinking behind him and the dim green ahead. All else was black, black as eternity. It was like stumbling through a coal mine.

His fingers trembled in the air. His knees jellied. His back prickled with cold sweat. God, did he need to pee.

Be strong. For Elle.

He knew she was making a run for it now. She was a helpless little speck in Tapp's dark prairie. Every second

221

counted. He hadn't yet heard any gunshots, which told him two important things: firstly, that she was still alive, and secondly, that their gamble had paid off and Tapp couldn't see in the dark.

His cell phone chirped – LOW BATTERY – and he jolted with frigid adrenaline, nearly falling on his ass.

He rounded the corner and the noise intensified as he found the source. A shuddering generator trapped in a cage of metal. Duct-taped dryer vents clumsily mated up with the exhaust port and snaked under the wall. Four red fuel jugs rested against it and a puddle glinted on the floor. The source of that radioactive green light was also there on the floor – two tubular glow sticks discarded among the candy wrappers like ethereal cave worms.

Next to it, he found a metal cabinet – head-high with two swinging doors – and his heart double-clapped. It was a gun locker. He threw open both doors, one crooked and shrieking, and saw in the murky light several rifles, including a black military M-16 or something close to it, standing rigidly upright. They smelled like oil, powder, and stained wood. These weapons were kept pristine, tucked away and lubricated with little square patches the way a hobbyist might jealously guard his model trains. James grabbed the black one, but the cabinet had a restraining bar and a loop of veined polymer through the trigger guards, like a bike lock, with three numbered rollers. He tried two random combinations and gave up.

His bladder was two seconds from detonating like a water balloon, and before he went any further, he needed to address that. Considering his other options and finding none, James quickly unzipped and urinated inside William Tapp's gun cabinet. The relief was revelatory. He made sure to target the M-16 and stepped back to avoid the back-spray. Under the drumming pressure-washer sound, he bit his lip and told himself not to laugh – *James, this is serious, life-and-death, people have died today* – but then he imagined the very real possibility of Tapp entering the building to grab a flashlight or something and finding him mid-stream all over his precious guns. It hurt to laugh.

He noticed a black platform thing on the cabinet roof with a Motorola logo on it. It was a recharging station, like the kind Elle plugged her iPod into. It had four radio ports where the receivers would stand upright and charge. Only one was occupied. James had one radio in his back pocket. Tapp had the other.

Who had the third one?

The Soviet, he hoped. He had just been in here, after all.

James zipped up, having already decided his next move. He knew that the snarling generator was in there for more than the shop light and radio charger. They'd gone through the hassle of buying it, maintaining it, and fueling it, so something important inside this little building required a constant supply of electricity.

Follow the electricity.

He grabbed both glow sticks, took a knee beside the rumbling generator, and found two extension cords knotted to the back. One led through a bare surge protector and crawled up the wall to that shop light clamped overhead. The other looped behind the gun cabinet now dripping with urine, under a card table, through another surge protector, and then plugged into the back of . . . something. It looked like a black plastic box, suitcase-sized, with a skinny carrying handle fattened with rolled electrical tape. Six antennas, resembling the thick plastic nubs of a wireless router, groped out the side. A tiny status light blinked a green heartbeat. On the side, stenciled in white: NETLINX.

You, he decided. *You look important.*

He lifted the machine and found it surprisingly light. The whirring internal fan changed pitch slightly. He honestly had no idea what this thing did – it looked like any other gadget in the control room of his old workplace, where engineers performed their arcane work under dimmed fluorescents. Could it be an internet setup? Not likely. Could it be some sort of signal encoder to mask their communication? Maybe. Or maybe the damn thing was just a cable TV box and an utter waste of his dwindling time. After an unsure moment, he unplugged the power cable and waited.

The NETLINX light flashed once, turned red, and died. Nothing else happened.

That was it?

He wasn't sure what he'd expected. The earth kept spinning. Gravity kept working. None of Tapp's gaudy end-of-the-world scenarios happened. He stood still in the dark for a long moment, listening to the din of the generator and the gentle pop of sheet metal contracting in the changing temperature. He considered powering the generator down as well, just to be certain, but that would kill the light and draw Tapp's attention sooner than he wanted. Queasy panic crept over him again, and he feared he was wasting time in here while Elle fled for her life somewhere up the valley. His wife might be seconds from death, pursued by one or both killers, and so far James Eversman's sole achievement was pissing on the sniper's gun collection. What next?

He paced. He returned to the door and checked the deadbolt. He opened a few drawers and found tools, bullets, emergency road flares bundled like dynamite (and more candy wrappers, enough freaking candy wrappers to wallpaper a house). He poked the steel targets with his foot. He rifled through gun magazines with sticky pages. His heart sank when he found himself looking at things he had already seen – a terrible mindless habit where he would check the same kitchen counter three times for his car keys – and paused in the center of the room, his fingers in his dirty hair, the amber glow of the floor shining up on him like an inverted spotlight. This couldn't be all. There had to be more.

What did I miss?

His cell phone bitched again – LOW BATTERY. He almost hurled it against a wall. He would later thank God he hadn't. As he pulled it from his pocket and powered it down to conserve whatever little charge remained, he noticed something striking on that little blue screen. The signal bar was full. Five bars out of five.

Cell signal was back.

That NETLINX box was a cell phone jammer. Like the kind SWAT teams used to shut down a neighborhood before a drug raid, or the military carted around in their convoys to disable cell-triggered IED's in Afghanistan. That was the reason for the damn generator. This entire area, Shady Slope Road and the fishbowl crater, wasn't a dead zone after all. Tapp had created one, with this gadget, to prevent his victims from calling the police. And now that gadget was turned off.

Tapp, I'm about to ruin your evening.

His battery icon was flashing empty – only a few minutes of juice left. Maybe less. He hoped it would be enough. He thumbed the buttons hard. Nine. One. One. Then he slammed it to his ear and heard his own furious heartbeat, a soul-crushing moment of silence, and then a puff of static as the call routed.

"Paiute County Sheriff's Station. What's your emergency?"

* * *

Tapp saw her.

Elle knew it somehow. It was her peculiar little sixth sense. She could always tell when she was being stared at, like at the Fuel-N-Food where she had first detected the Soviet's Cowboy's eyes on her as a vague uneasiness. Like sinister electricity in the air, gathering before the visible lightning strike. She couldn't describe it – it just *was* – and she felt it now, multiplied by a thousand. She imagined Tapp's scope on her back with his little crosshairs crucifying her while she ran. If you could call it running.

Every breath was agony. Crackling bronchitis gasps. She wished it were some sort of CIA torture so she could simply surrender to it. Whatever men feel when they're kicked in the balls, Elle was certain she felt it in her lungs. James had once tried to describe the sensation to her after she'd stepped on an unfortunately-placed garden rake in Home Depot, dropping him to his knees in the Yard Care aisle. *Imagine the exact opposite of happiness, and then set it on fire*, he had said, and now maybe she understood.

She was only three hundred yards up the prairie slope. She checked over her shoulder and saw the Soviet's torchlight still fussing around in the arroyo, patiently scanning every crack and crevice like Elmer Fudd while his prey escaped. She had eluded him by a comfortable distance for now. But what about Tapp?

"Elle."

She turned forward and missed a step, stomach fluttering.

It was Roy. She recognized his voice. She searched and found him in the darkness ahead. He was bent over with a hand tucked under his shoulder. A half shade of starlight glistened in his eyes but she could discern nothing else, and didn't want to.

"Elle," the sad silhouette said. "I'm so sorry."

She veered left and started running again, leaving him behind.

"Elle! Wait." Pattering footsteps.

Was he *following* her?

She ignored him and tried to put distance between them as slippery rage welled up inside her. She felt her cheeks burn and her throat jam up as she pumped her legs harder, her fingers tightened into white fists—

"Wait! I'm . . ." He gasped behind her. "This is important—"

She ran faster, suddenly not minding the pain. That asshole. He'd tried to kill her husband, and he might very well have succeeded for all she knew. She didn't want to look at him or hear him or even acknowledge him as a human presence. She wished he would not exist. And even here and now, in a darkly comic final insult, he was following her, drawing attention to her, placing two of Tapp's eggs in a single basket.

"I'm trying to help you. Listen to me." Even as his voice rose to a desperate hoarse shout, it shrank into the night behind her. "I had a head start and I *came back*. I came back and found you—"

She didn't care. She knew she should listen but didn't want to. She dug into a new stash of adrenaline, leaving this poor guilty wreck further and further behind. The crunch of his footprints faded.

"Stop!" Roy hollered, loud enough to draw an echo. It made her wince – even at three hundred yards, the Soviet had to have heard that. "I know who Tapp is. How he knew my name, my address, family, everything. It's bad, so much worse than we thought, if you'll just *fucking listen to me*."

She slowed and turned.

He came wheezing to her, the white text of his I PISS EXCELLENCE shirt almost-but-not-quite readable in the starlight. In his uninjured hand she saw a small square of paper. His body was quaking with gasps, as he lumbered to within arm's reach—

"What is it?" she asked.

He shoved the paper into her hand.

It felt like a receipt, but bigger. Thin paper, slippery and crackling. He started to say, "He—," but his voice cut out and she felt a rush of his body heat envelop her. At first it reminded Elle of urine, a splashing hotness, and then she blinked and realized it was slopped all over her, coating her eyelids, sticking in her hair, hardening on her lips with the taste of copper. She looked up and saw Roy was still standing but only barely. Most of the letters in I PISS EXCELLENCE were now gone. His hand was still on hers where he'd handed her that mysterious paper, and his fingers now squeezed tourniquet-tight, and in them she felt his heartbeat. A slowing metronome.

He tried to speak again. "He—"

His warmth scattered from the air and his blood turned icy on her skin. Elle's mind sluggishly processed this new information – *Tapp can see in the dark* – and knew she should be breaking away and running for her life, but what was the point of dying tired? There were only football fields of open ground in all directions. So she lingered in this dreamlike moment with the dying mechanic and for some reason, all she could think about were Roy's words after he'd chickened out of running for Glen's revolver, emasculated and hurting: *I'm not afraid of dying. I'm afraid of dying an asshole.*

She tucked the paper into her pocket, unpeeled his fingers from hers, and looked him in the eye.

"You're not an asshole," she told him.

She wasn't sure if Roy even heard. Tapp's second shot jerked his head backward, as if tugged by a chain, and when it recoiled back to face her it was deflated and leaking, no longer human.

* * *

Tapp experienced two distinct surprises.

The first was the woman. As the last neon bits of Roy Burke speckled the ground around her, she rocked on her heels, wiped little clam chowder chunks of viscera from her eyes, and turned slowly to face his night vision scope. She wasn't looking at Tapp, exactly – without first seeing a muzzle flash, she couldn't possibly locate him on the black horizon – but the gunshot had thrown around just enough sound to give her a general direction. She was helpless, blind inside his green x-ray, but her face turned to stone. She wasn't afraid of him.

Her lips moved in an exaggerated way, like she wanted him to read them. At this range it was impossible to know, but Tapp thought he saw: *My husband is going to kill you.*

Pretty cute.

It did raise a troubling question. Why had James chosen to stay in the arroyo while Roy and his wife fled? Had he been injured in the crash? Was he lying in wait to ambush Svatomir close-quarters for his Saiga 12? An armed James would be bad, but not terrible. A shotgun versus a night-scoped rifle at four hundred meters – yeah, good luck with that.

Tapp knew the hardest part, zeroing this new BlackEye optic, was over now. When you mounted a scope on a rifle you had to calibrate the crosshairs to zero exactly on the rifle's natural point of aim (layman's terms: where the bullet goes). Often the only way to do this was by shooting at a sheet of paper and then setting your crosshairs to the hole. His shortcut here had been a bore sight – a .338 cartridge-shaped gadget designed to lock inside the chamber and project a red laser dot. While he listened to James' hand-crushing story, he had read this dot at two hundred meters off the south wall of the bungalow (he thought he saw a flicker of movement behind the motor pool, but dismissed it) and adjusted the BlackEye for a loose sight-in. This, combined with the stored ballistic data on his handheld computer, allowed him to fire a six hundred and seventy-two meter center mass hit on Roy. A second adjustment for elevation and wind, and he popped the mechanic's head like a grape. Easy.

My husband is going to kill you.

No worries. Tapp would finish her off quick.

He was just crawling the BlackEye reticule – a bladed red chevron – up the woman's body and teasing the trigger with the very tip of his finger, when his Motorola crackled and he received his second surprise.

James' voice: "I'm in your shed. I just turned off your cell phone jammer."

20

"Sir?" The dispatcher hesitated. "Who are you talking to?"

James crouched on the concrete floor with the EMS dispatch lady in his left hand and Tapp, stunned to silence, in his right.

"Sir?"

He had already told her everything in a long, breathless spurt. He was shocked she'd understood any of it. It had taken three tries to enunciate Shady Slope Road. Twice she had urged him to slow down and breathe. He heard a keyboard click-clacking under her voice and it gave him a small comfort to know that this was being recorded. Somewhere in Paiute County, Nevada, there now existed a log of this nightmare.

So yes, the police were coming now, but how soon? How many? How many under-equipped Deputy Doogie Howsers or highway patrolmen would it take to fight a scoped killer on his own turf? Tapp was comfortably roosted and overlooked miles of open ground. He could see all approaches. He would spot them before they even knew they were at the right place and his supersonic bullets would smash windshields and perforate flesh like jelly. It wouldn't even be fair. It sure as hell wouldn't be a gunfight. It would be more of the same, more of Tapp's rigged game, while husbands, sons, and fathers walked themselves into the meat grinder. When the good guys finally surrounded him and prevailed, they probably wouldn't even have the satisfaction of gunning him down. Tapp would simply off himself on the hilltop with his last bullet. Like the lowest form of human life, the school shooter.

He realized it had been a long time and the killer hadn't spoken.

"Is . . . is Elle still alive?" he asked on the Motorola. He was terrified of the answer.

Silence.

Say something, Tapp.

The dispatcher had fallen quiet, too. He could hear her faint breathing as she listened. Nothing moved. The world dared itself to be still. The silence made James flinch in anticipation of whatever would break it. He tasted greasy nausea, rising in contracting tugs, while this awkward moment dragged and dragged. Somewhere on the north side of the building, a metal sheet warped in the falling temperature like a big drum.

"Sir?" the dispatcher asked again, but he ignored her and squeezed Tapp's radio until it trembled. He bit his lip to hold his jaw steady and felt a trickle of sweat run down the bridge of his nose. It clicked on the floor.

Please, you bastard. Say something.

The quiet was powerful now. It wasn't an absence of something. It was a presence. It thickened the air into Jell-O. Somewhere up the hill outside, close but not close enough, Tapp was recalculating his strategy, rerouting his plans to accommodate this unexpected new wrinkle. If he hadn't already, he might shoot Elle right now. He might try to broker a truce. Or, more likely, he might just

232

descend the hill, kick down the door, and execute James right here in his shed.

Please—

"Alright, James." The killer exhaled. His voice was utterly calm, placid, bereft of emotion. The polar opposite of how James felt. "Are you listening?"

He fumbled for the TALK button: "Yes."

"If you call the police," Tapp said, "I will shoot your wife."

The dispatcher again: "Sir, if you can hear me, *please*—"

James closed a fist around his cell phone to muffle the woman's voice and held a breath until his lungs bloated. He needed to decide how to answer Tapp's ultimatum. He thought for a few good seconds and finally closed his eyes and raised the Motorola to his peeling lips like it was a microphone. He knew there was no coming back from this.

"If you shoot my wife," he said quietly, "I will call the police."

Distant thunder rumbled.

His mind whispered: *Except I already did.*

"Okay," Tapp said.

"Okay?"

"Okay." The sniper coughed. "I have night vision and you have a cell phone. We have . . . a truce, then."

Another croak of thunder.

James was a god-awful liar. His cheeks were already burning, swelling into feverish blood balloons. How was it so easy when you were a kid? He was so bad at lying that he was almost physically allergic to it, and he hoped, *prayed*, that he was pulling it off right now.

"Well, hell." Tapp exhaled stiffly, like he was making small talk in an elevator. "This is . . . really awkward."

"Sir?" The dispatcher's voice chirped through his fingers. She sniffed, fighting back sympathetic tears: "If you can't talk right now, just press a button . . ."

"James?" Tapp said.

"Yeah?"

The dispatcher's voice peaked with alarm. "Sir, units are coming, okay? We're *going to help you—*"

"I'm going to kill you," the sniper said with metallic clarity. His voice seemed to meld into the circuitry to form a new sound, precise and inhuman. "Don't for one microsecond think that we're on the same level now. I am the end of your world. Start counting, because every one of your heartbeats is numbered. Every . . . mouthful of air, every electrical signal in your brain, every second of consciousness, all numbered. I can't tell you exactly what the numbers are right now, but I assure you, they're fuckin' small."

He'll kill Elle, James realized in a stab of terror. He would kill her the instant the police arrived. What else would he do? There was no other outcome here. *How could I be so stupid? This isn't a truce. It's a ticking bomb.*

Right now, somewhere close, the first responding police cruiser raced through the night, lightbar splashing red and blue, a screaming beacon visible for miles, just dwindling minutes and seconds from shattering this ceasefire. He had bought Elle time, but how much? How long until an incensed Tapp spotted police lights in his night vision, realized he'd been played, and shot Elle?

Shit, shit, shit.

He set the Motorola on cement and held his cell phone in both hands. "This is important," he told the dispatcher with a shiver in his voice. "How soon . . . how soon are they getting here?"

"I . . ."

"How much time do I have?" Another roll of thunder came as he spoke, closer.

"Oh." She smacked her lips.

"What?"

"Oh . . . Okay—"

"*What is it?*"

"Strange luck." She lowered her voice. "Sheriff's deputy just pinged back."

"How many?"

"We only have one, dear." The woman turned uncertain, as if she suddenly whiffed something rotten. "He's on patrol, on the Plainsway. He knows the area and he's . . . he said he's almost there."

* * *

It was just beginning to rain when Elle saw a police car at the rim of the valley. First came the pulsing lightbar, and then white headlights up and over the rise. Dust burning red in the taillights. She hit her knees, caught herself on her palms, and choked down a wheezing gasp. She had to blink before believing it was real.

The cop descended Shady Slope Road and flicked on his high beams. She hesitated there, half-crouched, the better part of a mile downhill and a few dozen yards west of the road. The lope of his motor flattened against the plains. She found herself moving automatically toward the road, to intercept the cop, without even thinking about it. The way mosquitos are drawn to a bug-zapper, and the parallel wasn't lost on her.

Why hasn't Tapp shot me?

The question of the day. The runners up were: How did this cop get here? Why hadn't Tapp shot him? And the returning classic: where was James?

As she half-ran, half-staggered, the rumble of deluge came sweeping in from the south, rattling the earth and splashing grit on her ankles. It instantly overtook her, the combined din of a million raindrops pummeling the Mojave floor. Brass marbles pounded the back of her neck, tapped her shoulders, and kicked up jets of dust at her feet like the bullet impacts back at the arroyo.

Already the first chills vibrated through her bones and she felt stranded in a dream. Nightmare logic took over, where things happened for no reason, locations shifted under your feet, and faces morphed like goblins. Nothing was real.

Where the hell was James? *What* was happening?

As the cop's headlights drew closer, a silent fork of lightning crossed the sky.

Roy's paper – allegedly the key to everything, the ultimate insight into Tapp's power – crinkled uselessly in her hand. She couldn't read it in the dark.

* * *

James found something eerie in the way his cell phone died. With a gentle pop, the EMS dispatcher was torn away mid-sentence. The feedback slurped away and suddenly he was sitting on the floor with a plastic briquette to his ear, alone under the machine-gun clack of rain on the metal roof.

Not alone, he realized. Worse than alone.

"James." Tapp surfaced again.

He picked up the radio. "What?"

"You lied to me." The sniper exhaled and flushed the connection with static. His voice shuddered and he sounded oddly wounded. Like a kid who had just tumbled off his bike, fighting tears to look tough for his friends. "I know that now. So now . . . now I need to admit that I lied to you as well. And it's only fair, now that your cards are down, that I show you mine."

Thunder growled, perfectly timed.

"Yeah? What now?" James forced a hollow laugh and tried to fathom how this day could get any worse, or how this blackened shadow of a man, with his childish puns and his one-mile kill shots and his goddamn *night vision*, could become anything more alien and horrible.

"You have a day job, James?"

"I used to."

"What?"

"Account executive. I mean . . . it's a salesman, basically."

"I have a day job, too." Tapp cleared phlegm from his throat. "Inside the shed with you there's a reflective road jacket."

"Where?"

"By the door."

"I see it."

"Look behind it."

James pulled it aside and saw a sandy brown uniform folded neatly over dark slacks. It smelled like seat leather and sweat. A black gear belt rattled on the wall with an empty holster, a canister of pepper spray, and a dangling shoulder radio on a spiral cord. The nametag, glimmering in the swampy light, read SHERIFF BILL TAPP.

"I know," the sniper said. "It's a *cop-out*."

21

Roy's mysterious slip of paper was a speeding ticket.

It lay flat on the road where she'd dropped it, blotting butterfly wings in the rain. Slanted handwriting in a spidery blue pen: seventy-four miles per hour in a seventy zone at two in the afternoon. Today's date. The bottom line, the recipient, was signed by one Roy Michael Burke, the man who died to pass it to Elle.

It would have been helpful, if she hadn't been handcuffed. Her knees sank into the muddied edge of Shady Slope Road. Squinting in the blooming headlights, she recognized Deputy Doogie Howser — small-boned, pockmarked with acne, black crew cut, disturbingly young to carry a gun. He had smiled at them before, while James asked about Glen Floyd's empty white truck and she buried her face to keep from snickering at his silly campaign hat. He was still wearing it. It still looked absurd.

He wasn't smiling now. He slammed his trunk shut and reappeared by the driver door with a radio in his hand — another black Motorola, confirming what she already knew — and halted by the headlights while rain bounced off his shoulders in glimmering beads. Wet soil squelched at his feet. He was staring directly up at the horizon as if he knew exactly where to look (he probably did), and after a pause, he squeezed his radio and asked with the small voice of a child disturbing a busy parent, "Do you have a plan for this?"

"I always have a plan," Tapp said. His voice lacked conviction, too.

Lightning slithered across the sky.

The sonic crash came immediately and the deputy flinched. "I . . . what happened?"

"Focus."

"Svatomir?"

"He's fine."

"He said he was hurt—"

"Your cousin is fine. Stop talking. Stop moving. Stop thinking." Another nervous fork of electricity touched down in the distance and Tapp licked his lips, dry as Velcro. His words came slippery-fast, clipped and snarled: "You wanted in? You're in. You wanted this. Punch God in the dick, or whatever it is you said. Remember that you wanted this, ever since you were five. So put on your big boy pants and *turn off your goddamn headlights* before I shoot them out."

Deputy Doogie Howser ducked back inside his car. "Yes, sheriff."

Sheriff. He's a sheriff.

The vehicle lights flicked off, reminding Elle of the section in every haunted house tour where the lights cut out and someone screams. Always, like clockwork. Dozens of Halloweens and she was never the girl who screamed. Not even now. Especially not now, with James watching.

James was watching, she reminded herself. Be tough.

As her eyes adjusted to the darkness she saw the deputy's silhouette step outside of his cruiser, his elbow on the door, wiping rainwater from his eyes. "It was a bad

239

call," he said through a chatter of teeth. "Mindy sounded shaken up. I don't think she'd ever heard anything like it before. Multiple baddies. A sniper. Shooting from a mile away. He told her everything. The exact location. So I solid-copy back to Mindy and say no – I'm not at the salt flats where I should be – I'm speed-fishing two minutes from that exact location. That sounds bad. And it's going to look worse on paper tomorrow—"

"Names?"

"What?"

"Did James give . . . names on his call?" Tapp sniffed impatiently. "Any names that might link to a missing persons? James Eversman? Glen Floyd? The Roy Burke you stopped?"

"Just . . ." The deputy fidgeted with the pistol on his hip. "Just yours."

The sniper said nothing.

Two hot gashes tore into the sky, illuminating a flash of suspended rain. For a microsecond the entire valley fell under an x-ray of stark truth. Then the night came rushing back and in its comfortable hold, Elle quietly rocked forward on her knees and slipped her cuffed hands under her feet. Then she tucked her wrists to her stomach, arched her back, tensed her calves, and shook muddy hair from her eyes—

"What's this?"

Suddenly the deputy was beside her (how did he move so *fast?*) and crawling his hand up her side as if to grope her chest with his little claw fingers – but he was going for the sandwich bag. Fingernails scraped her skin. Then like a Band-Aid, he tore it off mercilessly (*James is watching, James is watching*). She winced, her next breath came involuntarily, and she felt a rush of frigid air entering her body from an uninvited angle. Her mind was so flooded with panic that she hardly heard Deputy Doogie Howser's next sentence, delivered with gawking adolescent fascination as he

240

crunched James' duct-tape and plastic through his fingers and stared at it:

"Medics are God's foot soldiers."

James, please be watching.

* * *

Sheriff William Howard Tapp had built a reputation early in his career for being ill-suited to law enforcement work. The newer psychological evaluations and assessments (which he had luckily dodged back in 1979) referred to this as "social competence." Apparently there was an entire twenty pages to it, crammed full of one-to-five-scale questions he knew he would fail — *when stressed or uncomfortable, is your laughter noticeably louder than normal?* — to say nothing of the polygraph exam, which would be disastrous without a thumbtack in his boot and some serious prep time. On patrol, he had a hands-in-pockets awkwardness to him, a woodenness, that made interacting with the public excruciating. He avoided pulling motorists over the same way he avoided answering his landline at home (thank God for answering machines). Social anxiety? No. He wasn't anxious about interacting with people — he was utterly uninterested in them and their tiny problems. People were too much work. That was part of the reason he'd left the New Mexico Highway Patrol and moved to the nation's second-smallest county.

Fun fact: it only took eighteen votes to be elected sheriff here.

He blinked away rainwater, fighting it back as it trickled down his neck, pooled in the wrinkles of his ghillie fabric, and glazed his rifle in beads. It was everywhere. It would add another ten pounds to his camouflage suit and turn him into a walking towel, reeking like a wet German Shepard. He knew his BlackEye X3S was weatherproof (of course) but that didn't prevent a nervous twinge from shooting up his spine when he noticed the perimeter of the green lens frosting with moisture. He hated moisture. Moisture is a pernicious little bastard that seeps into the cracks of your guns and cancerously rots them from the inside out. He would never forget the horror and shame of uncasing his .270, flicking the bolt, and discovering the action to be rusted shut. That had just been cold condensation, too – this was honest-to-God *rain*. Tonight he would need to perform a full breakdown on his rifle and towel-dry every last pin and screw.

Somehow, focusing on the smaller problems made the bigger ones feel manageable. It was progress.

In the BlackEye's green haze, Deputy Sergei Koal looked like a gremlin with his stunted body and wide-brimmed campaign hat. He was barely taller than the woman, and even handcuffed on her knees she seemed to dwarf him. Ten paces from the darkened Paiute County cruiser, he had peeled something off the woman's chest – too small to tell at this range, given the optic's limited six-power magnification – and studied it before tucking it in his pocket for later. Then he crouched beside her, took a handful of her hair, and studied her like a hooked fish. "She's pretty," he said on his radio. "As long as I can remember, cousin always liked the brunettes."

"Play nice, now," Tapp said.

He let her head drop. "What's next?"

"You found nothing out here. Just rain and darkness. You'll spend all night looking. Then after sun-up, you and me, we'll both check it out so it stays off State Patrol's radar. We'll follow the ridgeline, work up some blistering sunburns. We'll call it teenagers, pranks, bad acid, whatever. No worries about the killer using my name. You can Google me, for Christ's sake—"

"Runners."

"Don't interrupt me."

"Drug runners could be our angle. We suspect the call was a distraction. To clear the way for . . . you know."

"Let me see your hands," Tapp said. "Any tremors?"

Deputy Sergei Koal obediently raised both hands with his fingers splayed, his flesh burning algae green in the night vision. Then he looked down sheepishly because he couldn't handle eye contact at any distance. Unfortunately, in all the ways that counted, he was the polar opposite of his half-retarded cousin. He spoke fast, thought fast, and flinched hard, like a windup toy on meth.

He's the speed of light, an African freakin' swallow, a greased-up cheetah racing down a goddamn laundry chute . . .

At this range Tapp couldn't discern if the deputy's hands were shaking, but pretended he could. "You're doing well," he said. "Did you check both burn pits like I asked?"

"No coyotes." Sergei looked ashamed. "No bones dug up."

"Now, kid, that's impossible," Tapp said, rubbing away the caffeine headache already coalescing behind his eyes. "And I'll explain to you *why* that's impossible tomorrow. But right now, we've got shit to do."

Another pulse of lightning exploded neon in his scope, overloading the optic for a split-second. Shadows scorched into his eye. Then came the thunder, a gathering roar crossing the crater, as if the sky were being drawn tight and split open.

Koal looked down at the wife. "She's . . . uh . . ."

"What now?"

"She's making a funny noise. Croaking. Like she's . . . breathing through a straw or something."

Tapp heard it too; a dry wheeze under Deputy Koal's voice on the Motorola. It sounded excruciating. His throat knotted up a little, involuntarily. If today had left any patience in him at all, he would have felt that poor woman's pain and express-delivered some .338 caliber euthanasia. Instead, Tapp calmly contemplated the new dimensions of this chessboard, caught some rainwater in his mouth, squirted it through his teeth in cold jets, and decided: "Hopefully she's still got a few more breaths left in her. Because as of right now, she's our ticket. Our hostage."

Koal tensed. "You mean there's *another one* alive?"

Tapp choked on a childish little smile, bubbling up from somewhere dark. He was winning again. He scooted forward on his elbows and levered his rifle down on the sandbag to focus the green lens on his ramshackle little bungalow, where the source of all of today's problems cowered inside.

"James Eversman. I know you heard everything in there. Step outside of my building so I can kill you. If you don't, I will . . . *butcher* Mrs. Eversman with my rifle in such a way that the Gore Museum staff could spend all day trying to reconstruct what happened, and still only get it half right. Piece by piece, limb by limb, I will shoot her into . . . little fleshy bits of firewood while my deputy applies tourniquets to every stump, to keep her alive and aware to experience every terrible second, while you listen. Your choice."

* * *

James felt dead already.

He sat cross-legged on the floor with the radio clasped in both hands under his chin. Rain drummed metal overhead and trickled through in waterfalls, slapping the cement and splashing him. Water sizzled off the hot light. The building had become a cave – cold, dark dripping. It took on a pungent wet odor, as if calcium deposits were forming dripstones around him. He was numb, utterly still. He couldn't even locate his own heartbeat.

He had listened to enough of Tapp's indulgent little monologue to know that Elle was going to die, and that he was going to die, and all hope was lost, but somehow, a strange little fragment from before snagged in his mind:

Turn off your goddamn headlights before I shoot them out.

He couldn't get it out of his head. He needed to think about how to handle this final ultimatum, how to surrender Elle's life and his own to Tapp in the most painless and humane way, but like a scratched CD, the stupid phrase repeated itself over and over.

Turn off your goddamn headlights before I shoot them out.

What did it mean? What was Tapp talking about? He scrutinized the tiny nuances of the killer's speech as it came around each time – the way the sniper clipped the last syllable of some words as if he was in a hurry, the way he drawled the first syllable of others as if he wasn't, the folksy way his tongue navigated the word *goddamn*.

Turn off your goddamn headlights before I shoot them out.

Finally he confronted the notion that he was picking up breadcrumbs dropped by his own imagination. His memory was imperfect. Every looped echo was just a corrupted copy, each one further from the real thing. This was procrastination, busywork, distracting him from what needed to be done.

Tapp's voice: "Thirty seconds, James. Then I shoot off her right arm."

He stood up and approached the door. It wasn't even a choice. He pressed one palm to the metal – still warm from the day, but chilling fast. It vibrated faintly with the outside rain, almost like electricity.

"Don't worry, James. She's tough. She'll keep . . . *shouldering* on."

The echo resurfaced, crowding out every other thought: Turn off your goddamn headlights before I shoot them out, turn off your goddamn headlights before I shoot them out, turn off your goddamn headlights before I—

"Twenty-five seconds." Tapp exhaled impatiently. "Here . . . hold the radio to . . . We'll make him talk to her."

James listened by the door in the silence.

A rustling click on the Motorola. A washing machine roar of tinny rain cycled through, and he was reminded of those fuzzy airplane black box recordings, congested with staticky pops and hisses, in the final seconds of free fall before impact.

"James?" Elle said.

He couldn't speak. His mouth turned to cotton.

"*James*?"

"I'm here," he struggled to say.

"Good news," she said tiredly. "The police are here."

God, he missed her jokes. He wished he could laugh one more time. He realized this would probably be the last smartass remark she'd ever make to him, just like the greasy steak burritos at the Fairview were their last breakfast together, and their last real argument had occurred by the gas pumps at the Fuel-N-Food with that stupid Roswell sign with five exclamation points. The last movie they'd ever watched together had been a forgettable horror flick with selfish characters that died badly in the end. Their last kiss had been in the wrecked Toyota, under the roar of the Soviet's engine, with his hands duct-taped to the shifter. Their last child never had a name. Everything was a *last*. He thought about the finite beats of his heart, counting down in his ribs.

"Fifteen seconds," the sniper said.

"Honey," Elle whispered. "What's the plan now?"

His cheeks burned and his throat tightened. "There's no plan."

"Yes, there is." She sounded irritated. His heart plunged when he noticed her voice had that familiar sucking whistle under it again. Her wound had reopened – she would be dead in fifteen minutes anyway, give or take. "You *always* have an idea. I won't make fun of it this time, I promise—"

"Ten seconds . . ."

"I'm stepping outside," James said.

"Please, don't do that."

"I have to—"

"No, you don't."

Violent thunder crashed overhead. The building warped and vibrated as his fingers closed around the doorknob. "I love you, Elle."

"Shut up."

"Five seconds . . ."

"I love you."

"*Shut up.*" She sniffed and he could hear her pulse in her breath, shuddering between gasps. "Don't you see? I'm with you. I'm ready. We're going to kill them all with your next crazy plan. Please, I just need you to tell me what to do, and I'll do it, okay?"

"Grab her arm," Tapp said. "Hold it . . . hold it out—"

"*Wait!*" James tugged the door – and it didn't open.

The deputy struggled on the radio. Scuffling movement. A sharp gasp—

Tapp fussed: "Fuckin' *hold her*—"

"Wait! I'm *coming out!*" He wrenched the door again, harder. It clanged, clicked. It was catching on something—

"James!" his wife screamed.

He remembered the deadbolt. He snapped the lock open as blood filled his eardrums, and the corroded squeal echoed twice (*too late, already too late, not enough time*) and he grabbed the door with both hands, gasped through his teeth and tugged the thing – scratching the floor, rotating as heavily and ponderously as a bank vault – wide open to reveal the darkness outside.

And the Soviet Cowboy.

He stood in the doorway like a gargoyle. Tall, broad, draped in that duster slick with rain and blood, reeking of French Roast hardened between teeth. His right hand was half-extended, as if he had just been reaching for the doorknob when James opened it. The shop light defined his cheekbones and turned his face ghoulish, eye sockets empty and unblinking, as his lips curled up to grin at James. A double-flash of lightning lit him up and revealed that today's blood loss had drained his skin into something pale and soggy, like dead oyster meat.

The struggle on the radio fell silent and Elle whispered: "Honey, if you tell me you have a plan to kill him, I'll believe you."

Tapp fired.

22

Tapp's eyelashes fluttered against the lens as he clacked the bolt up, back, forward, down. The wife was moving preternaturally fast, like security footage on accelerated playback. She had jolted upright on her feet, screaming, shocking weak little Deputy Koal, and head-butted the kid right in the front teeth. He reeled with both hands to his mouth while his campaign hat spun away like a hubcap, and the woman whirled, her wrists still cuffed at her stomach, and sprinted for the patrol car.

Wet gravel exploded beside her. She flinched but kept running.

An acceptable miss, Tapp told himself. His BlackEye wasn't fully zeroed yet. The atmosphere had turned into a maelstrom, his rifle bore had cooled, the hand-loads were a fresh batch from January (new primers), and a whole host of other unknowns had settled in. How could he expect to hit every shot he took in this weather? On a moving target, no less? Shit happened. He hadn't missed her by more than a meter anyway. Now he knew the windage – three clicks to the left.

She dove like a gymnast through the car's open driver door and disappeared behind the murky windshield. Deputy Koal pursued her with one elbow clasped to his jaw and his other hand going for the Paiute County-issued Glock 17 on his hip. He had her.

You could say he was going to . . . punch her ticket (*ha, ha, ha!*).

* * *

Elle hit the driver seat on her stomach. The car was dark, the windows blurred with rain, the seats sticky and damp and pungent with bleach. The scent reminded her of a stadium bathroom in that way something can be both filthy and nauseatingly over-cleaned. She elbowed up and saw a police computer – a blue monitor and a dirty keyboard with a missing spacebar on the center console. She checked the ignition for keys. No keys.

"You bitch!" The deputy was coming. "You *fucking bitch.*"

She was certain she would die there, either by gunshot or suffocation, and that was okay. At least she wouldn't die on her knees. Her head throbbed in waves of migraine pain and a warm line of blood ran down her forehead where his front teeth had cut into her scalp. How did head-butts work in the movies? Had she done something wrong? Because that *hurt*. She groped with her cuffed hands around the steering column, beside the driver seat, under the ancient computer. She needed to find the deputy's radio. Even out here in the badlands, cops must have radios built into their cars, right? If she could shout into it, someone would hear on the other end. Anyone.

"I'm gonna kill you." Wet footsteps, coming fast. "You broke my teeth—"

There it was! She found the receiver dangling on a spiral cord, and clasped the clicker and screamed – no feedback. No tinny echo. Was it even on? She saw gummy buttons on the console, indicating preset frequencies. There was an LCD screen above them, but it was the primitive kind you found on a cheap calculator. She couldn't read it without light. She tried slapping every button, mashing left to right with rising panic, but nothing responded—

"TURN AROUND, BITCH."

The driver door squealed open and cold water dumped down her back. She gasped and rolled over to see the deputy standing in a curtain of rain, his left palm cupped vise-tight to his jaw, his right hand darting for that sidearm holstered on his hip—

It wasn't there.

It wasn't there because Elle had it. A little squared black automatic, clamped in her wet hands, aimed up at him. She had plucked it from his holster fifteen seconds ago after she head-butted him. She had a good sense for holsters now, seared into her muscle memory, and it helped that the deputy's had been near-identical to Glen Floyd's.

His eyes widened.

She caught her dwindling breath and steadied the pistol.

The rain intensified.

"Your hat," she said through bared teeth. "Looks stupid."

Quickly, he hiked up his pant leg and went for a holdout piece on his ankle. She was quicker and shot Deputy Doogie Howser in the neck.

* * *

James closed the door the same instant the Soviet grabbed for it. He wasn't sure exactly what happened in the next second, but the second after it involved the door slamming almost-but-not-quite shut with the Soviet's sausage fingers crushed in the frame. The knuckles tensed like a dying spider curling its legs. The Soviet made that hissing noise again – like when James had stabbed him, that awful cold-blooded sound that summed up everything he hated about Elle's snakes – and emptied his lungs, sucked in another gasp, and hissed some more through his teeth. James screamed at him through the door, something he wouldn't remember.

After the second hiss, the Soviet pulled his hand and the door clicked shut.

James relocked the deadbolt and staggered back, his shoes squealing on leaked rainwater. Another crash of thunder shook the walls and crowded out the Soviet's snarl, and when the report drained away, he had fallen silent too.

Turn off your goddamn headlights before I shoot them out.

He had it now.

Light, light, light.

Light was Tapp's weakness. The cop car's headlights had interfered with the sniper's night vision optic, forcing its iris to adjust and readjust like one of Elle's cameras. Night vision wasn't a superpower. Like any other tool, there was a time and a place for it, and it either worked or it didn't.

He ran for Tapp's generator.

I'm going to make light.

The Soviet jangled the doorknob outside. Locked.

James thumbed the cap off the first fuel jug and left it twirling at his feet. He raced to the other wall, heaved the container over his head and sloshed gasoline on Tapp's workbench, his expensive ammunition reloading equipment, his candy wrappers, his scales and casings and reams of scribbled notes, soaking it all. Every inch of it. Bitter waterfalls ran down the drawers and spread black on the floor. He dropped the empty jug, scooped the radio off the floor where he had dropped it, and clipped it to his belt loop. It croaked and he heard Tapp's voice again, jarringly different now, breathless, vulnerable, nearly begging: "Stop, James. Stop. She's still alive. We can negotiate."

He ignored it, all of it.

I'm going to make a lot of light.

A gunshot boomed outside, like a bowling ball hurled into a marble floor, and the door latch exploded. The Soviet must have remembered that he had a shotgun. Shards of brass skittered across the floor and pinged off the far wall. The door sagged in its frame. The deadbolt still somehow held.

James hefted the second fuel jug to his shoulder and poured a glugging trail as he ran. The roof echoed thunder and the building shivered around him. He reached the center of the room, took a running spin under the yellow shop light, and hurled the container to the dark eastern wall. It tumbled over rows of humanoid targets, bowed like Muslims at prayer, and landed at the welding station where it coughed and quietly leaked between the two acetylene tanks. Flammable, the decal said. Or inflammable. Whatever.

"Stop," the sniper said weakly. "Whatever you're doing in there, please stop."

Sheriff William Tapp.

James grabbed the third jug and scooted it under the ring of light; he had plans for this one. He wiped sweat from his eyes, sucked in a breath, and tasted an overpowering wave of saccharine nastiness. It wrestled his gag reflex. All the gas fumes crowding the air. The world wobbled under his feet and he caught himself with one hand, suddenly light-headed, like five shots on an empty stomach, where you can pinpoint the exact spot you were standing when you transitioned from sober to drunk. James wasn't stopping. Not now.

You may own this entire county.

The Soviet fired into the door again, his multiple shots melting into a single freight train crash. He couldn't see the deadbolt from the outside so he was spraying the upper right section of the door, hoping to take it out by sheer firepower. He had almost succeeded. The lock warped and twanged, spraying chips under hot smoke. Bladed metal curled into flower petals. Buckshot pellets punched through and ricocheted inside the building, snapping from floor to ceiling. Candy wrappers puffed in the air like feathers after a pillow fight. A solvent bottle exploded near James and he slid to the floor behind the bench, covering his face. Then silence descended and the Soviet reloaded, one shell at a time. Click-click-click . . .

Even torn to a perforated sliver, the deadbolt still held.

Matches. James needed matches. He pulled drawers from the dripping workbench one by one, letting them crash to the floor and spew tools. In the deepest one he found something even better – those handheld flares, red as spaghetti sauce, stenciled EMERGENCY SIGNAL with taped seals and pull-wires. They were self-igniting and probably bright as hell. These weren't ordinary road flares. These were the things you lit up on a sinking boat to call in an airlift. He stuffed one in each of his back pockets.

You may be untouchable at a distance.

"James. We can negotiate."

The Soviet grunted and kicked the door, buckling it. Bruised metal groaned and the doorknob popped out and twirled on the cement. The man let out a frustrated huff, paced back, and kicked again, and again, and again, caving the doorframe a few inches further with every impact.

James held a roll of duct tape in his teeth, hit his knees, and dragged the smallest target from Tapp's heap – a steel plate, two feet by one, an inch-and-a-half thick, its bottom edges peeling flakes of rust on the floor. Scraping it into the light and letting it crash down flat, he saw it was blistered with thousands of concave bullet marks.

Importantly, no holes were punched clean through. It could stop a bullet at whatever incredible ranges Tapp practiced at, but up close? He didn't know. He lifted the thing to his chest, forty pounds at least, and drew looping circles of black tape around his torso, tightly bracing it to his body until he had exhausted the last strip. This new center of gravity pitched him forward but he caught himself, and crossed his arms over the plate, over the improvised body armor covering from his collarbone to his belly, and drew in a full breath. It was tight but he could breathe.

Up close, you're just a man.

He grabbed the road crew jacket from the wall – putrid yellow, glowering with reflecting pads – and threw it over his shoulders. It was fitted for the Soviet's bearlike frame and hung off him like a tent. Snapping buttons with one hand, he took a knee and sifted through clanging tools on the floor, pushing aside pliers, clamps, bolts, for the sharpest and deadliest instrument he could find: a flat-head screwdriver with a canary yellow grip.

Up close, I can kill you.

The Soviet rammed the door, rippling the wall. As he chuffed and retreated to make another charge, James palmed the screwdriver and stood up. He ran the slick blade through his fingers and scraped the back of his mind one last time to think of Elle, poor Elle whose time was ticking away right now. He remembered her green apple shampoo, her snorting laugh, a memory, any memory he could grab hold of, and found her on the Santa Monica Pier with her sunglasses dwarfing her face as she played with her hair against a vast gray ocean. *I'll save you*, he promised her.

After running for Glen's revolver and taking that unlucky ricochet, she had lasted ten, maybe fifteen minutes before losing consciousness.

I can do this.

I can kill them in fifteen minutes.
Whipcracks echoed up the hill. Tapp's rifle.

* * *

Elle scooted to the floor of the police car and covered her head. Pierced metal rang, the hood popped open and slammed shut, and fluids splattered over the windshield. The glass turned into a crystalline version of Starry, Starry Night and finally caved in as dirty white smoke billowed from the engine. She tasted ash and oil. Her eyes watered. She screamed until the gunfire stopped.

Had she been hit again? She didn't know. She patted herself down, wincing at the hot knife in her lungs. Arms, legs, body. No worse than they had been thirty seconds ago. Rain came through the empty windshield like cold pinpricks.

She was safe in there from Tapp, but that meant almost nothing. Her body was already filling with air, her lungs shrinking and tightening with every crackling breath. That familiar someone-is-standing-on-my-chest sensation was back, nicely complimenting the claustrophobia of the dark car. She knew she needed to clamp her hand over the wound to seal it and halt the flow of air. Too bad she was *handcuffed.* No amount of limb contortions would allow an airtight seal. The best she could do was tuck her right arm over it, half-covering the scabbed gash below her armpit and hopefully slowing the leak. Maybe she could purchase herself a little extra time; she didn't know. Every breath was accompanied by a persistent wet hiss. Every second, more sand streamed through the hourglass.

Keys. She needed the deputy's handcuff keys.

Too far away to reach, the deputy had died in a sitting position on the road, legs splayed, one hand still clamped to his neck where she'd shot him. His pant leg was still hiked past his sock but she couldn't see the holster in the darkness.

Too far. Tapp will kill me.

She set the gun on the seat and tried the police radio again. Dead air. One of Tapp's lucky fragments had taken it out; the LCD screen was fissured with icy cracks. Smoke was filling the car, pushing cloudlike through the windshield and curling through the air vents in wisps. Rainwater pelted her through it, turned dirty and ashen. She tasted charcoal, mesquite, whiskey. The smoke tickled her throat and she hacked a cough into her elbow, and when she looked up again, she saw the corpse of Deputy Doogie Howser had raised its head and was now looking at her.

She gasped and raised the warm pistol.

He smiled. She saw black staining his lips, running down his mouth and chin, forming a waterfall down the breast of his uniform. He didn't say anything – she wondered if he could still speak at all – and just kept grinning at her, like a hellish jack-o-lantern.

She curled her finger around the trigger.

"William Howard Tapp," he said with a full mouth. His voice had a gurgle to it. "William Tapp . . . is a demon in human skin."

She squeezed the gun until it rattled.

"Break that skin and he'll . . . drip out and pool and reform himself." His grin widened and dumped another dark mouthful of blood down his shirt. It splashed in his lap. "He hangs in the air and condenses inside people—"

"Give me your keys," Elle ordered.

The deputy reached for his belt and produced a small key ring. He looked back up at her with it jingling in his palm, and she saw the gears turning inside his little insect brain (shoot him, shoot him, *shoot him*) but it was too late. With a flick of his wrist, the keys hurtled into Tapp's dark prairie.

The last gasp of hope left Elle's chest, replaced by chilled air.

So close.

"He can't . . . die because he's a concept," the deputy said with increasing strain. Rising blood bubbled in his voice. "He's . . . a *contagious idea.*"

Then the kid slackened into shadow and dropped his hand from his neck, and she heard his blood jetting into the gravel like a water spigot. His final bit of damage done, he was dead for good now.

His radio, forgotten on the road by his ankle, buzzed feedback as someone activated the connection. She held the pistol to her body, hunched tight, and waited to hear the sniper's ugly, weedy voice again. Instead, she heard James, punching through the rain, as sharp and focused as a searchlight:

"Elle, honey, I have a plan to kill him."

She smiled a forbidden, guilty smile.

Get him, James.

* * *

"Fine. Great. *Fantastic.*" Tapp snapped the rifle bolt shut and wiped his chin with his wrist. "Let's see this plan."

Downhill in dripping green, Svatomir took ten paces from the bungalow. Then he slung his Saiga 12 over his shoulder, whipped water from his ponytail, and charged the door again. The crash came to Tapp a half second later.

"You're not cut out for this, James." He indexed the trigger and fought the heartbeat behind his ribs. It was violent, uneven, like a drum set tumbling down stairs. He forced himself to laugh and made sure the radio heard. "You listening? I . . . I said we can negotiate. What you wanted all along. Your bread and butter. I'm offering you the closest thing you'll see to an olive branch for the rest of your very short life, so don't . . . don't oversell yourself. For everything that's happened here, you're still a salesman. You still please people for a living. You're still that little kid watching his father beat the shit out of his mother with a—"

"I didn't finish."

"What?"

"I was interrupted," James said. "And I didn't finish."

"F . . ." Tapp missed a breath. "*Finish*, then."

"There was a gun my dad kept loaded by the door," James said. The radio connection filtered itself and became oddly perfect. All static, feedback echo, and background tone bled away until there was only James: "I grabbed it."

"And?"

"And I ran to the kitchen, to the scream, where he had her with her left hand flattened to the counter now, to break her other hand." He lowered his voice to a dry whisper, his words cleanly spaced: "And I shot him. In the eye. He didn't fall over. He just kind of sat down by the dishwasher. And I watched him die, for two full minutes, and we stared at each other and said nothing."

The connection clicked off.

Down the hill, Svatomir heeled back, lowered his shoulders like a linebacker, and charged the door again.

* * *

James opened the door.

The big man came barreling through the now-empty doorway over a rush of displaced air, wheezing with shock. Their shoulders brushed briefly as they passed – the Soviet going in, James going out.

And James was going fast. He ran three paces into the night with the third fuel jug in his right hand, glugging a trail at his feet. Then he took another running spin and hurled the container at the graveyard of broken cars, catching droplets in his eyes. Behind him he heard the Soviet's boots squealing, the man falling on the fuel-slick floor, his shotgun clattering on cement like kitchen pans.

He'd be back up in another second, turning to face James and shouldering his weapon for the kill.

James didn't look back. He kept running, ten yards from the building now. He heard the fuel jug land and splash by the front of the motor pool where Roy's Acura (and its full tank of gas) had been parked. He didn't turn to look at that, either; he was out of the building's safe shadow now. He was inside Tapp's scope. Right now, those hungry crosshairs were finding him, intercepting him like white blood cells zeroing in on a virus. He imagined the half second of delight Tapp was feeling right then – *there you are!* – and hoped it would dull the sniper's reflexes for another half second as he wrenched the first emergency flare from his left pocket and groped for the pull-wire with slippery fingers. Missing a step, losing momentum, he tugged once, twice, three times, until the world turned red.

He imagined Tapp's mild surprise: *Oh? What's this?*

Heat on his cheeks. Hissing sparks. The stench of damp fireworks. Around him splashed a twenty-foot radius of crimson light, of jagged shadows scattering and re-gathering with every step. He dug his feet in and whirled, slicing a fiery gash through the night, and threw the flare thirty feet toward the building's open doorway. Where the Soviet stood.

The Soviet was just bringing his shotgun up to fire at James when the flare came twirling at him, skimmed off the doorframe and flew past his left ear. He turned to watch the burning projectile bounce off Tapp's workbench and splash on the wet floor behind him.

He looked back at James.

James wasn't looking. He fell to one knee and covered his face.

The air ignited. Raindrops boiled away. Every molecule turned hostile to life. A wall of pressurized air (*Mount St. Helens-esque*, James managed to think) whipped his road jacket taut, and when he caught himself with an outstretched hand in the mud, his ears rang in answer to a blast he never heard.

* * *

White.

So much white. An instant nuclear flash.

Tapp's BlackEye X3S, which had a suggested retail price of $2,899, became a sheet of blank paper. He leaned back, his brow suctioned free from the eyecup, and he saw what the gadget couldn't. The explosion burned as bright as the sun for a moment, and then shapes took form and through seared retinal shadows he saw the bungalow's walls had disintegrated into a hail of sheet metal, thrown by a fountain of fire.

Think, he told himself. Think.

Instead he watched dumbly, slack-jawed, as the heat wave came rushing to him. He felt it on his cheeks and exposed knuckles, hot as a hearth oven even in the downpour. The report filled the air and blended into the next thunderclap. The fireball melted from orange to red before swallowing itself in a mushroom cloud, building to a hundred meters of cauliflower smoke. Flames leapt from the structure's black ribs, coiling in the suction of returning air to form a surreal tornado, a storm of swirling fire aching to meet the sky.

Think.

He eyeballed back to his scope. Still a white-out. Arctic white. Not the faintest hint of green. In the corner, flashing urgently: OVRLD. He hadn't opened the manual in months, but he suspected it stood for *overload*. Too much light. The image intensifier tube was burning out, photocathodes popping, two grand worth of circuitry in there sizzling like toast—

Think—

261

He couldn't. He felt like that little blinking OVRLD icon. His thoughts lost their bones and jellied into mush. He didn't even know where to start; everything had changed in a microsecond. So many plates had been hurled in the air and were now falling, and he only had two hands to catch them with – Paiute County's Deputy Sergei Koal slain by his own sidearm, the pillar of fire visible for miles like Mosby's jealous rendition of the Roswell crash, Svatomir burning alive right now, the emergency call to Mindy that *personally named him*. It overwhelmed him, but his mind stuck on that particular image – a dumb woman full of smart questions, her cow-like eyes as wide as dinner plates. There was no damage control for this. No cover-up would be elaborate enough. Tomorrow's light would reveal Sheriff William Tapp, the most reviled lawman in national history.

So, he had a head start on the manhunt by at least . . . what, four hours? More, if seventeen years here taught him anything about small-county emergency coordination. He considered the logistics of fleeing the law – eating, sleeping, scratching out a secret nomadic life in a world where every dumb bitch in a Dairy Queen could pull up his face on a smartphone – and that's where things fell apart. It sounded like a lot of work, and frankly, made him feel tired and old. He would much rather just take a dirt nap out there. To quote James Eversman in a moment of sensibility: *I'll be dead. Won't be my problem.*

He couldn't quite reach the long-barreled rifle to his head without sacrificing his grip on the trigger, but he could certainly brain himself here and now with his little target pistol. Of course, the .17HMR was an iffy kill caliber; small, high-velocity, zipping through meat like a laser beam with minimal deformation or trauma. What if he accidentally pulled a park ranger job on himself – a Glen Floyd, you might call it – and merely blew his ability to read and write out of the top of his skull? Or sentenced himself to a coma? That would be embarrassing.

The first debris-meteorites were landing now, touching down on his hill in flashes of ember. A big one, wreathed in fire, crashed down somewhere to his left. The air thickened with burnt powder, melted plastic, white-hot aluminum.

Suicide. He scooped up his thoughts like loose sand. Sure. Suicide would do well enough. He just had a few little things to tie up first—

As if on cue, another kernel of red light ignited at the foot of the blaze as James lit a second emergency flare. The salesman, the lanky white-collar guy with the self-deprecating shrug and the yellow Rav4 crammed with furniture, was coming to kill Tapp. This was it. It was *on*, as the kids say.

Okay, James. You ruined me. Before I go, I'll ruin you worse.

A scythe of sheet metal twirled over the sniper's head like a fiery windmill blade. Tapp didn't even flinch as he peeled off his headset microphone, and when the shrapnel banged into rock a few meters behind him, all he heard was his deceased, biggest fan:

You're a demon. You just don't know it yet.

23

James was starting to climb the sniper's hill when he heard Roy's Acura ignite behind him and the escarpment throbbed under another wash of light. A secondary blast thumped from the skeleton of Tapp's building, and then a third. He supposed there were more acetylene tanks in there than the two he'd seen, but it didn't matter now. He heard Tapp's library of ammunition and exotic gunpowder cooking off like machine gun fire, popping in ragged bursts. Thousands of candy wrappers rained down like a ticker-tape parade from Hell. Sheet metal came crashing down around him, warping and twanging, some glowing molten. His scalp and back tingled with second-degree burns and he recognized the dense stench of burnt human hair. Somewhere behind him, the Soviet was howling like a kenneled dog, his lungs full of bubbling fire, burning alive. James ignored all of it.

Elle is running out of time.

Get up there and kill him.

The grade steepened immediately as the land crested around the building in a harelip and became a wall of columned rock and scree piles. Granite emerged from the land like bones tearing through skin. Every step loosed a small landslide. Wiry brush tore out in handfuls. Even the rain worked against him as it ran down the hill in torrents, washing rock faces clean and spurting dirty water in his eyes and mouth.

His arm ached from holding the second signal flare skyward like an Olympic torch. It burned erratically in the downpour, hissing and snapping, dumping flurries of sparks. It threatened to die at any second. Weren't they supposed to be waterproof?

"Keep burning." He didn't recognize his voice. "Please."

Because it had been almost sixty seconds now and James wasn't dead yet, he knew his plan was working. It was like a horror movie – stay out of the shadows and the monster couldn't grab you. As long as he remained in the light, Tapp's night vision scope couldn't see him. Light beats darkness. The coughing flare, the reflective jacket, the burning building; so far, it was enough.

Up, up, up. Rock faces grew taller. Footholds fewer. He was ascending further from the well of orange firelight, or maybe the flames were already dying behind him. That would be bad. He didn't have time to turn around and check. He could only go forward. Only forward.

The flare wheezed and for a second, blackness rushed in on all sides.

"Oh, God." He sheltered it with his hand. "Don't go out. *Please.*"

Wet limestone under his feet, slick as ice. His knees slammed down and sickening pain shot up his legs. He lost the flare, groped frantically for it, and found it rolling in a puddle, gurgling and bubbling red fish eggs. He recovered it with both hands while his mind screamed at him: *I'm running out of time. Elle is dying. Not fast enough. He's——*

Ahead, something stirred in the darkness.

He shot upright and held the flare forward like a lantern, his breathing labored and his heart thudding in his eardrums. It was a flag. A yellow flag, triangular, flapping in the deluge, just like those meticulously spaced flags Elle had first spotted on Shady Slope Road, forever ago. He came closer, dousing it in red light, and read jotted black Sharpie: 150M. Somehow he knew immediately, instinctively, that M stood for meters. He was only a hundred and fifty meters away. So *close*.

"Tapp!" he screamed into the darkness. "I'm coming for you."

A dry gunshot popped in answer – James couldn't discern from where – and slapped into the ground somewhere close to him. He fought a jolt of panic. He felt thick globs of dirt stick to his face and as the fear subsided he fought something else, something unexpected – a shit-eating grin. Tapp had fired at him and missed. It was working.

Don't stop. Keep going.

Another shot cracked and landed somewhere behind him. This one was closer, disturbing the air above his neck like a fastball and peppering his back with rock chips. He shook it off, tucked his head and pumped his arms to cross a patch of level ground at a sprint. Already he could see the sniper's hundred-meter flag, coming fast.

* * *

Tapp slammed the bolt up, back, forward, down and ejected brass to his right. He clicked the scope to one-power but still couldn't locate James in the pulsing blowout of confused whites. So much light. So much changing light. The optic could open and close its iris on the fly to adapt to changing conditions like high beams and enemy torchlights, but not to this. The contrasts were too severe. He considered firing a third blind shot but every second James climbed closer, the range pulled in shorter, and his scope grew more cumbersome.

He hunched both legs to his belly, grabbed his rifle by the checkered grip and hand guard, and rose to a bladed rifleman's stance under a double-flash of lightning. It wasn't even remotely graceful but he didn't care. The chrome barrel was forward-heavy and tugged him on his toes. His hanging belly didn't help. His biceps were already burning under the weapon's twenty-four pounds and he could feel the growing tremor in his nerves. Rain bounced off the useless BlackEye scope, beaded on the barrel and ran down his tattered ghillie camouflage in streams.

James climbed closer. With that flare, he was a moving red beacon.

The marksman sucked the rifle to his shoulder to accommodate the .338 Lapua Magnum's punishing kick and estimated his point of aim. Firing downhill helped his balance and took much of the strain off his arms. He tracked James' path from the hip, swung the bore to match him like a skeet shooter zeroing in on a clay pigeon, and in a split-second he discarded everything he had mastered about the art of the rifle – the trigger squeeze, the sight picture, the half breath – and handled the thing like a shotgun. He slapped the trigger, the weapon barked in his slippery hands, and James kept coming.

He drove the bolt home and tried again. The scope had finally gone black (*Black*Eye – ha, ha!) because the processor had judged it to be daytime and automatically powered down to prevent damage. It was okay. Fine. He'd expected it. He was back in his confident rhythm. Cool, unhurried, with nimble fingers and an agile mind. There was such finality to this battle, a culmination of every terrific shot he had taken in his life, and it was a special exhilarating rush. He caught himself giggling and didn't try to suppress it. Why bother? Not even the sun lives forever.

Downhill at the base of the towering fire, he noticed a figure pushing through and staggering out. Wearing a coat of flames, palms out, it walked a few paces and collapsed in a blind, burning lump. Now Svatomir could join Sergei in nonexistence. Tapp couldn't let it distract him.

We're all dead.

We'll all be dirt by morning.

He wiped a dribble of saliva from his mouth and fired at James again, and thunder boomed overhead in unison.

* * *

A firecracker of chipped rock exploded in James' face as he passed the fifty-meter flag. Stinging shards buried themselves in his nose and lips. He felt a fragment rattling between his front teeth like a popcorn kernel and spat it out. He elbowed back up to his feet, rubbed blood and rainwater from his eyes – yes, his eyes were undamaged and he could still see.

He laughed. "You missed!"

But Tapp hadn't missed by more than a foot. His shots had inched closer ever since the first, and as the distance continued to narrow, it seemed inevitable that the sniper would regain the advantage. Even crippled by firelight, at close quarters a sniper rifle was still better than a screwdriver. That was probably why no armed force on earth outfitted its troops with screwdrivers. He couldn't even allow himself to think about how the hard part wouldn't be over when he finally clawed his way up into the sniper's nest – no, the hard part was just beginning. It would be like running a marathon and then fighting a bear. With a screwdriver.

His laughter faded. He realized that he was still going to die tonight. It had been a pleasant few minutes, pretending that any other outcome was still possible.

Keep going.

But he was losing momentum now. His limbs felt heavier. The flare sputtered and the red light flickered, inspiring another realization – as this engagement morphed into touch-and-go combat, broadcasting his exact location was becoming an awful idea. His natural night vision was absolutely destroyed. He could only see what the flare saw, twenty feet around him in a warping zone of red light. All else was blackness, black as space, cold and hopeless and indifferent. Tapp could be anywhere in it, moving, positioning, aiming, preparing his ambush like a craftsman measuring out wood before the first cut. This is what he does, after all. Orchestrate ambushes.

He sees me, James realized. *I can't see him. We're right back to where we started.* He swallowed nauseous terror.

Keep going.

But he was exhausted. His knees melted. His throat burned with smoke and hard breath. Blood ran over his eyes and glued his eyelids shut. His cheeks and lips stung with what felt like a face full of birdshot. If Elle were here she would have a remark for it, maybe something about looking like he'd gone hunting with Dick Cheney, but she wasn't. She was almost a mile away, dying alone.

Another gunshot boomed, tugging the jacket off his left shoulder. It trailed like a cape. He was numbly aware that a large-caliber bullet, the kind that would kill a buffalo, had come within an inch or two of ripping off his arm. By now he was used to being shot at. Whatever, right? He was close to Tapp. Maybe thirty meters? Twenty-five?

The rocks grew taller and he climbed on all fours. Scrub grass sliced his cheeks and raindrops pounded his eyes. He had to shield his face with an elbow, spitting clots of blood, climbing forward, only forward, nowhere but forward. In his other hand he held the screwdriver as an icepick, piercing soft shelves of earth and hauling himself up and over, like he was climbing a glacier wall.

Keep going. For Elle—

That was when Tapp shot him. It was true – you never heard the one that got you. Something monstrous slammed his body down flat and he heard the sheriff's wormy voice, crowing from uphill: "Oh, *no*! My night scope is back, James. My night scope is back and I can see your wife. Dumb bitch was safe in the car but now she's . . . she's crawling around the grass looking for something. Oh, no! I'm gonna pop her head off like a goddamn water balloon. Oh, no . . . oh, no . . . oh, no . . ."

He heard the deadbolt click-clack of Tapp's weapon. It was sharp, piercingly metallic, and it made him think: *Oh, Christ, I made it so close to him.*

I'm so close.

Then the floor dropped out and James was falling, plunging, becoming weightless, and all he heard was the ragged monster that was Tapp, half-wounded, half-hysterical, fading fast like water swirling down a sink:

"Why was my old AR15 like Bob Marley? Because it was always jammin'. Oh, no . . . oh, no . . . *oh, no, James . . .*"

24

Elle saw the keys.

Ten feet away, in the cone of illumination produced by the miniature keychain flashlight she'd discovered under the deputy's driver seat, they glimmered silver in the packed soil by the road's edge.

Coming closer.

She gripped the flashlight with her mouth as she crawled and the checkered metal scraped against her teeth. With her cuffed hands forward like a swimmer preparing a dolphin dive (much like running, she *hated* swimming) she pushed forward on knees and elbows, croaking dry breaths and feeling more cold and uninvited air ballooning her chest every second.

Closer. Then she could breathe again.

She didn't care that Tapp could probably see her in his night scope. She would rather probably die out here than certainly die in the police car. At least out here she had a paper-thin, *it's-not-impossible-it's-just-unlikely* shred of hope. She couldn't believe she was doing this, crawling through mud with a flashlight in her teeth and her tortured breaths whistling like a wet flute. Mud in her hair. Black fingernails. She must look like a ghost from a J-horror movie. She didn't even feel like herself. Not her real self, at least. She felt like the badass, blood-soaked version of Elle that James had imagined when he saw her eat shit on that hurdle track. Elle Eversman: the girl who *wanted it*.

What do I want?

I want kids.

I want kids with James.

I want kids so bad.

No matter if her uterus was made of arsenic, or Drain-O, or whatever the hell her problem was that baffled every doctor in California and kept her grandmother's Ark-of-the-Covenant crib empty and desolate inside a "baby room" that slowly morphed into a home office before finally being reduced to ashes. She would keep trying. They would keep trying. And for God's sake, she would name every one of them with James, because we're all nothing before we're something, and every chance of existence, even the tiniest and most blade-thin, deserves to be believed in.

Here lies Elle Eversman. She gave a damn.

Closer . . .

The handcuff keys reflected a ring of light and she let the flashlight drop from her mouth. Were her hands not clasped together, the keys would be close enough to reach right now, but she had to make one final lunge.

She did this and reached for them with both hands—

And she heard a *gunshot* over Deputy Doogie Howser's radio. Not the hollow knuckle-cracking pop of distant gunfire – no, this was booming, deep, close. It was as powerful and unsympathetic as a car accident. Every detail smeared and her mind whiplashed from the roof of the Whimsical Pig with James, to the speeds of sound and light, to a single juddering train of thoughts, tugged by the slamming beats of her heart:

Gunshot.
At me.
Move.

* * *

Rarely did a shot feel so right to Tapp. The trigger broke as cleanly as the tick of a pendulum. He hardly registered the recoil against his shoulder, or the thunderclap report, or even the warm cloud of rich smells – charcoal, gunpowder, rainwater sizzled to steam – and he was already unseating his hand from the grip to work the bolt while leaning back into the BlackEye viewfinder. He found her again in his green world, doubled over and crawling, unaware that the end of her life was less than a second away, racing toward her at thousands of miles per—

She dodged it.

She had started moving the microsecond his trigger broke, and she was now completing her somersault. She hurtled sideways and the .338 Lapua Magnum round skimmed over her shoulder (maybe slicing off a centimeter of skin, but probably not) and touched down with a spray of wet dirt.

She fucking dodged my shot.

She couldn't have seen the distant pinprick of the muzzle flash; she was facing the wrong direction. It couldn't have been dumb luck, either. There was a purity of intention to her movement. She had somehow known exactly when Tapp had fired and removed herself from the bullet's path.

He clacked the bolt home and prepared a frustrated follow-up shot.

But now Elle Eversman had sprung to her knees and was groping for something in the soupy green beside the deputy's body, silhouetted in curls of smoke from the destroyed car. Then she thrashed upright with something black in her hands. It was too grainy, too low-resolution to

273

make out in the six-power BlackEye at this range – and then she raised it to her mouth, and he knew at once that it was Deputy Koal's radio. Suddenly he understood everything.

Radio waves.

A radio wave travels faster than a bullet. The instant his primer struck, the gunshot traveled twenty meters down the hill to James' stolen radio, passed through the Motorola eight hundred meters away at Deputy Koal's feet, and reached the woman's ears three-quarters of a second before the bullet. That's how she knew. For a sweet moment, he was relieved – overwhelmingly relieved – that he hadn't actually missed. He was off the hook. James, in a truly impressive final sacrifice, must have died with a stiffening finger wrapped around the Motorola's PUSH TO TALK button, to secure his wife one last shot (ha-*ha*!) at survival.

Then Elle spoke into the radio and Tapp heard her crackling voice: "James?"

It came from *right behind him*.

He froze.

He took in a half breath and held it, stemming back a wall of nervous pressure in the back of his throat. Then he closed his eyes, willed his heart into a tight rhythm, and methodically scanned his senses, through the gentle patter of the rain and the dripping rocks, the settling flood basins, the flexing grass, the low rush of distant wind, and recognized . . . wait . . . maybe . . . yes, there it is . . . the audio shadow of someone standing behind him, over him, with trickling rainwater tapering and beading on a bladed point.

Tapp had been ready to die before, but suddenly he wasn't. Suddenly he was terrified, and words burbled in his throat as he started to say, "Please—"

But fingers had already twisted his scalp, his head wrenched back to face the sky and a pierce of reflected starlight, and simple, childish fear was the second-to-last thing to go through William Tapp's head.

25

Checking the sniper's pulse was redundant but James did it anyway, and when he was certain it was over, he let the scarecrow wrist drop. There was surprisingly little blood. He wanted to sit down and rest, but he needed to go back to Elle. He had to see her. So without even catching his breath, he turned and began to descend the hill.

What do you remember?

You came on the radio. You said you'd killed him.

He tugged off the yellow road crew jacket and dropped it behind him, rumpling like a tent in the wind. Then he tore off the last snakeskin peel of duct tape and let the steel plate, pockmarked with thousands of old bullet impacts (and one new one), clang down to the rocks at his feet. He didn't feel any chest pain yet, but he would later learn that the kinetic force of that cigar-sized .338 Lapua Magnum round exploding off his makeshift body armor had liquefied the skin over his sternum into a black blood blister, and beneath, bruised five ribs and cracked two. None of the medical staff would believe him when he told them he hadn't felt a touch of pain until he was inside the ambulance. All he could think about at that moment was Elle, and her weak electric voice, growing weaker every second.

I don't even remember what we talked about, James.

Anything. Anything to hear your voice. I didn't care. I . . . I'm pretty sure I asked you what your favorite tree was.

I think I said maple.

You did.

He passed the remains of the building. Bonfire embers under a collapsed skeleton. The motor pool was scattered like blackened toy cars, and the Soviet's jeep was parked close enough to the explosion that it was now burning with the bodies of Ash, Glen, and Saray inside. Glass melted out of the windows in ropy brown curls. With the firelight on his back he realized he was still carrying the sniper's screwdriver in livid knuckles, stained with blood, so he dropped it, too, and although he would later describe exactly where he had done this (at the arroyo's edge, just left of the trestle), the investigation never found it. One cop would later remark with sagging shoulders that the desert was a vast place, bigger than acreage can measure, and some things just hit the ground, fell through, and kept falling.

Then you stopped talking to me.

"Elle?"

He broke into a sprint. The trestle was behind him now as he followed Shady Slope Road's long crawl uphill. Somewhere around there he lost a shoe.

I was so afraid. I had to find you. Nothing else mattered.

He came up on the police car, tangled in smoke-swirls and backlit by a strip of naked sky. Although he had crossed over a half mile of Mojave land, for some reason this final fifty yards or so took the longest. He broke into a sprint and it was dreamlike, like running underwater. His hoarse breaths raced out over the plains to vanish into a vast darkness.

He found her curled up near the car while halfhearted flicks of lightning skimmed the horizon. She wasn't moving. Her muddy hair covered her face. Panic rising now. He remembered very little of this, just rolling her over under camera-flashes of distant light, and holding her small hands and whispering her name like he was waking her from a nap. Another awful moment stretched and cemented into forever.

Then through a crack in her hair, her eye opened, looked up and found him, and he felt her breath on his cheeks. He began to laugh and so did she, stupid giddy laughter, like they were daring the darkness to produce another William Tapp.

What were we laughing about?

I don't know.

They watched the last lightning and counted seconds until the thunder – but there was no thunder, and finally, nothing but a churning sky and handfuls of gritty sideways rain. Around then the second responder arrived, a state patrolman named Denny Hatcher, who cut through the pass all the way from Highway 93, and his headlights came down the road like white POW camp searchlights. James didn't believe they existed until he saw their shadows playing across Elle's face, because she was the only real thing in his world.

* * *

It started with a modest printout of a half dozen names safety-pinned to a bulletin board in the Las Vegas department's second-floor lobby. The list grew by two or three names a day as dental records returned with matches to decades-old missing persons' reports – mostly late-night abductions from homes and accident scenes. Idaho. Washington. Louisiana. Texas. A great many from Nevada and New Mexico, where travelers were funneled to Shady Slope Road via false detours. Every time the spool of wasted life looked to be finally waning, another DNA test would net a match and another cluster of names would appear – most recently, an entire family slain last year, including a little girl aged ten. Overnight it became an unofficial shrine of sorts that the local affiliate cameras would never see, the bench underneath stacked with candles and chalky flowers strung in bouquets. Some days the detectives lit the wicks on their way in and wax pooled rainbow patterns on the linoleum. The janitors didn't dare touch it. The list was appended from the top, so the first-identified victims, bodies most intact, were at the bottom of the paper, now three pages and unfurling like a calculator receipt:

> SARAY HARRIS
> ASHLEY HARRIS
> LEROY BURKE
> GLEN FLOYD

Here James stood, and every time he glanced back at the paper, he swore he would see JAMES EVERSMAN and EILEEN EVERSMAN in their designated places. He couldn't imagine being the one who broke this chain of violence, and it was much easier to simply believe he hadn't.

Fifty-seven. Counting you.

The identified number had reached thirty-nine, as of new results that morning – but a sergeant James had met for coffee the day before supposed it would never reach fifty-five confirmed victims. The swathe of murders was too vast, spanned too many jurisdictions, and pierced too deep into the past. Too many partial remains, pulverized by fire and time, would never be identified. Others would never be discovered at all; lives and faces and dreams sealed under shoveled sand. And for what?

Sheriff Tapp was, by all accounts, a screw-up. Mosby regulars described him as a fussy little potbellied man – something like Friar Tuck in uniform – deeply uncomfortable with human interaction, and apparently that worked both ways (*Christ, he was like the social equivalent of tear gas,* said one highway patrolman from Prim). He had been elected two years ago with a whopping haul of eighteen votes. His two-man department was an inefficient, unchecked mess. He had amassed over sixty thousand dollars in credit card debt, mostly from online purchases of shooting gizmos with long, technical names and five-star customer reviews. Never married, rejected from the armed forces for medical infirmity back in the seventies. His single-unit under the Mosby water tower had the look of a college dorm in September, all scrubbed for the incoming freshmen – his walls bleached, his floor bare, his fridge stocked with apple juice and energy drinks, his twin bed dutifully folded and pressed with a tucked pillow awaiting his return.

Tapp wasn't a demon, but he wasn't quite human, either. He was something. No wonder the Koals – two dim and childlike men – were drawn into his orbit.

He was *something.*

Elle took James' hand and her breath tickled the back of his neck as she whispered: "Let's get gone."

It was five past seven. The building hummed with gurgling coffee machines and unlocking doors. The city outside was still pewters and grays but the sun would bring color. She tugged his hand again, impatiently now, and as he gave in and left the shrine behind him, he resolved to do that sheriff a final and ultimate insult: to forget him completely.

* * *

The horizon unfurled a roll of blacktop.

Elle sang along with every song in a fearless way, and when the last radio station crackled away she sang a few from memory. Some James had never heard. Some were from her best friend's band in college. One, in particular, he recognized because it was the song she had described from her prom, her favorite – something about *finding you in the dark* – the one they never got to dance to. It somehow had never even played at their wedding, even though it was on the playlist. She sang it twice, and he pitched in on the final chorus, and then she fell into a warm silence with her head on his shoulder.

The road hummed. He was waiting for her to say something – something to confirm a strange little hunch he had nurtured ever since leaving Las Vegas.

She didn't. By the end of the first day I-40 had led them to Flagstaff, Arizona, where they stopped in a dive bar with a stuffed rattlesnake in the window ("Eastern Diamondback," she had whispered as they passed it). Dollar beers, shrill karaoke and greasy fries. They laughed about things from college, her old boss at the reptile store, and of course, the laxative brownies to which they owed their adventure together. As the night blurred they talked about Glen Floyd and whether they had done right by him in his final hour, and the last thing Elle had told Roy after he came back for her – *you're not an asshole*. She swallowed tears and wished she had said something different, something sweeter or more profound, but James reckoned that in this world not being an asshole was somehow good enough. The crowd was thinning out now, and he drank while Elle restricted herself to Diet Coke, which he noticed. They made love in the rental Audi and slept in the back seats. Dawn broke through the windshield and their necks ached.

The next day went fast – Winsbrow, Gallup, Albuquerque. Hours rushed by and the desert swept away like a tugged blanket. The ridges flattened as the rocks retreated back into the land and the world turned over to reveal soft sheets of something they hadn't seen in weeks – the color green. He clicked off the air conditioning and unrolled his window. It felt momentous, as if they were re-pressurizing a space shuttle returning from the edge of the universe. He expected her to say it then, but she didn't.

So he held his tongue as the blue markers ticked and the day faded. A state line passed without ceremony, and then another. The sun lowered behind flattening agricultural basins and flashed mottled orange behind rising deciduous trees. Shadows grew and deepened until they were silhouettes against sunlit wheat, racing past at seventy miles an hour. Finally, she said it.

"Names." She cradled her stomach. "Let's name this one."

THE END

If you enjoyed this book please leave feedback on Amazon, and if there is anything we missed or you have a question about then please get in touch. Thanks for taking the time to read this book.
Our email is jasper@joffebooks.com

www.joffebooks.com

ABOUT THE AUTHOR

Taylor Adams directed the acclaimed short film *And I Feel Fine* in 2008 and graduated from Eastern Washington University with the Excellence in Screenwriting Award and the prestigious Edmund G. Yarwood Award. His directorial work has screened at the Seattle True Independent Film Festival and his writing has been featured on KAYU-TV's Fox Life blog. He has worked in the film/television industry for several years and lives in Washington state.

EYESHOT is Adams' debut novel.

Look out for further books by Taylor Adams coming soon.

Follow him on Twitter @tadamsauthor, find him on Facebook at www.facebook.com/tayloradamsauthor, and check out his author page at www.tayloradamsauthor.com